It starts
when a quiet boy
stalks the women
who mocked him in his dreams.

It ends
with a deranged killer
face to face with the
homicide detective's own daughter.

STRANGLER
A nightmarish novel
of a madman's reign of terror.

STRANGLER

T. Jeff Williams

For Tom and Eileen,
Who were always with me

STRANGLER
A Bantam Book / January 1979

ISBN 0-553-12305-X

Published simultaneously in the United States and Canada

Bantam Books are published by Bantam Books, Inc. Its trademark, consisting of the words "Bantam Books" and the portrayal of a bantam, is Registered in U.S. Patent and Trademark Office and in other countries. Marca Registrada. Bantam Books, Inc., 666 Fifth Avenue, New York, New York 10019.

PRINTED IN THE UNITED STATES OF AMERICA

1

The red-and-white soup cans in the supermarket blurred and seemed to stretch into infinity. Twenty more cases of soup to be stacked lay waiting in front of me. A large lady with an overflowing cart wanted past.

"Have you ever seen so much soup in your life?" I asked her. "That much soup is revolting."

I looked at her for an answer but she only gave me a nervous smile and turned back down the aisle. Probably going to tell the manager.

I turned back to the soup cases and began opening them. Inserting my knife blade under the carton lid, I drew the steel toward me and wondered if that slowly ripping carton could feel anything. I was cutting the sides to make the boxes open like morning flowers when I heard the squeak of crepe soles on linoleum. Mice closing in. Only it wasn't mice. It was Mr. Franklin coming to watch me again. I spun about and faced him.

"What is it, Mr. Franklin?"

"Sonny, just what are you doing? You've been standing in front of these boxes for fifteen minutes and done absolutely nothing. Nothing." Mr. Franklin reminded me of three balls stacked on top of each other; round belly, round chest, round head.

"I've been sorting things out, Mr. Franklin," I replied calmly.

"There's nothing to sort. Just stamp the price on each can and put it on the shelf. What could be easier?"

"I don't want anything to go wrong. It's not as easy as it appears," I said.

Franklin slapped his forehead and I clearly heard something break. He looked at me without saying anything and I knew he was trying to control me with this look.

"Sonny, you're a nice young man. How old are you, twenty? Practically a grown man. Not the biggest kid around, but big enough to do a day's work. So mark these cans and put them on the shelves *now*. No more excuses."

"I'm doing the best I can but I can't work with you watching me all the time."

"Watching, he says. If I don't watch you, nothing gets done. You just stare into space. You come to a dead halt. Or read some weird book about the stars. Do that on *your* time, not mine."

Still he watched me and I knew he was waiting for me to get to work, but that would leave me unprotected and he would spy on me again.

"Please leave me alone, Mr. Franklin, and the job will be done."

"Look, Sonny, I know you need the job. So do it. No more talking." He turned and bumped into a woman pushing a cart and pulling a small child. I heard him apologize and move away as if nothing had happened. With him gone I quickly stamped and stacked two cases of soup as I had promised. But as I started the third, the feeling returned to me. He was watching from somewhere, I knew it. I turned, but no one was in the aisle. That was strange in itself. People should be here. Folding my knife, I dropped it in my pocket and walked around to aisle fifteen. Only the big lady with the overflowing cart. Maybe she was working for Franklin. I went to aisle fourteen and looked down it. There was Hilda, the senior checker, pretending she was dusting the racks of Pampers. Casually I strolled past her with a friendly nod, then cut over to aisle thirteen so she couldn't see me, and walked directly to the checkout lines.

I peered around a stack of Arrid Extra Dry on sale and saw Franklin in his glass cubicle. Immediately, he looked up and directly into my eyes, as I knew he would. It proved he had been waiting for me. His jowls turned red and he bolted from his cubicle and stood in front of me with his finger extended in rage.

"That does it! How many times do I have to tell you to do a job? Here you are sneaking around like some kinda nut. Well, buster, you don't help me and I don't help you. Turn in your apron. You're fired. I'll pay you right now."

I stood outside the glass-framed office beside the express lane and watched him type my check. Mother would be livid when she heard of this. I could already hear her shrill voice, "What's the matter with you? Only three days on this job and fired?" She wouldn't listen to my side.

Outside, the September sun hammered on my head. The valley was too hot for this time of the year. Something was wrong. Too hot and too bright. The bright light was a fright, I thought, or is it the fright light that's bright? Don't be ridiculous, I told myself, and felt the heat rise through my striped running shoes. I had bought them so I could run again, get ahead of the others like when I won the cross-country races in high school. Only two years ago, but it seemed forever. And now it was too difficult to run. It took too much concentration.

My battered '65 Volkswagen was an oven inside. I rolled down the windows and sat for a moment pondering my next move. I could go back in and apologize to Mr. Franklin. Maybe if I told him of my problems he would give me another chance. Maybe he would work with me and help me, but I knew he wouldn't. He was like the others. Sweat trickled down my back and stained the football jersey I got on sale in Penney's. I fired the engine, which sounded like it had terminal lung cancer, and chugged down the street.

I drove aimlessly, wondering why Franklin felt it necessary to spy on me, until I hit Sixth Street. This would lead me through sagging downtown San Miguel to Helen's house. I brightened, knowing it would help to talk things out with her. She was the only one who really understood my thoughts. I drove through town without looking at the two-story brick buildings with glassy window-eyes. It is an old town in an old wine-growing valley, and like everything else around here the place was dying when it should be living.

I was soon out of the town's center and driving past the tree-shaded old homes on the east side. Helen's house was easy to spot. Her father, Bill Marshall, was the biggest contractor in town and owned an elaborately restored old Victorian that rose behind a long expanse of lawn. The Marshalls were rich, which we Sillses were not; old man Marshall always made that clear to me. Helen's pinched-faced mother still resented the fact that Helen and I had dated in high school. She always said her daughter would go away after graduation, go to the City, or at least to Socorro Junior College here in town, but Helen did neither. I knew the Marshalls blamed me, but Helen could make up her own mind. She just didn't want to be a socialite and I liked her for that.

She must have seen me pull up, for when I reached the porch steps she came out the screen door and stood watching me with arms crossed beneath her small breasts.

I gave her my brightest smile but she didn't respond.

"What are you doing here?" she said coldly.

"I just came by, that's all."

"To apologize to me?"

"For what?" I was surprised.

"For what?" she cried. "What do you think? For attacking me like some animal, that's what."

I had to squint to see her clearly above me. Sunlight shimmered on the white porch. "Oh, that. Yeah, well, I'm sorry." It was coming back now.

She came down the steps and appeared to be softening. "If I told my dad about that, he would come after you with a gun." She kept her dark eyes locked accusingly on mine.

Helen was not bad, but not pretty either. She wore her black hair pulled back tightly, which gave her face a strained look. She had not been the most popular girl in school, never a cheerleader or prom queen, but she was smart and I appreciated that in her. Our brain waves clicked well.

"You attacked me, and for no reason, Sonny Sills." She remained on the step above me just so she could look down on me. "I only said I wanted to be an airline stewardess and you started yelling that they were snobs. Then you said all women were snobs."

"You started pushing me in the chest with your finger," I replied. I didn't want to think about that night, how the anger suddenly flared and overwhelmed me.

"That sure didn't give you the right to start grabbing me!" Helen lowered her voice and looked back toward the house. "Sonny, I have several bad bruises on me." She held her breasts lightly and leaned toward me. "Why did you do that?" she said softly.

I sat on the bottom step and pulled a blade of grass. It felt cool and clean when I bit down on it. "I don't know, Helen. Really. Something snapped. Just so much piling up on me, I guess." I pulled another blade of grass. It gave a small cry as it came away.

"I'm out of a job again," I murmured.

She was beside me on the step now. "Oh, Sonny. What happened this time?"

I looked up. My blue eyes on her black eyes, looking for derision but seeing none. "It was like the others. The manager didn't like me. Didn't trust me. Nothing I did pleased him. He was always creeping around on his crepe shoes trying to catch me at something. He wanted me to make mistakes so he could jump on me." I felt my chest tightening. "This time it was a Mr. Franklin. He would say, 'Go open some cartons of soup.' So I would. Then he would be down at the end of the aisle, not saying anything. Just staring. Spying. Just like old Simons at the shoe store. Ferguson at Ace Hardware. All the same."

I pulled another blade of grass and ignored its squeak of pain. Helen's hand touched mine, cool and restraining.

"What are you going to do now?"

"I don't know. Go home, I guess. Got to tell Mother."

"What will she say?"

"Oh, you know. It was all my fault. It always is."

Her mother's voice called from within the house. "Will you please help me with this?"

"I'll be right in," Helen said without moving.

"Now, please," Mrs. Marshall insisted. I stood up to leave and Helen watched me.

"Will you come back soon?"

"Helen!" Mrs. Marshall again. Probably watching from the window.

I moved across the lawn that seemed to be a green ocean. "I'll try, Helen. If I can get myself together." I turned and sprinted across the lawn just to feel the wind.

The word "together" was still circling my mind when I pulled into our place at the end of Hawkins Lane. Samuel Hawkins was my mother's grandfather and it was he who built the ranch. Once it had been more than five hundred acres of prune orchards. My mother's father made it succeed. He kept the prune trees and made a profit when others were tearing out their orchards to plant vineyards. But when it came to my mother, an only child . . . well, I don't want to think about that right now. I parked in the shade of the arbor that extended from the porch over part of the circular gravel driveway. From the weed-filled flower garden, once my mother's joy, the elves watched me. Their plaster eyes were bulbous, and their cheeks, once painted a robust red, were now faded and cracked. Seven elves. I hate every one. I climbed out of the car and paused to enjoy the coolness of the arbor. Wisteria vines writhed through the latticework overhead and covered much of the screen porch that led into the house. I lingered outside because I was afraid to enter. I would rather go out to the pumphouse and climb into the loft that was my new sanctuary. Up there I was safe; down here I was vulnerable.

"You're home early."

My mother's disembodied voice. I started violently and faced the deeply shaded porch. She was barely visible behind the dark screens, just a pale blur watching me.

"I didn't see you in there," I said.

"I heard your car but couldn't imagine it would be you." Her voice was dry, like the rustle of winter grass. "Why are you home so early?" she insisted.

When I didn't reply she turned and entered the house. "Come along, Sonny," she said.

I passed through the screen porch that my grandfather had kept light and airy and into the old adobe-walled house. Mother waited in the living room, where the shades were pulled as usual. She said it kept the house cooler but I knew she didn't like light. She stood in the middle of the room and clutched her blue cotton robe across her. The robe had no belt and she had to hold it to prevent it falling open. She was a stout woman, just over five feet tall, and her black hair hung lank and straight down her back. A network of red veins on her pale cheeks gave her the false image of health.

"Sonny, what are you doing home now?" She took a step toward me and I could see her puffy ankles above the blue slippers I had given her for her fiftieth birthday.

"It's not so early," I said and walked around her to the television set.

"Leave that off," she said. There was a pause as I stared at the black screen. "You been fired again, haven't you?" she said. "Look at me when I'm talking to you!"

I turned. Her voice seemed to come from a great distance. It had done that several times in recent weeks, and I couldn't understand how she did it. "They were spying on me again, Mother. Just like before. Only this time it was worse. I wanted to tell you yesterday what they were doing to me but I couldn't. I wanted to keep the job, you know I did. I know how much we need the money. But everything I did was wrong. And Mr. Franklin spent all his time sneaking up on me, or sending someone else to spy on me."

She said nothing for a moment, just compressing her lips and then pushing them out. In-out, in-out. Finally she spoke: "Sonny, why do you feel people are spying on you?"

"I can't explain it, Mother. They just are, I know it. If you were there you would see them."

"This is the third job you've lost in the past three months. What's the matter with you?" I felt myself shrinking as her voice rose around me. "How are we going to eat now? You know I can't go out there and work, not with my arthritis. I can barely walk. I had to put up with the pain from the time you were a baby until you finished high school. I was even willing to suffer more, keep working while you went to junior college so you could get a really good job. But did you go? No. You wanted to go to work. Now what's it all coming to? Nothing." She leaned toward me and I could see the spittle that always formed in the corners of her mouth when she was angry.

"Mother, that's not true. I wanted to go to junior college but you said your arthritis hurt too much. I *had* to go to work."

She pulled her robe tighter about her and glared at me. "I could have lasted another two years. After all I had been through with you to that point, I could have lasted. I made it all these years without your father, I could have made it a few more."

Sickness stirred in my stomach. "You always bring him into these arguments. He has nothing to do with it."

Now Mother waved both arms and her robe fell open to reveal her sagging breasts and protruding stomach beneath her blue cotton nightgown. "He certainly does," she yelled. "He got me pregnant and then just couldn't wait to leave. He talked big about marrying me and taking over the farm until he found out I was pregnant, and then, pouf! Gone. Just ran off and left me with a—"

"Stop!" I shrieked. "Don't tell me that again. Don't say that word. Never again. You throw that at me every time. It's not my fault. It's yours! You're the one who was . . . was whoring around."

My mother stared at me and her face turned chalky. Her voice came out choked and hoarse: "Don't you ever say that. Don't you ever. God forgive you." She began to cry and covered her face with her hands.

"God forgive *you,*" I said, and started for the door.

"Where are you going?" she called after me. I paused at the front door and listened to her shuffling toward me. "Sonny, don't leave. Your mother loves you. She needs you now. Stay and talk to me."

I pulled the door tight behind me and ran to the VW. "Leave me alone, you lying bitch," I yelled. I had to get away before she caught me. I gunned the car around the driveway, spewing gravel everywhere, and for a moment considered smashing into one of the leering elves. Then I was on the road, headed toward town, toward the freeway that sliced through the town. Drive anywhere, just get away. The nausea within me faded, but not the anger. I felt it pulsating in my chest and roaring in my ears. A roaring of voices, like someone trying to reach me. I've heard it before. Two nights ago I awakened when someone called my name. The voice came from a great distance but I heard it clearly. Afterward, when I lay in the darkness of my room and held my breath to hear more, there was only silence.

With the roar in my head subsiding, I turned west on Seventh Street toward the freeway ramp. I didn't know where I was headed and didn't care. Nothing mattered. There were so many Franklins in the world, the kind of people who smile when they meet you but then work behind your back to destroy you. Helen's mother was the same. And she would bend Helen until she acted the same way. Helen could have stayed to talk with me, but she had to run right in to her mother. And my own mother! Why wouldn't she talk to me? I wanted to make her understand it was not my fault, but she wouldn't listen.

At the freeway on-ramp the car in front of me braked suddenly as if to pick up the lone hitchhiker, then gunned forward again. The hitchhiker, thumb still extended, turned back to me and I started to drive by the long-haired hippie. But it wasn't a boy, as I thought. It was a girl with tawny hair, blue workshirt, and cutoff jeans. Her eyes locked onto mine and demanded that I take her with me. She seemed to look right inside me as if she could steal something away. How could she do that? I pulled over and waited for her to half-run, half-walk to my VW.

I could tell she didn't want to seem too anxious, but then again she didn't want to miss the ride, either. She opened the door and looked in to check me out. I smiled at her.

"How far are you going?" she asked. Up close she looked younger than I first thought, maybe sixteen.

"How far are *you* going?" I countered, and knew I had said the wrong thing. I could see her eyes calculating, wondering why I would ask such a question instead of just saying where I was going. She hesitated, so I quickly added, "I'm going only as far as Potterville, about thirty miles north of here. But if that will help, you're welcome." I smiled at her again.

Still she didn't move to get in. Cars were accelerating past us on the ramp.

"Come on, if you're coming," I said, and put my hand on the stick shift. She made up her mind then and threw her little yellow duffle bag into the back seat and climbed in. I studied her as she closed the door. Her hair was long and light-colored, a honey blond, and she had some small pimples on her cheeks, but that didn't hurt her looks. It certainly didn't detract from her brown and probing eyes. She relaxed and leaned back in the worn seat as we gained speed on the freeway. Her blue workshirt, knotted in front, exposed a tanned strip of belly above her cutoffs. She draped her nylon jacket over her long tanned legs.

"Where did you come from today?" I asked to end the strangeness.

"Oh, wow, would you believe it's taken me half the day to get here from the City? Only an hour away, but I've spent at least five hours on the road!" She brushed her hair back and turned toward me, willing to talk.

She was about to continue when she stopped in mid-word and stared at my eyes.

"Hey, you really have unusual eyes. It's not just that they're so blue. What is it?" She paused and then fixed on my right eye. "Wow, great. I really like that extra pupil."

"It's not an extra pupil," I said brusquely. "It's just a dot on my iris above the real pupil."

"But I like it. Does it bother you when someone asks about it?"

"People have asked about it all my life. I get tired of it."

"You shouldn't worry. Be proud of it. It makes you different. You have a nice face when you smile." She became flustered. "I mean, you should smile more often. It really lights up your face."

"That's what my mother used to tell me." I changed the subject. "How come you had trouble today? You should get rides easily."

She gave a nervous laugh and adjusted the coat to cover more of her legs. She had very pretty legs but ugly old white tennis shoes. "The first ride I got was with this old man, like, he was in his forties. He told me all about this houseboat he has on the marina and would I come down and spend some time there with him. I tried to tell him no way, but when we crossed the bridge he whips down to the marina anyway. He really came on strong and told me, 'You're not so innocent, you know where it's at.' "

I laughed, a derisive snort really, to show I was on her side against this freaky ancient.

"Are you innocent?" I asked with a smile.

She cocked her head defiantly. "I'm not innocent, but I do things my own way." She resumed her story. "So when we got to the docks he made this big pitch again to come on board with him, just to sip a little wine he says. I told him my people were expecting me. He actually tried to pull me down to his houseboat, but I put up a scene, man, and he split. Then I had to get out of the marina area and back on the freeway and start over." She sighed. "And then there was a whole bunch of short rides. Like this one."

"You didn't tell me where you were headed," I said.

"Hampton. Still quite a ways," she answered. Her eyes studied mine. "You're only going to Potterville?"

"I guess," I said. "Mostly just driving. But Hampton is about a hundred miles from here. Pretty far."

She didn't say anything to that and we drove north through the prune orchards and vineyards. The vines were heavy now with great purple grapes that swell under the pressure of your tongue until they burst and seem to bleed.

"Are you from Hampton?" I asked.

"No, from the City. I'm staying in a commune up there. Just seven of us. We're going back to the earth, you know what I mean? Getting away from the poisons in the city and going back to what's natural and pure. So we work the ground and read." She threw back her head and gave a pleasurable laugh.

The sun was low and filled the car with a red glow. "What do you read?"

"Oh, wow, books that open my mind. Books like they don't tell you about in school. We're all into Taoism, and Henry, he's sort of our spiritual leader, he's reading Hemingway to us. We just finished 'The Short Happy Life of Francis Macomber.' It's so great. Have you read Hemingway much?" she asked while turning more toward me. The jacket slipped away from her legs. Her face was golden in the final sun.

"Francis Macomber," I mused aloud and tried to place the story. Something clicked in my mind. "Oh, yeah, wasn't he a rich guy who goes on a safari with his wife?"

"Right, and—"

"—and Francis Macomber is a coward because he runs from a lion he's supposed to shoot and—"

"—and in the end his wife can't stand him because he is a coward and so she shoots him and—"

"—and claims she was shooting at the lion. Right! Now I remember." We laughed over how we had told the story together. Something was still clicking in my mind. "Do you think she was really aiming at the lion or just wanted to kill Macomber?" I asked.

"Even if she didn't, Macomber deserved to die. He was rotten to her. And he was a coward and a spoiled bastard."

"How do you know he was a bastard?" I flared. "There's nothing in there about him being a bastard." The anger that had quieted in my chest after leaving home was burning again. And my mind clicked repeatedly, like a computer searching for something missing and terribly important.

"I'm just talking about the kind of a guy he was, just a rotten bastard. If she didn't kill him, then the lion should have. Henry taught us to see an awareness of women's rights in the story. The woman was used and put down, but in the end she asserted herself."

"Maybe it was Mrs. Macomber who was the real evil," I countered. "She was like a lioness on two legs, always stalking Francis. Ever think that Macomber was only doing his best but got cut down from behind just when he was about to succeed?" I felt the heat rising in my chest. The girl watched me uncertainly.

"And remember what happened to Hemingway? He got sicker and sicker in his mind. Nothing helped him. Maybe he knew all the time that some lioness would cut him down, just like the lioness did to Macomber." Just like my mother did to my father, I wanted to add, but didn't because that would be beyond her. The girl had already given up the argument and was staring out the window. Her eyes were golden, like a bright agate I once had as a child. She seemed afraid to talk now, while I, on the other hand, suddenly found a release in the conversation. Still, I didn't want to push her, so I changed topics.

"You know," I began, "maybe you're having trouble traveling today because your sign is negative. Are you a Leo?"

"Leo! Never. I'm an Aquarius." She turned toward me, curious again, and curled her legs catlike on the seat. "Are you into stars too? Astrology has to be right on, don't you think? I mean, look at the way the tides are run by the moon. Look at the way the sun makes flowers turn and bend. Forces from the planets just have to be pulling on us too."

"Absolutely," I said. "The sun and the moon represent the opposing forces."

"Right on." She was smiling at me. "That's Taoism."

"Sun and moon, good and evil, man and woman." I turned on the headlights as darkness crept in behind the sun. "These opposing forces can tear you apart. Some people just can't hack it." Was I talking to her or myself? The yellow divider lines on the highway snapped and winked at me and my mind spun to keep up the pace.

"Everywhere around each of us are forces that oppose each other. Reason against intuition. Man against woman. Reason is masculine and pushes straight ahead. Intuition is feminine and it just envelops and traps. Do you see that?" I asked.

"Oh, wow, this is really my day," she said, shaking her head.

My palms were wet where I clenched the wheel. I forced myself to lean back and breathe deeply. "Sorry," I said. "I guess I came on a little strong." She didn't reply.

"Look," I said. "There's another way besides astrology to learn about yourself. You know anything about numerology?"

She brightened somewhat at this. "A little." I could tell she wanted to know more but was afraid to set me off again. She just looked at me, at my right eye.

"Your date of birth tells you almost everything. What's yours, and I'll tell you something about yourself."

"February third, 1959."

I calculated out loud. "That's the second month and the third day. So add a two and a three to 1959. That makes it 1964. Then you add those numbers, one plus nine plus six plus four. That's, uh, twenty. Add that again, two plus zero. . . ." My voice trailed off while my mind raced around her being a two. Was that why I picked her up? Destiny? I don't pick up hitchhikers, but here I am with a girl who has the feminine number two. The bad number two.

"Two plus zero is two," she said.

"What?"

"I said that makes two. I'm a two. What does that mean?" She sounded curious and unconcerned, but I knew that was deceptive. She was just trying to draw me out, then trap me. I wouldn't tell her everything.

"Well, two means . . . two is feline, I mean feminine. It just means you are very feminine."

"Is that all?" Her eyes watched me closely, scrutinizing my face but always coming back to my right eye.

"There's much more," I said evasively. We were in Potterville now. It is a tight little town with tight little frame houses inside tight little picket fences on each side of the freeway. Did I want to let her out here? Or keep her and find out what she was really thinking about me? My mind still clicked and searched, but for what? And what was behind those lioness eyes that quietly measured me?

"Tell you what," I said. "Let me go by my cousin's place and give him some money I owe him, and then I'll drive you on up to Hampton."

"You don't have to do that," she said. "I can catch another ride."

"That might not be so easy. It's not your day, remember? Besides, it's getting late. And I've got nothing better to do. A long drive would do me good." I turned off the freeway at the south exit and she made no further protest as I drove east on Canyon Road, which followed the twisting waters of Crab Creek.

"My cousin has a cabin not far out of town. This will just take a few minutes," I said. How could my voice come out so calm while my brain raced? I was amazed at myself. I had no cousin out here. Didn't she know that? Couldn't she see into my mind? It was dark now, as houses of Potterville fell behind. Few cars were on the road. Everyone was home stuffing food in their faces or sitting mindlessly before their televisions.

"Do you have a heater?" she asked, and pulled the jacket over her shoulders. Why did she want to know that? It wasn't that chilly out. The heat she radiated filled the car and made tiny bubbles of sweat burst on my forehead.

"Lioness."

"What?" I said.

"I didn't say anything," she replied, and looked at me again.

But I heard it very clearly. Lioness. The same voice that came to me last month, and came to me last week, the voice that came from nowhere, just arriving on the wind. It was a voice that frightened me, a voice that would not go away even if I refused to listen to it.

"Lioness." Again! So clear even over the rattle of my engine.

"No!" I cried.

"What are you talking about?" the girl asked, while watching my every move.

"Just thinking out loud," I muttered. We were well beyond the summer cabins now, and there just ahead was the rough track that led up to the abandoned Turpin mine. I turned up it without a second thought. The wheels occasionally slipped as we bucked up the rocky road. The girl said nothing until we topped out on a leveled area of rock tailings and the headlights caught the broken beams at the entrance to the mine.

"This is it?" she said in disbelief while she peered through the window at the blackness.

"He's got a cabin just back up the hill." I got out. "Come on, it will only take a minute."

"I'll wait here," she said, and pulled the jacket tighter around her shoulders. I knew now that she sought to deceive me. She would wait within, waiting to envelop me.

"Don't let the lioness trap you," the voice warned me. He was right. I walked around to her side and opened the door. My left knee jerked spasmodically and I wiped my palms repeatedly on my Levi's to keep them dry. But my voice was surprisingly calm.

"Come on. I'd rather you didn't stay here alone in the dark," I said, and my heart thudded, because it was going to be now and I had to be ready. She would fight, and she could kill me. Her face, only a white blur in the starlight, turned toward me and I could not see her eyes, which was bad because I couldn't tell what she was thinking. She didn't say anything, but slowly, like a lazy cat, turned in her seat to get out of the car. She stood beside me and I was surprised she was almost as tall as I. I closed the car door and took her arm lightly as if to guide her in the dark and then suddenly I was behind her and both my arms were around her, pinning her arms so those silver claws would not come tearing at me. I squeezed hard, lifting her off the ground.

"Oh." The breath came out of her in a sharp exhalation and she buckled forward, her feet scrabbling at the rocks. "Oh, Jesus—what are you doing! Oh, don't, please!" Her head was twisting about and she was trying to pierce me with those cat eyes but I wouldn't let her. I squeezed again, and still holding tight, toppled her forward onto the ground. She went down fast, and when we hit the ground she lay stunned. My arms were pinned beneath her and I could feel one of her breasts in my hand. I knew that I would win and that breast would never again suckle another lioness.

Straddling her back, I whipped the nylon jacket from her shoulders and bound her arms behind her. She started to twist and fight before I finished, but I leaned forward and hissed in her ear that I would smash her head with a rock if she didn't stop, and she did.

I rolled her over there on the rocks and grabbed her mane in both my hands and thrust my face into hers, sucking in the breath of the huntress, stealing away her air. I opened my mouth and took her throat lightly in my teeth as if to rip it out, and I could feel her tremble violently. Elation surged through me because I knew that I had captured the lioness before she could hurt me.

"You almost had me," I cried at her. "You thought you would catch me, and you played so innocent, but I knew! I knew you weren't innocent, I knew it. You made a fatal mistake and told me. And you pretended not to know about the stars and the power of numbers and—"

"Oh, sweet God, please let me go!" Her voice came in a sudden, piercing cry. I clapped my hand over her mouth, and she tried to bite me but I was ready. I seized her throat tightly with my left hand and squeezed until she stopped, frozen in terror.

"Don't scream. Don't cry out and I won't hurt you," I hissed in her ear. I was lying full upon her and I could feel the spasms of fear ripple through her body. "Don't say anything," I said again, and slowly rolled off her. I removed her shoes first and then ran my hand up her leg to the button on her cutoff jeans. As I released the button she drew her knees up, and strangling noises came from deep in her throat.

"Please, please don't hurt me. Don't do it." She

rocked her head back and forth and in the starlight I could see tears glint in her eyes. But I knew it was just another feminine trick and I clamped the fingers of my left hand around her throat again. She was silent except for the whimpers. My heart raced and I wanted to stop, but it was too late now. If I let her go she would kill me. Punish her first. I unzipped her shorts and tried to slide them off her but she kept her knees up, tight together. I had to use both hands to straighten her legs and pull her cutoff jeans down. I sat on her ankles now and reached forward to remove her white panties, pulling them down slowly, inch by inch to make her suffer as she had made men all over the world suffer. When I pulled them free she rolled on her side and drew her knees up protectively.

Unexpectedly the clearing around the mine filled with a soft light as a lone car rounded the bend in the road below and its headlights bounced off the trees. Suddenly she screamed and rolled away from me. She struggled to her feet while I remained paralyzed by the unexpected light. Her screams tore at my ears and I saw her run toward the road below in awkward, stumbling steps with her arms still bound and the rocks cutting into her bare feet. I started after her as the car lights swung around the corner and the clearing darkened again. Then I heard the car slow, and I froze, ready to run the other way. Maybe the driver had seen something or even heard her and was coming up the old mine road. But then the engine accelerated again and I realized he had only braked for the curve.

Now the darkness seemed more intense than ever. I stood completely still and held my breath, listening for her movements, but I could hear nothing other than the terrible thudding of my heart. Then, at last, I heard her. She was off the rocks and into the underbrush on the slope below the mine. I raced after her and fell heavily. A rock tore my hand, but I didn't feel it. I had to catch her. I reached the edge of the clearing and stopped to listen again. Nothing. Not a sound. She was lying somewhere out there, a wounded lioness. She would be stalking me now, slavering to tear me to pieces. I could feel those long white teeth sinking into my skin, pulling it away in chunks while her eyes, brown and calm, watched me. As I walked slowly forward I knew the fear that had gripped Macomber; but I would not let it overcome me, let it rob me of my masculinity.

I stopped again and held my breath while I listened. Still nothing, but I knew she had gone this way and was hiding. She could not be far, unless she had found a path and slipped silently through the brush. The fear of that possibility started me moving again, but within a few feet I drew up short. There she was, just ahead! I could see her lying next to a tree, all but invisible except for the pale blur of her face in the starlight. If she had ducked her head and covered it with her hair I would not have seen her. But a lioness could not do that; by instinct she had to watch and wait for her chance to pounce upon me. I walked slowly toward her, my body crouched, my mind worried that she had freed her arms and her silver claws were now unsheathed. I was only a few feet from her when the lion bitch snarled, deep and throaty, and sprang toward me. We met head-on, grappling beneath the dark oaks, and her rank smell of death filled my nostrils. Her arms were unbound, as I had feared, and she raked at my eyes, but I caught her arms and threw the lioness on her back.

"You goddamned man-eater," I yelled, "you will never again kill man." She screamed and lunged at my throat with her teeth. Then I was on her, forcing myself between her legs, thrusting deep, and I could hear her cry in pain. I thrust again, a white-hot sword, and she shrieked, which was good. She had to suffer and understand that all the pain she had brought on man would now be returned in full. She bucked and tore at me but I only thrust harder and faster and faster until I exploded inside her. Abruptly I could feel weakness washing over me, shades coming down over my eyes, and I knew that to hesitate now would be fatal. Her powers were working on me. I had to act instantly. I took her throat in both my hands and squeezed with what strength remained. No warning, no caressing of the neck, no words, just a deep, powerful squeeze. I felt my thumbs bite deep into the skin, and something inside her throat snapped audibly, and then she was bucking wildly beneath me, her back convulsing and heaving until I was thrown to one side. My God, she was powerful! Her knees came up again, hammering at me, and her claws bit deeply into my back and neck. I ducked my head close to hers to prevent her from clawing out my eyes. Would she never stop? I bit even deeper with my thumbs until her frantic twisting weakened, then stopped with a final tremor in her legs. But I knew it was a trick. She was only pretending to be dead until I released her, and then she would be on me again. I held her throat until my fingers were numb and without strength. I eased the pressure and there was no movement. I lifted my head from beside hers and her eyes were wide and staring at the dark branches overhead. The mouth was open, fangs bared, but now useless. I rose to my knees over her, my heart still thudding. I was drenched with perspiration, sick with exhaustion. But I had won! I had defeated the lioness, something that Francis Macomber and Ernest never had been able to do. I had done it!

I rose to my feet, swaying slightly, and started to leave. I sat down again and looked at the lifeless face with a shudder. She had almost trapped and castrated me. If she had succeeded, I would have walked around the rest of my life less than a full man, while others pointed and smiled and the girls held their hand over their mouths to hide their laughter. Now that could not happen. But what to do with the body? I could just leave it. No one came up here, and it might never be found. And if she were found, so what? You can't take prints off a body. There was nothing to link me with her. We were complete strangers. I felt sure that no one saw her get into my car, that no one noted what she looked like and wrote down my license number. There are thousands of hitchhikers. Who pays attention to them? Again I rose to leave, but something troubled me, something seemed unfinished. Yes! The lioness should be thrown back into her lair as a final irony! The mine! It would be perfect. Let her languish, useless, in her lair. I pulled her into a sitting position and then rolled her onto my back in a fireman's carry. God, she was heavy. I stumbled and nearly fell several times as I struggled up the slope below the mine. Once I reached the leveled tailings it was easier, though I was sure my ragged breathing could be heard for miles. As I walked to the car to get my flashlight, her free arm bumped against my legs and I had the eerie sensation she was alive. My flashlight showed the mine shaft went straight into the hillside for about thirty feet, then turned to the left for about twenty feet, and there it ended. It was cold inside and water dripped from the ceiling. The black rocks glistened in the pale beam of my flashlight. I dropped her in the farthest corner of the mine shaft.

Again I paused, still sensing I had forgotten something. A trophy! The successful hunter needs a trophy. I couldn't very well skin it, as the boys had done for Francis Macomber, because the lioness was still in the guise of a woman. Something glinted in her hair, and I bent to see. It was a hoop earring in her pierced ear. I fumbled with the clasp until it came free, then turned her head and took the other one. What about the body? Why not take everything, leave the lioness figuratively stripped of her skin, of that gray hide she loved to preen? I bent to unbutton her shirt and found my fingers were trembling violently.

Despite the cold air of the dripping mine shaft, perspiration still streamed down my face. It seemed forever until I had removed her shirt and bra. Already her body felt cold when I touched it. I placed one of her hands in the small stream of water that ran along the mine floor. Then, without reasoning why, I put one earring on her breast. Finally I kicked her legs apart to leave the lion bitch vulnerable. She deserved nothing better.

Outside, I quickly gathered all her other clothes and stuffed them under the front seat of the car. After a panicky moment when I thought the engine wasn't going to catch, I drove down the narrow, rocky track with my lights off. It was painfully slow going, but no one must see me leave this area. There were no cars when I reached the road, and as I sped home I kept gulping the night air. I couldn't get enough to feed my lungs and quiet my racing heart.

It was around eleven when I finally swung into the yard of our old farmhouse. My lights flashed over the seven dwarfs who crouched and watched from the weeds. Were they smirking at me? Averting my eyes, I drove past them and followed the driveway back toward the barn and the pumphouse. First my lights picked out the redwood barn with its doors falling from the hinges, then swung onto the two-story pumphouse. I killed the lights and the engine simultaneously and sat listening in the darkness. One lamb at the far end of the pasture bleated twice and then was quiet. The chorus of tree frogs behind the barn was in full voice. Nothing unusual. Just one light from the house. That would be Mother in the living room watching television, as she did every night until early morning. She couldn't hear me drive in over the television noise; she wouldn't even know I was here. I gathered the girl's clothing from the floor of the back seat and entered the pumphouse. To the right of the doorway was a ladder nailed to the wall, and I quickly made my way up to the loft and into my sanctuary. Inside, I turned on the light and lay on the floor until my mind suddenly flooded with what I had done. I killed a girl! And raped her! Why? Did she make me do it?

Sitting upright again, I looked at the clothes before me. I hadn't forgotten anything. But why did I do it? Who was she that had such power? Seeking answers, I rummaged through her duffle bag and found her small purse. I snapped open the wallet and looked at her driver's license. She smiled up at me from her picture as I read the statistics: Roberta Ann Thomas. Sex: F. Hair: Bld. Eyes: Brn. Height: 5′7″. Weight: 120. That's all there was left of Roberta Ann Thomas, just a picture and some typing on a card.

Music. I needed music to help me understand what was happening. Beethoven would know. He would give me insight. In a moment the opening rush of Beethoven's Fifth flooded my little space. The music seemed to swirl around the bare walls that once housed a great water tank which my grandfather sold after submersible pumps came on the market. There wasn't much up here, just an old piece of carpet I had found in the barn, and some lug boxes to hold my books and tape recorder. The music soothed me and helped me understand what had happened. Lioness! She had been the lioness! The voice told me so. A wild beast running loose among men. That's why my mind clicked at the story of Francis Macomber. The real lioness was his wife, not the animal that charged through the grass at him. And there were many lionesses still running loose. Or was it only one that kept changing forms? A gray lioness stalking the land dressed as a young girl? How would I know? What girl could be trusted not to prey on me?

I shook my head to clear it, but nothing helped. Before me, the clothes lay scattered on the rug, and slowly I carefully laid them out. It seemed important to spread them at one end of the loft exactly as she had worn them. I buttoned the shirt and tied it in front, then tucked the filmy brassiere inside. I arranged the cutoffs and shoes below the shirt and then dug in my pocket for the earring, which I placed just above the collar as if on her ear. Everything looked complete. Now I would listen to Beethoven again, and later, much later, I would see Mother.

2

Dan Eriksen put down his pen with exaggerated care as he saw the new secretary, Nancy Hall, approaching his desk with another file folder under her arm.

"You've got to be kidding," he said. His voice was rough, like someone had sanded his throat. "You're not kidding," he added as she placed the file alongside others that covered his desk.

"Compliments of Lieutenant Nye," she said with a cheerful smile.

"What makes you so happy?" Eriksen grumbled.

Bill Darby, his younger partner, spoke through the open doorway that connected their two small offices. "She's happy that she's not the senior homicide detective and you are. You get to do all the paperwork."

Darby leaned against the door and put another stick of gum in his mouth while he looked Nancy over.

"Both of you should be happy there are so few homicides this year," she said.

"This year is a long way from over," Eriksen said morosely. "And thirteen murders this year isn't exactly nothing for Socorro County. That doesn't even count accidental deaths or the old farts in the rest homes that keel over."

Nancy shrugged and started to leave, but Eriksen's voice stopped her. "What's this Jackson file for?"

"Lieutenant Nye said you had a court appearance on that this week and he wanted you to bone up."

"So I will do the right thing in court and make Conrad look good so he can get himself reelected?" Eriksen said.

Nancy said nothing, but raised her delicate eyebrows in confirmation. As she left, both men watched her walk toward her desk in the middle of the detective bureau.

"Man, I'd like to screw her," Darby said. "Oh, oh. Here comes the Socorro County saviors."

Eriksen looked up to see Sheriff Conrad heading toward his office with Lieutenant Nye in tow. He could see why Conrad was elected on his first try for public office. Six-feet-four in his Tony Lama cowboy boots and waves of silver hair over his square face, he looked like a sheriff from central casting. Nye, on the other hand, was a rotund five-foot-six man with sagging jowls. Chief of Detectives Nye kept an unlighted cigar perpetually in his mouth. He ate one cigar a day.

Both of them crowded through the door and overflowed Eriksen's office.

"You came to tell me I didn't have to do any more paperwork, right?" Eriksen said.

"This is no time to be funny," Nye said.

"Afraid we have a bad one for you, Dan," the sheriff

said. He pulled up a metal chair and sat down. "We just got a call on a 187. Some kids found a girl dead in a mine shaft up near Potterville."

"Is somebody rolling already?" Darby asked.

"Yeah, that's Blanken's sector. He should be pulling in there any moment now," Nye said.

"Oh, joy," Darby said, and snapped his gum. "Bigfoot Blanken. Good-bye, evidence."

Eriksen stood up and slipped on his suit jacket. He reached back to make sure it hadn't caught on the handle of his .357 Magnum. "Does the identification team know where it is?" he asked.

"We've already told them. It's in that old Turpin mine on Canyon Road east of Potterville," Nye said.

"Right." Eriksen started around his desk, but Conrad stopped him.

"Dan. This girl is a white female juvenile. She was found stripped naked. Maybe raped."

"All right," Eriksen said, and started for the door again.

"Listen, Dan, this isn't just some little nigger gal that got herself gang-banged and then dumped," Conrad said.

"So?"

"So the first Tuesday of November is less than two months off, and I don't want this nice little white community to start jumping down my throat."

"I know, you want an instant solution."

Conrad rose and patted Eriksen on the back. "I know you'll do your best, Dan. You always do, you and Bill here." He strode back toward his office, with Nye following.

Eriksen and Darby drove rapidly north toward the old mine, with Darby complaining about the need for a larger clothes allowance and Eriksen thinking of the added paperwork and court appearances this case was going to entail. He overshot the mine road and had to back up and try it again.

As he rounded the top of the hill beside the mine, the first thing they saw was Deputy Larry Blanken talking with two teenagers. Blanken broke off and came toward the car.

"Those are the kids who found the body. ID techs are already inside. The girl's naked as a jaybird. Nice tits on her," Blanken said with a laugh. Eriksen just looked at the deputy, who was several inches taller than his own six feet. Blanken had a noticeable sag over his belt line, which made Eriksen self-conscious of his own battle to keep himself under two hundred pounds.

"Let's talk to the kids," he said to Darby.

"I've already interviewed them. Got the notes right here," Blanken said.

"We'll talk to them too. Just for practice," Darby said.

"Christ, it's hot." Eriksen peeled off his dark blue suit coat and loosened his tie as he walked to where the two youths stood by their dusty Ford. A boy about eighteen came toward him, followed by a pale, dark-haired girl. Darby jotted down the particulars while Eriksen questioned them.

"We went into the mine, see. Just looking around," the boy said excitedly. "Once you get around the corner in there, it gets pretty dark. We turned the corner and I seen something laying up ahead but I couldn't make it out very well. Then we got a little closer and I thought it was a store dummy, see? And then I got real close and it was dark and I touched it to make sure it was just a dummy, and wow!" He rolled his eyes. "It's a dead woman." The girl was furiously biting her nails and grinning excitedly.

Everyone loves a body, Eriksen thought sourly. He took Blanken's steel flashlight and entered the mine, with the others following. He had to duck slightly as he made his way into the hill for thirty feet before making a sharp turn to the left. The air chilled noticeably, and dripping water spotted his shirt. He turned the corner and saw Harris, the deputy coroner, standing with two ID technicians. Another was snapping pictures. A heavy rubber bag lay unzipped beside the girl.

Harris, a stockily built deputy with a gray crew cut, kept his light on the girl. "She's been strangled, Dan. Maybe raped, too. We'll let the pathologist confirm that." They all had to move out of the photographer's way, then Harris continued. "Hard to say how long she's been dead, maybe just a day or two. The air in here is so cool and damp it kept her well preserved."

Eriksen studied the girl through eyes gray and cold as a winter pond. "What have you found?" he asked.

"Not much. All her clothing is gone. She had pierced ears. Whoever did it apparently took one earring and left the other on her left tit. Weird bastard. Quite a bit of leaves and dirt in her hair, which indicates she was killed elsewhere, maybe just outside, and then dumped in here. The bruises on her arms indicate she was probably tied. But not with rope. Didn't leave a narrow mark. Maybe some of her clothing."

One of the technicians bent and slipped a plastic sandwich bag over each hand. "We'll get some fingernail scrapings," Harris said. The technician then placed a larger plastic bag over the girl's head to hold the debris in her hair. Eriksen thought she looked grotesque, as though she had been suffocated in the bag. The technicians lifted the body into the body bag and zipped it shut. Eriksen made no move to help. Dead bodies disgusted him.

Harris held up a bag with the earring in it. "We won't get any usable prints off this," he growled.

"Goddammit," Eriksen said. "What kind of an asshole would do something like this?"

"Either someone who's crazy or one mean son of a bitch," Harris said.

"Or both," Darby added.

"She's a pretty girl," Eriksen said. "Was."

"Maybe she went out with some dude who thought he was going to get a great piece of ass and when she wouldn't put out, he snuffed her," Darby said.

"It does appear she was raped," Harris volunteered.

"Maybe she brought it on herself," Darby said.

"And maybe she didn't," Eriksen snapped. "No girl, no matter how much of a whore she might be, deserves to be raped and then strangled."

"All right, don't get worked up," Darby said.

"Let's go," Eriksen said shortly. Outside, he told Darby and Blanken to search the area while the technicians finished photographing and measuring. Eriksen approached the two teenagers, who waited, pale and nervous. Watching the body being loaded into the technicians' van had killed their earlier excitement.

Eriksen dug a Camel out of his shirt pocket and wished he had a shot of bourbon to go with it. "What brought you up here?" he said to the boy, and saw the youth's nervousness increase.

"Uh, we just came up to look around," the boy said. "Just fooling around."

Sure, Eriksen thought. You came up here hoping to screw that little X. He unconsciously used the police identification letter for a female. "What took you into the mine?" he pressed.

"Just looking around. I never been in there before," the youth replied.

"Did you find anything that might have belonged to the girl? Any piece of clothing? Jewelry? Anything?" He looked hard at the boy, then at the silent, wide-eyed girl.

The boy said they had found nothing. Eriksen asked if they knew the girl. Both shook their heads, and Eriksen told them they could go.

"Hey, Dan." It was Harris, standing at the edge of the railings that spilled away from the mine entrance. Eriksen walked over. Darby stood below the slope in the oak trees and looked up with a triumphant smile.

"Looks like he did her in down here. Leaves all torn up. Looks like the same stuff that's in her hair. Blanken even found a leaf with come all over it."

"Oh, goody," Eriksen said. He watched as the others scuffed through the oak leaves looking for any other evidence. He was about to join them when he heard a car in low gear grinding up the hill to the mine. Eriksen saw it was Fred Thomas, a reporter from KSM-TV. Thomas was all right, better than most, but his pushiness got on Eriksen's nerves. The reporter came toward him, trailing a cameraman and a sound man. Eriksen waited stolidly.

"We just heard," Thomas said. He was of medium height but with a thick build that made him appear shorter. "What happened?"

"Couple of kids found the body of a girl in that mine."

"She still in there?" Thomas asked hopefully. He had a microphone in his hand and was ready for an interview.

"Nope. She's bagged and in the van and we're about to leave. You're a little late, Fred."

"Can we talk to you about it, on film?"

Eriksen shook his head. "Deputy Blanken here was first on the scene. He can give you the best picture."

Thomas bored in. "The girl was white and probably raped, is that right?"

"We'll let the pathologist determine if she was raped."

"How will this affect Sheriff Conrad's bid for reelection?"

"I wouldn't know," Eriksen said, and turned away. Thomas moved toward Blanken, and Eriksen watched the deputy flush with pleasure at the chance to be interviewed on television.

They combed the area for another twenty minutes but turned up nothing.

"What do you think?" Eriksen asked as they drove back to San Miguel.

"Could be a lovers' quarrel."

"Why would he take the clothes?"

"To hide her identity," Darby said as he unwrapped another stick of gum. "He put her in the cave thinking she would never be found."

"But he left one earring."

"Or just dropped it," Darby countered.

Eriksen watched the fields of ripening grapes roll by for a moment, then said, "I don't like it. Something weird about it, and weird deaths are a pain in the ass. There's no logic to them."

As they pulled into the Sheriff's Department, Eriksen said, "Get the prints off to the FBI and see if they have her on record. Get Dickey-Boy to put a smiling picture of her together from the Identikit, something we can distribute to the papers. I'll start through the files of our known sex offenders for a possible."

They entered by the side door, and Eriksen stopped to give Nancy the cassette with his taped report on it. "Will you give this top priority, please?"

"Every detective in here thinks his report is top priority," she said, and then smiled at him. Eriksen was surprised that her eyes were blue. He didn't associate blue eyes with raven hair. "But for you, I'll do it now," she added.

He headed for his office, and she called after him, "The sheriff wants to see you."

"Now?"

"If not sooner."

Eriksen noticed she had a long, curving upper lip, which he liked in women. Cynthia's lips were fuller, tending to be pouty. He stuck his head in Darby's office.

"After you get the prints off, find out when they're going to do the postmortem. You be the witnessing officer." He knew Darby wouldn't mind that. Darby once bragged he got an A in biology the semester they had to dissect frogs. Eriksen turned and went down the hallway to the front of the building and pushed open the sheriff's door without knocking. Harry Nye was already there.

Conrad waved him to a chair, then leaned back and put his yellow boots on his desk. Eriksen knew they cost eighty dollars a pair.

"Is this going to be a tough one, Dan?" Conrad asked.

Eriksen lit another Camel before answering, and felt the smoke bite deep in his lungs. "I really don't know, Sheriff. It could be. First we've got to get an ID on her."

"When can we expect that?"

"Darby is moving the prints now. And Dicky-Boy is putting together a picture for distribution to the press."

"I'll get copies made of that, and you can give them out at the press conference," Nye said.

"You going to give us someone for the phones?" Eriksen asked Nye.

"I suppose I could give you Slater from burglary. You think we'll get many calls?"

"Well, with only eighteen thousand population, San Miguel isn't exactly a metropolis, but it's got its share of whips, and they'll start claiming they know who did it or that they did it themselves."

"What are you doing now?" Conrad interrupted.

"I'm going to start with some known sex offenders. We'll contact our snitches on the street. But I'll tell you now, Sheriff, there's damn little to go on. It was too rocky in and around the mine to get any footprints, and the road up there is too rocky for tire prints. We got one possible tire track from the dirt where the mine road hits Canyon Road, but both the kids who found the body and Blanken ran over most of it."

"Jesus. We put Blanken at the farthest end of the county where he will do the least harm, and still he fucks things up," Nye said.

"I want to be posted on every move," Conrad said as he pointed a finger at Eriksen for emphasis. "I'm speaking to the DAR ladies tomorrow and I want to reassure them that their own pussies will be safe."

"Half of them probably wish this cocksman would come around," Nye said with a laugh. Eriksen left them.

He started for the files, then picked up the nearest phone and called his wife.

"Cynthia, I'm going to be late again tonight."

"What is it this time?" Her voice was faint. It angered Eriksen that she never spoke directly into the mouthpiece.

"Another murder. A young girl. The sheriff is uptight about it."

"You were going to take Denice to cheerleader practice tonight, remember?"

"I know, honey, but I've got to get right on this one. It's not a nice one. The girl was strangled and raped."

"I don't want to hear about it," Cynthia said. There was a pause; then she said, "I guess I can take Denice."

"I guess you'll have to."

"If you would fix her bike, she could take herself, you know."

"Yeah, I know. Look, I've got to go now. See you later." He hung up before she could protest. Cynthia would light a cigarette and have a cup of coffee while on the telephone with him or anyone else who would listen. Her number-one entertainment, Eriksen thought as he started through the files.

At five P.M. Nancy brought him his copy of the homicide report she had typed. Eriksen heard her murmur something sympathetic as he plowed through the rap sheets. As she walked away, he looked up long enough to notice how nice her legs were.

By eight o'clock, when Darby came in to tell him the FBI print check was negative, Eriksen had three possibles. At the top of the list was Billy Carmichael. He slid the yellow sheet on Billy across the desk to Darby. Billy Carmichael, age thirty-eight, twice convicted for child molesting, twice to see the psychiatrists at Atascadero, twice released on grounds he had recovered.

"Billy is also a troller," Eriksen said, "the kind that likes to go up and down freeway ramps looking for nice young chicks hitchhiking. He likes them young. The younger the better. He was sprung from Atascadero only last month. Let's see if he knows anything about this girl."

They drove through the glowing evening light to the address Carmichael had given both the Atascadero Hospital officials and his parole officer. It was a low, white ranch-style house in a fashionable suburb on the northeast side of San Miguel. Eriksen advised the dispatcher of his location as he wheeled into the driveway.

Repeated ringing of the doorbell, however, brought no response. Eriksen and Darby were about to leave when a slender brunette in her mid-thirties rounded the corner of the house and came toward them. She was wearing jeans and a sweatshirt and carried a trowel in one hand.

"I'm sorry. I was weeding in back and wasn't sure I heard anything or not." She brushed back a lock of hair. "May I help you?"

Eriksen identified himself. "We're looking for Billy Carmichael. Is he here now?"

"Why? Is there something wrong again?" Her eyes swung between the two detectives.

"We just want to talk to him on some routine matters. He gave this as his address," Darby said.

"Yes, I know. I'm his sister. I'm Mrs. Phillip Strong. Anna. Billy just isn't here right now."

"When will he be back?" Eriksen watched her as she nervously tapped the trowel against her leg.

"Well, he comes and goes. I . . . I don't always see him." She smiled nervously.

"Mrs. Strong. It is important that we see Billy immediately. When he is not here, where is he?" There was an unfriendly rasp in Eriksen's voice that made the smile fade from the woman's face.

"Is Billy in trouble again?"

"We just need to talk to him. Now," Eriksen said noncommittally.

She looked at the thick lawn beneath her feet. "Billy has been . . ." Her voice was very low.

"Pardon me?"

She tossed her head back and raised her voice: "I said Billy has been staying with a girlfriend. She has an apartment over on Third and Oak Street." She looked beseechingly at Eriksen. "It's the same girl he was staying with before, the one with the daughter. Carol Gordon. I didn't want him to go back there. I told him not to. But Billy said he was cured and that was all over. But it can't be. He needs more help."

Eriksen was dumbfounded. "You mean he's staying with the same woman who reported him last time? The same one who got him sent away for a year?"

"Yes. I told him not to go back, and he said he was cured. And he said she needed him. They would work it out. But I don't believe it, I don't." He could see the tears gathering in her eyes.

"What's the address?"

"It's above the Oak Street Market. The first apartment on the right at the top of the stairs. You will help him, won't you? He can't help himself."

Eriksen cursed as they drove back into town. "There

is just no explaining people. How does a guy get to be a punk like Carmichael in the first place? And why do the shrinks let him go when he isn't ready? And why in hell would this Gordon broad let him back in?" Eriksen shook his head. "I ought to quit this and spend the rest of my life fishing."

Darby grinned. "You couldn't. Pretty soon you'd see one fish eat another and you would be down there trying to book him."

The Oak Street Market was a two-story building, run by an old couple that eked out a living selling a few basics to the rundown neighborhood. They sold more beer and wine than anything else, Eriksen guessed. A few more bucks were made renting some apartments overhead. Years ago, the top floor had been a large family residence but now it was cut into four small apartments. The twenty-five-watt bulb did little to reveal the stained walls or the torn linoleum on the stairway. Just as well, Eriksen thought. People here might get sick if they could see what they were stepping in. At the top of the stairs, he knocked on the door while Darby stood to one side, ready. There was the sound of footsteps inside, a door closing. Then latches on the apartment door rattled and it opened a few inches to reveal a pair of eyes magnified behind thick glasses in a round face topped with pale, lank hair. "Yeah?" the man said.

Eriksen clicked off the description in his mind: Billy Carmichael, age thirty-eight, five-feet-five, 210 pounds, blue eyes, blond hair. Eriksen held his badge before Carmichael's face and said, "We want to talk to you, Billy."

"What about?" He made no move to open the door farther.

"Can we come in, Billy?"

"What do you want to talk to me about?" Billy's pale eyes watched them.

"About a girl that was murdered. And raped. Now, do you want to talk here or down at my office?" There was an edge in Eriksen's voice.

Billy blinked. "Just a minute." He closed the door,

and Eriksen heard the bolt being thrown shut again. Darby moved up.

"Shall we go in?"

"Give him a minute. Besides, we don't have enough cause to kick his house down."

The door opened again and Billy Carmichael, wearing baggy trousers and a sweaty T-shirt that clung to the rolls of his midsection, waved them into the tiny kitchen. He sat on a metal chair beside the wooden table and pulled another one out with his foot for Eriksen. Darby stood in the doorway.

"I'm clean, Sergeant. I ain't done nothing wrong. They said I was better, and that's why I'm out."

"You were released August 20. Where did you go then?"

"Carol came and got me. Carol Gordon. This is her apartment. She came and got me and we drove back. That's all."

"Drove back in what?"

"My car. I got a Volkswagen. But Carol has been using it since I've been gone." Eriksen stared with slate-gray eyes at the man, who kept wiping his stubby hands on his pants.

"What's this about a girl being murdered?" Carmichael asked. "You don't think I had anything to do with this, do you?" There was fear in his eyes.

"Did you?" Eriksen asked.

"No! Jesus, no. I been here all the time. I tried to get a job, but I ain't had no luck. Ask Carol. I ain't done nothing wrong."

Eriksen lit a cigarette with elaborate care while looking around the kitchen. A stack of washed dishes sat on the drainboard. "Where is Carol?"

"Oh, she had to go out. To get some groceries," Carmichael said. Eriksen blew a thin stream of smoke toward the fat man.

"You still like little girls, Billy?" Eriksen asked.

"Yeah—I mean, no. Not like that anymore. That's all over, Sergeant. I got cured down there. I'm better now. That's why I'm staying here. To prove it."

"How about women's jewelry or clothing, Billy? You

like to keep some women's clothes around just to feel now and then?" Eriksen watched the fat man closely.

"What is this shit, Sergeant? I ain't done nothing wrong. I had nothing to do with any murders." His lower lip wobbled as he talked.

"That's good, Billy. If you have nothing to worry about, you wouldn't mind if we looked around, would you?"

"You got a search warrant?"

"No," Eriksen said, and stubbed out his cigarette. "We don't have one because we felt sure you had nothing to hide from us." Eriksen stood up from the table. "Okay, Billy? Or shall we take you downtown and talk to you while we get a warrant?"

Billy hesitated, then heaved himself up. "All right. You can look around in the living room but not the bedroom. The little girl is in there. Sleeping. And she's been sick, so I don't want her bothered."

Darby was already in the living room, leafing through a stack of magazines on the couch. "Look at this crap, Dan." He held out a well-thumbed magazine that was filled with pictures of nude young girls. They seemed so innocent, laughing and playing on lawns or beside swimming pools. The girls were innocent, but not the magazine. The pictures all stressed the young girls' vaginas.

Billy watched from the kitchen doorway. "They're just magazines about nudist colonies. Nothing wrong with that. No law against having that."

"But who would be interested in pictures of nude young girls not even in their teens, except people like you?" Eriksen threw the magazine on the couch and opened a cracked wardrobe in the corner. It contained a few dresses and shirts on hangers and some bedding. Nothing unusual.

Everybody heard the muffled sob at the same time. Eriksen and Darby looked at each other to confirm they had heard it, trying to place it. Billy edged toward the closed door that led into the only bedroom.

"What's going on in there, Billy-boy?" Darby asked, and moved toward the door. Billy stood in his way.

"It's the girl. I told you she was sick. That's all. You can't go in there. You don't have a search warrant."

Eriksen moved up and shoved Carmichael aside. It was like pressing on a damp marshmallow. He pushed the door open and heard Darby catch his breath behind him. "Son of a bitch."

Spread-eagled on the double bed that almost filled the small room was a girl about twelve years old. Her wrists and ankles were tied to the corner bedposts. She was completely nude. She was a slender, pale girl with reddish hair fanned out on the bedspread; her breasts were just beginning to form. The girl did not look at them as the door opened, but stared unblinking at the ceiling.

"You guys just can't go busting into an apartment like this. You gotta have a search warrant." Billy was whining now.

"Shut your face, Billy, before I put my size-twelve foot down your throat," Eriksen rasped. He turned back and entered the room. The crying came from the far corner, and he had to round the bed before he could see what it was.

In the corner, on the floor, with her face buried in her hands, sat a woman wearing only a yellow slip. Eriksen turned to Darby and pointed at Carmichael, who now stood with his face against the wall.

"Cuff that asshole, and call the juvenile section and get someone over here." He pulled at the ropes holding the girl, but they were double-knotted and would not come loose. He cut the girl free with his pocketknife and wrapped her in the bedspread. Eriksen leaned over and spoke softly.

"It's all right now, honey. I'm from the sheriff's office. We're going to take good care of you."

The girl made no move. She uttered no sound. Her eyes remained locked on the ceiling. In the corner the woman snuffled in her arms.

Eriksen spoke to her. "Get up and put on a dress." When she did not respond, Eriksen repeated his command with heat in his voice. This time she rose, her thin face red and streaked with tears, and went to the closet, where she took a blue knit dress off a hook and slipped it on. She stood in the corner, staring at the floor.

"Are you Carol Gordon?"

She nodded.

"Is this your daughter?" Again she only nodded, and Eriksen felt the disgust churn his stomach.

"Why in hell was she tied up like this?" he snarled. "How can you, her mother, stand by and let it happen? What have you and Billy been doing to her?" Eriksen felt like grabbing her by the throat and pitching her down a flight of stairs. "How can you stand by and watch this with your own daughter?" he repeated.

Her voice came out muffled, as if she could not fully open her mouth. Eriksen saw she was biting down hard on her knuckles. "He made me let him do it. I didn't want to, but he said he would leave me and never come back again. And he promised not to hurt Melissa. Not hurt her."

Eriksen felt himself turning cold. "Not hurt her? What the hell do you call this?"

"Well, he didn't . . . you know. He just made her play with him. You know, in her mouth. I didn't like it, believe me, but I don't have nobody but Billy. I never did. He's the only one that's been good to me. And he never really hurt Melissa. Just played with her. And just sometimes he would tie her up like this, but not too tight. He only did it when he said I couldn't give him enough pleasure, you know."

Eriksen handcuffed her and sat her on the couch. He and Darby were going through the drawers and closets when Sheila Fenwick, the juvenile officer, rang the doorbell. She looked like she was just out of high school.

"What have you got?" No nonsense from Sheila.

"Oral copulation," Eriksen said. Sheila made a face. "The girl is in there on the bed. I put some clothes out for her. I don't think she has been raped, but she needs to go to a hospital first for a complete exam. And she's in shock."

The doorbell rang again. It was a San Miguel police officer who had been advised of the developments.

Eriksen identified himself. "We came to talk to Carmichael in connection with that 187 we had today. We found this. We're on your turf but we need to keep him."

"Take both of them and shove them in a toilet as far as I'm concerned," the officer said. "You're the deputies and you got jurisdiction in town too. If you guys are going to handle it, take it all. I'll be seeing you." With that he left.

While Sheila dressed the still-silent girl and prepared to take her to the hospital, Eriksen and Darby went through the drawers and closets. There were two drawers of women's underclothing; all the clothing seemed to belong to the girl and her mother. Eriksen turned to Darby.

"We'll have ID come down and pick everything up and really go into it. But let's take him in first. Read him his rights."

Darby pulled a worn card from his shirt pocket and rapidly read through it: "You are hereby advised of your right to remain silent, and you do not have to say anything unless you choose to do so. Do you understand? Answer yes or no."

Billy stared at him. "What's this about?"

"Do you understand? Yes or no."

"Yes, but . . ."

"Anything you say may be used against you in a court of law. Do you understand?"

"Yes." Billy Carmichael was breathing heavily and staring at the floor. His glasses glittered beneath the overhead light.

"You have the right to have an attorney present with you during any questioning now or in the future. Do you understand?"

Eriksen, listening to Darby's monotone, found his mind drifting away. Goddamn child molesters, he thought. Worst creeps on the face of the earth. The trouble is, there are millions we don't even know about. Fathers or uncles or cousins or boyfriends who do unspeakable things to defenseless little girls. Or boys. And the mothers let the creeps do it because they are just as sick or they don't want to offend their man. We book them and a few days later they're out on bail doing the same thing. Then it's weeks before they go on trial. Delay, delay, delay by the defense. Delay by the judges. Then maybe they get sent to some overcrowded mental hospital, like Billy did, and pretty soon they're back molesting children again.

Darby finished and pulled Carmichael to his feet.

"Away we go, hero. You too, Mrs. Gordon."

"What are you booking us for?" Carmichael asked plaintively.

"Child molesting, for openers," Darby said.

Eriksen moved close to Billy, and he could smell the man's fear running from every pore. Time to lean on him a little. He blew a stream of the blue Camel smoke into Billy's face, making him close his eyes. "Billy," he said softly, "we found a girl murdered today. Strangled. And she had been raped. Why, Billy?"

Carmichael's round little eyes bugged behind his thick glasses. "Jesus, Sergeant. I never murdered no girl. Never! I been here all day. Ask Carol. We ain't even left here for the past three days."

Eriksen winced inwardly at the thought of the girl being tied to the bed with this creep hanging around her for three days.

"Billy, you know we're going to put you away for life for this. In the slammer, too, not in the nice clean wards at Atascadero. You're going back to the big house with all those mean cons in there. And you know what they think of child molesters, don't you, Billy?" He watched as Billy's chin began to tremble uncontrollably.

"You know what they do to your type, don't you? You're going to get raped yourself. Butt-fucked, Billy, butt-fucked until you fucking bleed to death!" Spittle ran down Billy's chin and he began to cry.

"Now, I want to know why you killed that girl yesterday. Who is she and where did you meet her?" Eriksen's voice was hard and raspy.

Billy sank down to the couch; his head bowed, and his body shook with spasms of weeping. "I don't want to go back. I don't want to. They'll kill me. They will! They'll kill me."

Eriksen put one finger to Billy's forehead and pushed it back until he could see the fat man's face. "The girl, Billy. Why did you do it?"

"I didn't. I didn't, I don't know anything about that. Please, don't send me back. I won't come back alive. I'd rather kill myself."

Eriksen looked at him in disgust, then ground the cigarette out on the floor. He turned and saw the juvenile officer in the other room watching him. Her eyes were wide and her face was very pale.

"Let's take them in," he said to Darby. "We'll book them and continue this conversation in the morning."

It was eleven before he finished taping his report. He put the cassette on Nancy's desk and turned out the lights. His stomach felt nauseous from the hours of coffee and cigarettes. He wanted badly to pour himself a slug of Jack Daniels and sink into his easy chair. As he drove home he wondered if Cynthia would be awake. And sober.

She was waiting up for him, sitting at the end of the couch she had just had covered in a green floral print. He detested it.

"Have a bad night, dear?" she asked. He nodded and glanced at her. She was drinking something, probably brandy, but she looked all right, he decided. He went into the kitchen and poured himself three fingers of Jack Daniels in the bottom of a short glass, dropped in two cubes of ice so cold they stuck to his fingers, and splashed a little water on top.

"Do you want any dinner?" she asked as he sagged into his easy chair.

"I don't think so. I'm going to read over a couple reports and then go to bed."

"It must have been awful. I saw her picture on the TV tonight. And they had some film of you walking around. You looked very good. Just like you knew what you were doing."

He gave her a quick glance, but she looked innocent enough. Her hair, which had been so cheerfully red when she was younger, was now auburn but still shone in the light. Her face and neck were still slender and helped divert attention from the weight she had gained around the bust and hips. She was still a good-looking woman, Eriksen thought. He drained his drink and stood up.

"I'm going to look over those reports in the morning. You coming to bed now?" he asked.

"Later, I think," she said, and swirled her brandy.

He turned and went upstairs, suddenly exhausted.

3

His face felt stiff in the morning, as if he had gone to bed half-drunk, but Eriksen knew he was just tired. There was no reason to be; he was only forty-two, and had years of good work ahead of him. That thought depressed him slightly and he went outside to get the paper. Spider, their deaf Airedale, lay beside it on the grass. Eriksen walked over and touched the shaggy dog with his toe. Spider jumped, then pushed his gray muzzle into Eriksen's hand.

"Ol' dog," he said affectionately. "Can't hear anymore but can still hunt a little. Maybe we'll get out for some pheasant before too long, or at least to the coast." The dog watched his face with alert hazel eyes and Eriksen wondered if he could teach him to lip-read. Spider could learn sign language, anyway. Eriksen bent and gave the dog the finger.

"Learn that one and give it to your friends."

He walked back inside, reading the story of the girl's death. The paper played it big on page one, but it was pretty much what the sheriff had released. There was nothing about finding the earring. That would be useful to weed out any kooks who wanted to admit to it, or to pin it on the actual killer. The story emphasized the sheriff's inability to identify the girl. And such a story was going to stir up the community, Eriksen knew.

He poured himself a cup of coffee, enjoying the silence of the house. Cynthia and Denice were not up yet, but they would be before long. He sat at the table and dug the autopsy report out of his briefcase. He had not had time to read it yesterday. As he began, he could see the small white room with the doctor bending over the body on the stainless-steel table and talking into a small microphone pinned to his smock while he made swift openings with his scalpel.

The terse report called her Doe, Jane, 5′7″, 120 pounds.

> *1. Disease or condition directly leading to death: asphyxia due to strangulation.*
>
> *2. Homicide: place of injury unknown.*
>
> *3. How did injury occur: attacked by unknown assailant.*
>
> *4. Pathological diagnoses: a. Superficial abrasion and contusion anterior neck and hemorrhage in right stylohyoid muscle, thyroid gland, on thyroid cartilage, and behind left horn of hyoid, consistent with manual strangulation. b. Mucosal denudations in vagina consistent with aggressive sexual penetration. c. Perimortal abrasions, contusions and lacerations, head, trunk, and extremities.*

The report added that her ears had been pierced and she had been wearing light makeup. Eriksen sighed; just another unidentified female who had been raped and murdered. There were dozens of them across the country, maybe a dozen every week, and many of them would never be solved.

He was about to get more coffee when Cynthia appeared in a housecoat, with her hair loose. She lit herself a cigarette and then brought the coffeepot to him.

"Can you drop Denice off at school on your way this morning?" she asked.

"What happened to her bus?" It would mean going out of his way.

"She wants to go early today for some practice session with the other cheerleaders."

Denice burst into the room. "Yeah, Daddy. We're going to be the best cheerleaders ever, even if we are only for the freshman team." She banged down into the chair next to him in a rush of clean smells and flying blond hair. Fourteen years old, a freshman in high school, and a cheerleader. She had the world by the tail.

"Hey, Daddy. You looked great on TV last night. You were heavy."

"I'm puttin' on weight but it's not that noticeable, I hope."

"Oh, you know. Heavy, man, heavy. Tough, far-out." She laughed at him with her clear blue eyes, Nordic eyes she had inherited from him. "That means neat, in your old-fashioned language. Did you really say things like 'neat' when you were in high school? Only dumb kids say that now." She attacked the bowl of cereal Cynthia set before her.

"Who killed that girl?" she asked.

"I wish I knew. Why don't you ask your friends and find out for me?" he said with amused sarcasm.

"All right, I will. You'd be so embarrassed if I found him before you did. They would make you turn in your badge. And probably hire me." There were times when her total self-confidence galled him.

"Do that," Eriksen said. "I'll retire; then you can support me and pay for all the new shoes and dresses."

"I don't think a new dress would help you, Daddy." She jumped up from the table and headed upstairs to get her coat. Eriksen watched her go, noting she already had the same well-developed body as her mother, bosomy and curvy in all the right places. And she would probably be fighting to hold that figure at forty, like her mother was right now.

As he prepared to leave, Cynthia gave him a light kiss on the cheek. "Try and get home early tonight."

"I doubt that," he said. "I'll almost certainly be working late until we get a good lead on this."

"And then there will be another murder, won't there? Finish one and start another. Then stay late again."

"It's the name of the game," he said.

"I suppose," she said, and gazed out the window. "But what about me?"

"What?" Eriksen said. He was trying to finish the paper.

"Nothing." She turned and yelled up the stairs. "Denice! Get going or you'll be late again."

As they drove toward school, Denice chattered about practice and the first game of the season. "You will come, won't you, Dad? There's five of us, but Cheri and I are the best. And there's this really good-looking guy. He's a linebacker, and Cheri says he might ask me out pretty soon."

He listened with only half an ear until they arrived. "Tell Mom I'm going to Cheri Donnato's after school for more practice," Denice said, and then she was running in leggy strides toward the school.

When he arrived at work, Darby broke off his conversation with Nancy and followed him into his office. "We got some feedback from the Criminal Intelligence Bureau in Sacramento. I wanted to see if this MO fit anybody they had a hot lead on. But it was negative."

Eriksen hung up his jacket, loosened his tie, and lit a cigarette. "What the hell do I wear a tie for?" he asked Darby. "Look at you. Wrinkle-proof knit leisure suit and a gold shirt. Why don't I wear that?"

"Because you're our leader. And you're too square."

"Yeah? You just be careful some fag doesn't give you a little kiss and tell you, 'Oh, I just love that gold shirt on you, you savage, you.' "

Darby was still thinking of a reply as Eriksen turned to business. "What have you got this morning?"

"I've got court. A prelim hearing on that Richardson case. The hit-and-run."

"All right. And Carmichael will probably be arraigned sometime today. You better handle that one too."

Darby frowned. "How about you do that and I'll start nosing around on the girl?"

Eriksen ignored the request. "What about that dirty biker we found with the pomegranate head?"

"Yeah, Flint. The way it looks now, he and the other bikers took their old ladies to the Boar's Nest for amateur strip night. The chicks get ten bucks for a turn on the bar. He was apparently trying to take the money from some of the ladies when the others decided they were tired of him and took some chains to his head. That whole gang is now up in Oregon. I've advised the Oregon state police of that."

"So, we're stymied on that for the moment. Okay, you handle the court scenes today and I'll see what else we can come up with on the girl." Darby was about to protest again when Eriksen's phone buzzed.

Nancy's voice was in his ear: "A Mr. Cahill insists on talking to you." He could see her from his desk, swiveled toward him. Considerable leg showed beneath her black pleated skirt.

"Just what I need," he growled. "Put him on." He was looking at her eyes and found it strangely intimate to be looking at her from a distance while talking in her ear and listening to her breathe.

There was a click and a querulous voice asked: "This is Detective Erskine, ain't it?"

"Eriksen," he said shortly. The old geezer always had him confused with the television FBI hero. "What can I do for you, Mr. Cahill?" He didn't really need to ask. Cahill called him periodically with breathy tips on how to solve the latest crime.

"I've had a dickens of a time getting through to you, boy. Seems like every person these days is so important they's got to have themselves a *seckatary*. Now, it's very important that I get through to you, Erskine, because I got some information you'll be wantin' pretty bad."

"What's that, Mr. Cahill?" He got out another cigarette. It wasn't easy to cut the old man off.

"Well, m'boy, I know something about the murder of that gal the other day. The one that's been in all the papers and the TV." He pronounced it *tee*-vee.

"What can you tell me, Mr. Cahill?" He started sorting papers on his desk as he talked. He jotted down Cahill's name with the date and time. Just for the record.

"Well, I can't be giving out information like this over the phone. I'm probably tapped, you know." He paused. "I mean my phone's tapped. Not me." He cleared his throat loudly into the phone, and Eriksen winced. "Now, tell you what, Erskine, I'll meet you down at the coffee shop near my place and I'll spill the beans there." He cackled at his joke. "Not really."

"I'm pretty busy, Mr. Cahill. Tell me what you know, now."

"Can't do it. They'd get me for sure." His voice dropped to a hoarse whisper.

"Why don't you come on down here, then? We'll give you good protection."

"Well . . ." The thin voice sighed. "I'll try, because you are going to need this information."

"Right. Thanks, Mr. Cahill." He hung up before the old man could start up again. Cahill believed he knew something about every murder in the county, but Eriksen realized he was just a thin old man living alone on the edge of town, trying to make contact with the outside world, trying to keep what was left of his sanity. Maybe that's what we're all trying to do, Eriksen thought, just hoping somebody out there will listen to us. He found himself looking at Nancy Hall's legs again; she seemed to be moving them a lot. He got up and shut his door. He had to think about something other than those legs. He rubbed his lined, weathered face. Things were going to get worse. The phone rang again.

"Eriksen . . . hello?" he answered, then held the phone closer to his ear and listened. There had been the soft sound of a woman's voice, then nothing. "Hello?" he repeated, and then heard a throat being cleared on the other end.

"Yes, This is Mrs. Thomas. Mrs. Robert Thomas. Whom am I talking to, please?"

"This is Sergeant Eriksen, Homicide."

"Oh." There was a pause.

Eriksen was becoming impatient. "May I help you?"

"I'm calling about my daughter." Eriksen was now alert. "I saw a picture in the paper this morning that looked like her. But I'm not sure. It was just a drawing."

"Where is your daughter . . . I mean, when you last saw her?" Eriksen asked.

"She has been staying in a commune near Hampton. I called there this morning . . ." She started to cry. ". . . and they haven't seen her. She should have been there yesterday."

Eriksen took the number and the location of the commune. Could Mrs. Thomas come by and see if she could identify the body? Yes. Today? Yes, she would come as soon as she contacted her husband. They would be up there from the City, in an hour.

Eriksen met them when they arrived, somber, middle-class working people who were shaken at the prospect of confirming their fears. There was little conversation as Eriksen drove them to the mortuary. Identification took only a few minutes: the refrigerated box being slid out on silent rollers, the sheet pulled back, then the terrible twisting of the father's mouth and the sobs of the mother. Eriksen drove them back to his office, got them some coffee, and took all the details on their only child.

Mrs. Thomas stared at Eriksen and finally said, "Who . . . would do something like that? Roberta had no enemies. She was a very loving, gentle girl. Who would do that?"

Eriksen met her bitter eyes. "We haven't any clues right now. We're talking to restaurant people along the way to see if they had seen her; we're checking out known rapists and child molesters; I will go to the commune today. We'll check all past boyfriends. It's a matter of putting together a puzzle, Mrs. Thomas."

She looked at him with a mixture of hope and disbelief, and then the two left as silently as they had come.

It was noon, but Eriksen didn't stop to eat as he drove north to Hampton and the commune. It took him a while to find the old and rundown farm tucked into a narrow canyon shaded by large oaks. When he pulled into the yard he saw a bearded young man, shirtless, and a long-haired young woman, also shirtless, brushing a cow. Assorted dogs played in the packed dirt of the front yard. No one looked up as he got out of his car. He saw another youth in the field, resting on a hoe and watching him. As he walked toward the pair brushing the cow he ran his eye over the small frame house with sagging porch and saw another person watching from what appeared to be the kitchen window. He couldn't tell if it was male or female, only that it had long hair. He stopped a few feet from the cow. The girl was on the other side and he couldn't get a good look at her knockers. He thought of angling around that way more but decided that would be too obvious. For Chrissake, get on with it, he told himself.

"My name is Eriksen, from the sheriff's office." He flipped open his wallet and showed the blue-and-gold badge. Neither of the two looked at him but the cow rolled its eyes and blew loudly through its nose. "I'm here to talk about Roberta Ann Thomas," Eriksen said.

No reaction. He walked closer, took a long look at the topless girl, and decided she alone was worth the whole trip.

The cow began backing away and the gangly young man who towered over Eriksen turned and spoke: "Your presence is disturbing our karma." The youth had a frizzy blond afro, matching beard, and round spectacles perched on a beak of a nose. When he talked he kept his head tilted back and peered down at Eriksen like a wrathful minister addressing a ten-year-old boy who had spit on the church floor. Eriksen considered busting him one on his beak but instead entwined his thick fingers in front of his stomach and flexed them. There was an audible ripple of popping knuckles.

"Roberta Thomas, who has been living here, was found murdered yesterday. Now—"

"Yes, we know that. We saw her picture on television."

Eriksen felt anger growing in him. "Why didn't you call and identify her for us?"

"You represent death and violence, and we wish to live in peace and tranquillity here. We want no intrusions."

"Wonderful. But someone intruded on Roberta's serenity and I'm investigating that. Now, we can all talk here, like ladies and gentlemen, or we can go back to my office in San Miguel, where I guarantee you will find no serenity."

The youth, who reluctantly identified himself as Henry Pearson, spoke disdainfully of Roberta. "We really didn't know her well. She wasn't a regular member of the commune. Like, she wasn't truly in search of the Way. She often went home to her parents on weekends."

"Did she have a car, or use one of yours?"

"We allow no machinery in here. She always hitchhiked."

"Where were you yesterday and the night before?"

Pearson appeared indignant that he or any others should be considered suspect. Tiring of the games, Eriksen ordered all of them onto the porch of the house and questioned each one individually. He was disappointed when the girl who had been brushing the cow put on a shirt before speaking to him. The whole thing was a disappointment. All of them had spent the past three days and nights at a neighbor's ranch loading bales of hay. Eriksen knew, even before stopping there, enroute home, to confirm their stories, that it would check out. It was after five when he arrived in San Miguel. He considered stopping at a bar for a bourbon or two but decided he had better talk to Billy Carmichael again.

A note on his desk instructed him to see the sheriff as soon as he got back. Conrad, who usually left at five sharp, was still at his desk.

"You get anything up north?" he asked.

"It looks like a washout."

"Nye sent Slater down to the City and he saw five young men who used to date the girl. All of them had tight alibis. So you know what I think?" Conrad lit a cigar and leaned back.

"I think," he continued, "that Billy boy next door is looking better and better. He says he was in the apartment all the time, but his old lady told Darby today that he went out every evening for several hours. She thought he went to a bar but wasn't sure which one."

"So we'll have to check that out." Eriksen had a sudden thought. "Did Carmichael make bail today? Is he out again?"

"No. The judge ordered him held for a thirty-day psychiatric evaluation."

"All right. That gives us time to work on him."

"Work hard on him, Dan. He's a prime suspect. I'd love to hang his ass."

"So would I, if he did it."

"That's the idea," Conrad said as he rose to leave. "Just get me a little evidence to show he did it. That'll stop the jitters in this town. People are nervous, you know. The DAR jumped all over my ass today, and I don't like that. I told them we'd have this wrapped up immediately. So get with it, son."

At the county jail behind the sheriff's department he checked his .357 and two speed-loaders with the duty sergeant, then rode the elevator to the second floor. The jailer led him through a series of barred doors and then down the corridor of cells. Inmates in blue denim trousers and white T-shirts lolled on their beds or stared lethargically at him. Two men in adjoining cells were playing chess with their faces pressed against the bars as they strained to see the pieces on the board. Several radios blared soul music.

"I hope they get this jerk out of here before long," the jailer said. "The word is out on him already. He got punched around a little yesterday by his cellmate, so we've got him in a cell by himself. But that makes the others more crowded. If we let him exercise with the others, he'd probably get snuffed."

Eriksen found Carmichael lying on his bunk, his face to the wall. He could hear the fat man-boy snuffling. He refused to acknowledge Eriksen until the detective snarled, "Goddammit, Billy, get over here. I want to talk to you."

Billy removed his thick glasses and wiped them on his sweaty T-shirt, then shuffled over to the cell door. He stood back about two feet, staring at the floor.

Eriksen came to the point: "What about that girl you raped and killed yesterday, Billy? You going to tell me a little about it now? Let's go down to the interrogation room, have a few smokes, and get it all down on tape."

Billy shook his head in slow and steady swinging motions. He looked like a grandfather clock. "I'm sick. I need help. You gotta help me. They're gonna get me, they're all gonna get me if you leave me in here." Eriksen could see the tears running down his pallid cheeks.

"You tell me about that girl and we'll get you out of here, Billy."

Billy raised red-rimmed eyes that swam behind his thick lenses. "I didn't kill no girl. I didn't rape and kill that girl. No shit, Sergeant."

"All right, Billy, will you agree to take a polygraph test on that?"

"A what?"

"A lie-detector test. If you're innocent, you'll pass it. That will help you." Eriksen already had his doubts about Billy. The scumbag wasn't man enough to rape a girl who would fight back in the slightest. He had to have them all tied down. A polygraph would help settle the matter.

"Yeah, yeah, I'll do it. That'll prove I didn't kill that girl. And then will you get me out of here?" He stepped forward and took hold of the bars. His moist fingers touched Eriksen's, and the detective backed away, wiping his hand on his pants.

"All right, I'll be up to get you tomorrow."

"No! Tonight! Now!" Billy's voice filled with fear again. "They're going to get me tonight. They told me so. They said . . . they said they were going to rape me. Please, get me out of here now!"

"Tomorrow, Billy," Eriksen said, and walked away. He heard the man-boy yelling, "Now! Now!" and then begin crying.

He arrived home in time to hear Walter Cronkite tell everyone that's the way it is. He poured himself a Jack Daniels and sat down to watch the local news. Fred Thomas led the show with a roundup on the death of Roberta Thomas and an interview with Sheriff Conrad, who spoke in reassuring tones.

"Just because some leads have led us to a dead end does not mean that we have drawn a blank on this case," Conrad said while staring right into the camera. "My top detectives are working round the clock on this case, and if I can, I'll assign even more men to help them. But I want to stress that I do not believe that this killing was done by someone in our community. You must remember that the girl was not from around here. She did not know anybody here. I think the evidence will show that she was either killed by someone she knew in the City, or she may have been picked up while hitchhiking and killed by someone mentally disturbed. Someone just passing through."

Eriksen eyed the silver-haired sheriff over the rim of his glass. Horseshit, he thought. It was no accident that the girl was killed and dumped at the Turpin mine. The road up there was not marked or well-known. Only someone familiar with the area would go there. Whoever it was, was still around. He listened carefully when Thomas raised a question on Billy Carmichael.

"I can only say we are considering every possibility, and Mr. Carmichael still remains a possibility. I can't go beyond that. But I want to add that there is no need for alarm in our good community. The San Miguel Police Department is working closely with us, and I'm sure we'll soon end this matter."

"Oh, goody!" Eriksen said aloud.

I sat in the living room near my mother and tried to listen to what the sheriff was saying, but it was difficult. His voice alternately rushed at me and then receded, waves of sound. Did they really know something and weren't telling? That's what the police did. They always pretended they didn't have any leads and then all of a sudden they knocked on your door and took you away.

The voices rose around my ears again and it took me a moment to realize it was my mother speaking.

"Don't put your hands up to your ears when I'm talking to you. Do you hear me?" Her eyes glistened wetly as she stared at me.

"What?"

"I said I was surprised they had been able to identify that girl so quickly."

I stared at the television. "You mean Roberta? They know who she is now?"

"That was her name. I didn't think you were listening. Roberta Thomas, or something like that."

"I missed part of it. Did they say who killed her?"

"They don't know. The sheriff thinks maybe she was hitchhiking and some psycho picked her up."

"Well, girls shouldn't be out on the streets like that anyway. She wasn't very old, was she? Why didn't she stay home with her parents? What was she looking for? She was out where she could be picked up like a . . ." I broke off.

"Like a what, Sonny?" Mother said dangerously.

"Nothing."

"Like a what, I asked."

"I don't want to talk about it anymore!" I shouted, and stood up.

Mother shifted moods instantly. "Oh, Sonny, don't always become so angry. Come here and give me a kiss. I feel so blue tonight."

I turned away and watched some new figures appear on the screen, but Mother insisted. "Come on, Sonny, give Mother a kiss. Kiss and make up and never argue again." I sat next to her on the couch and gave her a peck on the cheek. Her skin was cool and I could feel on my lips the downy hairs that grew there. Even as I touched her she stiffened and withdrew from me.

"Isn't he a nice-looking man?" she said.

"What?"

"See? There's the detective who is trying to find the killer."

The camera showed a man walking with head bent, obviously looking for something. Slowly the man grew larger on the screen until there was only the face, which was flat and lined like a slab of cedar. His narrow eyes kept moving, searching for something. I felt cold. Don't find me! Find the voice. That's who did it. Find the lioness, she's the real evil. No, no, you've found her, you should know she was evil. Don't look for me. It's not me that is wrong! So don't be spying on me.

"Sonny! Sit up. For God's sake, you're practically falling off the couch." Her voice boomed, as if she were speaking from inside a steel drum. "If you're not going to look for a job tomorrow, I want you to butcher a lamb for us. We're almost out of meat again." Exhausted, I only nodded.

In the morning I crossed through the dark and silent house and walked to the sheep pens behind the barn. The air was warm and heavy. Brown air lay upon the toasted coastal hills and there was no breeze to carry away the smog. The sheep were in the far pasture and I was sweating by the time I reached them. I got behind them and slowly drove them toward the corrals at the barn. They went reluctantly, some trying to ignore me while they grazed, and some running heavily to one side to escape. Why? Did I smell of death? Angry and frustrated when I got them into the corral, I quickly singled out a lamb and set to work to catch her. She knew she was the target and cowered behind the other sheep, backing deep into a corner while I closed in on her. Then at the last moment she would dart across the corral and almost disappear in the cloud of dust being stirred by all those quick cloven hooves.

Finally she stayed too long in one corner. I made a feint to one side, and when she darted the other way I sank my hands deep into her woolly coat and threw her on her side. The lamb bleated in terror and her eyes rolled while I tied a piece of rope around her neck. Dragging the condemned beast, I went to the gate and freed the other sheep. The lamb bolted after them but I brought her up short with the rope. Fighting me all the way to the barn, she kept her head down and forelegs braced. Once inside, I turned and grabbed the woolly beast about the body. I felt the heat waves of fear pulsate from her, and her smell was cloying, like an unclean woman. She cried aloud, a sudden bleat that echoed in the barn, but I clamped one hand around her neck and cut the cry short. The creature struggled beneath me, but I felt my strength grow until it reached enormous proportions. This lamb was now completely at my mercy, and I knew what I had to do. Both hands tightened about the animal's thin neck.

She lay still for a second, then bucked violently. As I tightened my grip, the lamb's eyeballs began to swell from their sockets. Her mouth opened and her tongue protruded. She was going, she was going, she was going, and I felt my strength rise to a climax as the animal surged beneath me. The animal was lifeless in my hands, but still my head roared. There was no release for me. This was no answer. The lamb was no lioness. I giggled at the comparison. A lioness in sheep's clothing? Or could it be a sheep in lioness's clothing? No, only the women were the deceivers. And receivers. Men-receivers. With my mind circling these new words, I quickly skinned and gutted the lamb, then hung it in the root cellar to cool. In the silence of the cellar I could hear the electrical current in my body. The transformer in my head hummed smoothly, pumping alternating current to electrodes at my fingertips. The sensation was exhilarating. I returned to the house, and changed and showered. It was nearly two P.M. now. Where had time gone? If you didn't watch every second, all the seconds would run away. I would run with them.

The house was silent when I left. Mother would not be up for several more hours. I was too charged to sit still, so I drove away in my VW. I really had no idea where to go, just somewhere away from the house, from my thoughts. But how can you run from thoughts? They follow everywhere, always listening. It's those thoughts that eat away at a brain.

At the stoplight the man in the next car turned and smiled and said distinctly, "Lioness." I leaned out the car to hear him better, but he gave me a weird look and hurried on. "The lioness is still out there," said a voice. I try so hard to hear exactly where the voice comes from, but it's on the wind, or riding currents from my brain.

"All right, all right," I shouted. But I didn't really understand. I drove aimlessly for another hour, listening, but there was nothing more from inner space. Still disconcerted, I found myself parked in front of Helen's house. As I walked slowly across their Pacific

Ocean of a lawn, with my hands thrust deep into my pockets, I told myself Helen would help me. Mrs. Marshall answered the door.

"Helen is quite busy now, getting ready to go out. Perhaps you could come by another time?" she said, and arched her brows.

"Who is it, Mom?" Helen yelled from the stairs.

Her mother gave me a disgusted look and turned away. "Sonny."

"Hi, stranger," Helen said as she came out on the porch. I never went in the house. "What have you been up to lately?"

"Nothing much," I said. "I just came by to see how you're doing." I heard a voice laughing somewhere in the distance.

"I've got a job, Sonny," she said excitedly. "At the Blarney Stone restaurant."

I knew the place. It was a popular truck stop just off the freeway north of San Miguel. "What are you doing, cashier or something?"

Helen looked slightly crestfallen. "No, just a waitress." Then she brightened again. "But I meet lots of people. Lots of truckers. I've only been there one night, and already six guys have asked me out. Can you believe it?"

"Why would they want to go out with you?" I asked.

"And what is that supposed to mean?" she said, and gave me a hard stare.

"Well, I mean, they don't even know you. Why do you think they want to ask you out?" A synapse clicked along my spinal column and pushed me on. "Just for your conversation?"

She was silent for a moment, then said, "I've got to be going to work." She pointedly waited for me to leave.

"Look, I didn't mean to make you mad. I'm just trying to tell you that there are some pretty rough guys that go in there. They ask you out because they want to screw—"

"Sonny!" I couldn't tell if she was horrified or just angry. "I don't want to hear that kind of talk."

"It's the truth," I shouted.

"What's the matter with you? You act like you've been drinking or popping some pills. What's with you?"

"Nothing. I'm just looking out for your best interests."

"I can look out for myself. So if you're finished, I've got to be going now." With that she flounced into the house.

I drove away with the anger churning inside me. We didn't even really talk. She didn't give me a chance to ask her to go with me. She could have come with me right now, but she didn't want to. Instead of saying so openly, she chose to deceive me. Bitch. So who's whispering in her ear? The lioness, the gray lioness? She could be anywhere now.

In the early evening I went to a movie by myself. I don't recall what I saw. My mind continued to overcharge, and I couldn't stop wondering why Helen turned against me today. No reason! She just turned catty. It must be the lioness. She's around again, prowling for men. Evil bitch! She's got to be stopped once and for all. People around me began whispering and giggling during the movie, and I knew they were talking about me. Probably because they were with friends and I was alone. Groups always like to confirm the outsider.

It was just dark when I came out of the theater and stood there on the sidewalk, confused with reality. Laughing people, young girls with long hair and beads wearing faded Levi's jostled about me, and I saw some of them looking back with smiles. Maybe Helen had told them she had turned me down tonight and to look for a skinny guy with strange eyes all by himself at the movie. I moved carefully down the street toward the next block to my car. I could feel the connections clicking in my body, the tiny pops of a synapse as the nerve impulse leaped between neurons. It was like I had been plugged into the wall. I had to be careful that I didn't electrocute someone just by touching them with my wired fingers. At the street corner, where a group from the movie was waiting for the light, I saw a girl with hair that crackled with electricity. I could hear it. The light changed and the group moved like a centipede, with me caught among the legs. I found myself next to the girl with the charged hair. She turned and bumped me, sending a current through me. I must have jumped and cried out, for she turned to face me with an apologetic smile and said, "I'm sorry."

I smiled back my very engaging smile, and I could see her eyes waver on mine, confused but fascinated by the second pupil in my right eye. "It's all right," I said, "I feel flameproof tonight."

"What?" She laughed.

"Your hair is electrically charged and the sparks fell upon my soul, but I didn't burn. Just singed a little."

"Wow. That's a new line." She turned to the girl beside her and they burst into giggles.

"But it's true," I persisted, moving closer. "You have been trailing a hot current for a block now. I had to be very careful where I stepped." Even as I spoke, I knew it was wrong. She would not understand. She turned toward me again, and her smile was gone.

"That's right. You better watch your step." Her friends, who listened to the exchange, laughed and bunched tighter around her, like yak bulls forming a ring around threatened cows. I slowed down and watched the herd move farther away.

I had passed my car while talking to her, and now I retraced my steps, still wondering where to look for the lioness. It couldn't have been that girl; she was not cunning and enticing. The gray lioness was still out there in the night, waiting for me. She was too well hidden tonight. I drove home, still angry, and fell into bed exhausted by the fruitless search.

4

It was nearly eleven in the morning when Eriksen arrived at the office. His head felt like someone had drop-kicked it last night. Feeling mean enough to kick a kid, he opened his cubicle office and then went down the hallway to the coffee machine and punched in his thirty cents. That made him even angrier.

"Goddamn ripoff. Can't even be happy with a quarter, but now they gotta bleed me to death. And make me come up with two coins," he muttered. He took another aspirin from the small bottle in his jacket pocket and tromped back to his office. He had sat drinking and thinking too long last night. Neither one is good for a head, he thought.

He shuffled papers on his desk for fifteen minutes and decided he'd better pull himself together, when Nancy appeared with another mug of steaming coffee.

"Here. This is fresh from the percolator. Why did you go down and buy your coffee? And why do you look like an ogre?"

"Because I am one. Every time I have to go to court I wish I could turn into King Kong and stomp every courtroom into matchsticks." He sipped at the fresh coffee and swore as he burned his tongue. "Why do I do such work?"

"What's the matter?" Nancy asked, leaning against the doorjamb with her arms crossed beneath delicately rounded breasts.

"I had to go to a hearing this morning to testify in that Wilkes case. Did I testify? Did I help send that punk to the slammer for fifteen years? No, because that goddamn judge didn't show up. We sat around there for nearly two hours before his secretary bothered to call and tell us his honor was tied up and couldn't make it. Justice. If people in this country really knew how justice worked, there'd be a revolution."

"Maybe they do know and just don't care," she replied.

"The judge was probably planning a luncheon date with the prosecutor so they could sit around and decide how to settle the case. And it's not only them; defense lawyers are just as bad. They drag out cases forever. They're not interested in what's right; they just want to earn bigger and bigger fees. In court they spend days and weeks trying to tear down a decision we only had seconds to make. We have to make instant decisions in the field under great strain. Then the lawyers sit around with the books and try to undo it all. They deal with theory; we deal with reality." Eriksen broke off abruptly and grimaced over his coffee again. He felt slightly embarrassed at his outburst and glanced up at Nancy, who watched him with wide eyes.

"Have you had enough of my preaching?" he asked.

"I don't mind. It's good for you to get it out of your system right here."

"Get it out before I go into a courtroom and punch a judge?"

"Yes. You wouldn't do very well in jail. You're not the type."

"What makes you think that I'm any more honest than the next man?" Eriksen said mockingly, but he knew it was a serious question.

"Because you have such a sweet, cherubic face," Nancy replied.

"I won't even tell you how many punks I've booked for murder who had the nicest faces you would ever want to see. Some were absolutely angelic. It's getting harder and harder to tell the bad guys from the good. The line is very thin, you know. Just because I'm an officer of the law, am I good?"

"I don't know if you're good or not, Dan," she said with am impish grin. "But before we become too personal I better tell you that a Mr. Cahill is waiting to see you."

Eriksen rubbed his weathered face. "Old man Cahill. That's all I need. Tell him I'm not here."

"I did, but he said he would wait all day for you. He says it's important."

"Everything Cahill has is important." He groaned. "All right. Send him back." He was studying papers on his desk when he saw the frail old man round the corner past the secretaries and head toward his small office. Cahill walked with a decided list to his right and used a rubber-tipped cane to keep himself upright. Despite his eighty-odd years he moved swiftly to Eriksen's office, closed the door, and fixed him with a beady look from his hooded and sunken eyes.

"Are you bugged, Erskine?" Cahill demanded.

"Not by electronic sources." Eriksen allowed himself a thin smile.

"Can't be too careful, boy. Lot of people would stoop to anything to get my information. You might not even know this place is bugged."

"What can I do for you, Mr. Cahill?" Eriksen felt his impatience growing.

The old man set his weathered felt cap on the desk, revealing a gleaming head laced with a few strands of gray hair. "It's about that murdered girl," he said in his thin voice. "I'll not beat about. I'll come straight to the point." Thank God for the little pleasures in life, Eriksen thought.

Cahill continued, "I know who killed her, Erskine. I know. I don't know her name. But I seen her."

"Her? You're saying a woman killed the girl?" Eriksen asked with eyebrows arched.

"Why, sure. Them was two lesbians fighting it out. And the one who did it lives right near me. She moved in with a bunch of hippies into that old Walters ranch just south of me. I seen her. She wears man's clothes all the time, cuts wood like a man—"

"Lots of women wear a shirt and jeans all the time. And besides, Mr. Cahill, maybe it is a man with long hair."

"Well, if it is, he sure has got big tits." Cahill cackled over this and cupped his hands in front of his chest to convey her proportions.

Eriksen stood up to indicate the session was over. "This is the old Walters ranch, you say." He wrote it down but knew he wasn't going to check it out.

"That's right. Just south of me on Hawkins Lane. No one else down that road except old lady Sills and her boy. You find that girl and talk to her." Then Cahill held up a thin hand and spoke in a whine. "But don't tell them I sent you down there. She would come over and chop me up for sure. You just see how she handles an ax and you'll know."

Eriksen opened the door and ushered the old man to the reception area, all the while assuring him he would look into it. When he returned to his office, Harry Nye was sitting in Eriksen's chair, looking over the papers on his desk. Eriksen felt a flash of anger that the chief of detectives would leave him standing in his own office.

"What progress on the Thomas girl, Dan?" Nye gave a quizzical smile, like a teacher anticipating the correct answer from a star pupil.

"No progress to speak of."

The smile tightened on Nye's face. "It's been three days since the body was found."

"I know damn well when it was found, Harry. I'm just telling you that beyond knowing her name and background we don't know anything. We've checked out her boyfriends and the punks up at the commune where she lived, but they are all clean. None of them was anywhere near this area the night the autopsy indicates she was killed."

Nye tapped his pencil on Eriksen's desk. "The sheriff is getting impatient. He's meeting the League of Women Voters tomorrow to tell them progress has been made. He wants something that says we're getting close to a solution."

"Something to keep them off the sheriff's back, you mean? Make him look good for reelection?" There was a rasp in Eriksen's voice.

"We want to show them the department is on top of this case and that there is no cause for concern. That's all." Nye's voice was placating.

"Tell them the truth, that we don't know shit."

"I don't think that would go over too well, Dan." Nye rolled the cigar in his mouth. "How about saying we've eliminated numerous suspects and are continuing to tighten the noose? That we're working carefully because we don't want to upset the case."

"That would be fine, Harry, just fine. Now, if you'll move, I'll get on with my work."

Nye rose lazily from behind the desk. "Remember one thing, Dan. There's an asshole out there somewhere who killed a girl and might do it again."

"The sheriff told us not to worry, that it was just some psycho passing through," Eriksen replied. He couldn't keep the sarcasm out of his voice.

"We know better, don't we." Nye said, and left.

Eriksen spent the morning going through all the reports and notes on the Thomas case, looking for something he had missed before. He found nothing and turned to the paperwork that had piled up on his desk for the past three days. It was after four when he remembered Carmichael. He dialed Bill Burke, the polygraphist in the ID section, who grumbled about the short notice but said he would be ready in half an hour. Eriksen headed for the jail.

The jailer on the second floor chattered about how busy things were.

"We got a whole mess of people in here last night. No way I could keep your man Carmichael in a cell all by hisself. So I put him in with three others in a four-bed cell. You know, that asshole cried and cried when we moved him."

When they reached his cell, the jailer yelled at Carmichael that he had a visitor. The other three, two blacks and a Chicano, were playing cards on the floor. One of the blacks, a thin man with a massive afro, looked up at Eriksen.

"I sho hope you come to get that dude outta here. He's a badass mothafuka. Cried all night, man. Kept saying 'Don't butt-fuck me, don't butt-fuck me.' Shee-it, man, no way I'm goin' lay my big beautiful dick on that dude." He laughed as he threw down a card, and the others chuckled in agreement.

The jailer opened the door and walked toward Carmichael, who lay tight against the wall with his head buried in the corner. It was then that Eriksen saw the thick glasses at the foot of the bed near Carmichael's foot. One lens was shattered. Eriksen moved inside quickly, stepping over the protesting card players. The jailer was shaking Billy; the rolls of fat on his side jiggled beneath the T-shirt. Eriksen took one meaty arm and turned the fat man on his back. Billy's face was smeared with half-dried blood, his eyes glued closed by the blood he had left there as he wept away the final minutes of his life. His pudgy hands were clenched tightly, as if trying to hold on to something that was slipping past him. The jailer turned and ran for help as Eriksen bent closer to confirm his fears. Billy's wrists were gouged terribly by a piece of glass from his spectacles.

The three cellmates were standing now, staring with wide eyes. The black with the wild afro snapped his fingers. "That mothafuka done killed hisself! Jist like that."

Eriksen backed out of the cell and closed the door, then lit a Camel while he waited for the other jailers to arrive and remove Carmichael. Billy was a man killed by his own fears, he thought. Eriksen felt something akin to sympathy rise in his chest, but then he thought of the girl tied to the bed, staring with dry and empty eyes at the ceiling, and he decided it would have been better if someone had sawed Billy's balls off with a dull knife. He wondered then if he had driven Billy to suicide, if it had been his talk about Billy going to the slammer where the veteran inmates would take one look at his soft body and his background and then gang-bang him.

It was after eight before he finished taking statements from the others in the cell and the ID team had finished up there. He felt drained. The sheriff's office released a brief statement to the press, and then he was deluged with calls. The first one came from Fred Thomas, who kept hammering at why a key suspect was not given better protection. Eriksen took six calls and then told the operator he was out and would take no more. He left the office at nine and considered swinging by the Hilton for a drink. The bar had a happy hour every evening, which drew in many of the junior-executive types and attractive secretaries. He had seen Nancy there two weeks ago during one of his infrequent visits. She had been with two other girls, apparently also secretaries, but had not seen him. He wondered if she often went there. It would be nice to talk to her sometime in surroundings other than the office. Tonight he decided it was too late and he was too tired. He headed home.

Cynthia was in the kitchen when he entered from the garage. "How did it go today?" she asked.

"Pretty quiet," he replied. It was her standard expression of interest and his standard reply. She had been more curious after they were first married, but his details of death, of trying to describe to her what a man looked like after he had shot himself under the chin with a twelve-gauge shotgun, cooled her interest. He knew she couldn't relate to his work, and he didn't blame her. No one could unless they had seen and lived it themselves.

He poured himself a liberal shot of Jack Daniels, dropped in three cubes of ice, and sloshed a little water in the stubby glass.

"Where's Denice?" he asked.

"Out in back. Playing with Spider. She said she was going to teach him to read lips." She watched him as he started out the door. "Do you want anything to eat? I saved your dinner and can warm it for you."

"Maybe I'll have some soup later. I want to unwind first." He was halfway out the door.

"Would you please fix Denice's bike? I'm going crazy driving her back and forth to Cheri's home. She's either coming or going every day to Cheri's to practice cheerleading. It can't be that big of a job to fix a flat tire."

The door closed, but she heard him mutter, "All right, all right." Cynthia turned back to the counter, where she was mixing a chocolate cake.

She poured the batter into a pan and then went to the window to watch Dan and Denice. In the twilight they were playing catch, occasionally letting a ball go for Spider to chase, and then both giving the dog hand signals to come back, because it couldn't hear. They turned and started toward the house, and Cynthia went back to her cake. She wanted a drink, but Dan was so scornful when she drank just a little too much; so tonight she promised not to drink. And tomorrow she would not drink. One day at a time. Even though he still drank every evening.

Denice burst in through the door, flushed and beautiful. "Did you see us, Mom? Dad dropped more balls than I did. And now he's going to fix my ten-speed. Are you making another cake? You're going to get fat if you keep doing that." She laughed and ran into the living room to watch television. Eriksen fixed another drink and padded into the garage to fix the tire. A half-hour later he was done and returned feeling satisfied with his small accomplishment. If he had just fixed it when it first went flat, life would have been more simple for everyone, he thought. He finished his bourbon. But who wants a simple life?

He set his soup and toast, along with another drink, on the coffee table in front of the television. Denice and Cynthia chattered about the first football game coming up and the cute boys on the team. Eriksen could concentrate on neither them nor the TV program. His mind kept returning to the Thomas girl, then shifting to the way Nancy's dresses swirled about her legs. He was thinking about how Nancy would look undressed when he became aware that Cynthia and Denice were no longer talking. He looked up to see Cynthia watching him, her brown eyes solemn. His face remained impassive while he wondered if she could read his thoughts.

"What?" he said.

"I just asked what progress is being made."

"On what?" He hadn't heard anything she asked him.

"On finding the killer of the Thomas girl." Her voice carried exasperation. "Sometimes it seems like you aren't even there."

"Why does everyone want to know 'What progress, what progress?' " he said angrily. "We had thirteen homicides this year before Thomas. But no one is interested in those. What's so special about this one?"

"Just because it's not going well, don't take it out on me."

Eriksen was contrite. "I'm sorry. And you're right, we aren't making any progress. And now this jerk Carmichael goes the suicide route and the press is yelling about losing our prime suspect because of lousy jail security."

"Some reporter called here today. He said he wanted to interview me."

"Who was it?" Eriksen asked intently.

"I don't know. I forgot his name."

"Well, tell them to stay the hell away. I'm not going

to have them coming to the house, especially to see either of you. If they want information, they can get it from the sheriff. Make that clear to them."

"I will," Cynthia said, and brushed back a lock of her hair. "But you know everyone is talking about this killing."

"Why are they jumping on this?"

"I don't know. Maybe because it's so indiscriminate. It seems like it could happen to anyone. A lone girl gets picked up and is raped and killed. No one ever saw the killer."

"It just takes one ride with one nut," Eriksen said.

The sun was low and its beams cut horizontal swaths through the chinks in the old pumphouse walls. Those rays were dangerous. It was important to keep away from them. Just this afternoon while I was absorbed in the sounds of Beethoven, a light bolt struck me on the chest and sent a shot of pain through my entire body. To escape these shafts I lay close to the floor with my face upon Roberta's clothes. The fourth movement swelled around me until the great sounds burst inside my head, a crescendo that symbolizes Beethoven's triumph over his enemies. We are the same, Beethoven and I, always struggling. The music stopped and the silence was ominous. I pushed closer against the blue shirt and could still smell the faint perfume she wore. Or was that just the odor of her body? As I lay there wondering, a whisper came from the shadowed corner of the loft.

"Sonny." It was so faint. I said nothing.

"Sonny, it's time again." The voice was stronger this time, riding airwaves into my ear.

"Time for what?" I whispered back.

"You know."

"No, I don't." I wouldn't surrender easily. And where had I heard that voice before?

"You know what the gray lioness did to us, don't you? It destroyed us. And she's still out there, Sonny." The voice rode a tube of light into my ear. If I could break that tube, the voice would stop, but I couldn't move. That's why the lightrays were so dangerous.

"She's waiting for you. Be careful," the voice said, and grew fainter as it spoke, until it was gone.

A synapse snapped above my right elbow, which indicated I could move. I rose to my knees and smoothed Roberta's clothes, but not before slipping my hand inside her shirt to feel the current pass between my fingers and her silken bra. Time to move.

Mother was up when I walked into the dim living room. She puttered about in her blue robe while adjusting the television set. It seemed she never even bothered to dress anymore.

"How is my little baby? I hardly see you anymore. Are you all right?" she said in a voice that ricocheted around a steel drum.

"I'm fine, Mother."

"Where have you been?"

"Oh, just out and around."

"Up in your loft again?"

"Yes." Why was she interrogating me like this?

"Are you hiding from me up there? Why don't you enjoy the house with me?"

"I just like to be by myself sometimes to think." That thinking was dangerous. My mind spun so rapidly it seemed I could hear the whine of overheated gears.

"Have you been looking for another job? We can't live on love, you know," she said with a giggle.

"I've looked, but no luck, Mother." I sat down on the couch and she joined me. It wasn't necessary for her to sit so close.

"Have you really been looking, or out chasing the girls, hmmm?" she asked, and watched me wetly.

"No, just trying to find a job. Nothing else."

"Now, Sonny, you can tell Mother about the girls. I know a fine-looking boy like you has lots of dates. You're just so secretive about it. Come on, tell Mother."

"Well, I saw Helen yesterday."

"Helen Marshall? That rich girl? She's too stuck-up for you, Sonny. She's not your type."

"I've always liked her, Mother," I said. The synapse in my right shoulder connected to the spine with an audible snap.

"You just think she is, but believe me, she's not really your type. One of these days you'll find just the right girl, and then I know what will happen. You'll come and sit right here and tell me you're going to get married and you're going to go live somewhere else. But I'll understand." She leaned her head against my shoulder.

"You make it sound like I'm getting married tonight," I said.

"It's coming soon. I can tell. But don't you worry about your mother. You just go ahead and leave me. You don't have to worry about me getting around this big house by myself. There's always the telephone if I injured myself or got real sick."

"Oh, Mother." The generators within me were turning now, and the current was building.

"When you want to leave, you just go. I can get along." She reached up and pulled my head down to her breasts, and I felt safe among those pillows. I moved closer, burrowing deeper, then felt her stiffen and push me back.

"Get me a glass of wine, Sonny," she said flatly.

I sat up, once again vulnerable. "Why do you do that?" I asked.

"Do what?" She wasn't really listening now, just watching the evening news.

"Nothing." I rose and got the wine. "I'm going out now," I told her.

She turned back to me at this. "Going out looking for a job at this hour? Or going on a date with some girl?" I watched her take a drink of the wine and saw the bright red drops on her lips glitter until her tongue slid out and destroyed them.

"Just out," I said.

"Is that any way to dress? Just old jeans and a T-shirt with a beer can on it? Your father was a sloppy dresser too, and look what happened. He—"

"Mother! I don't want to hear about that," I shouted.

"It's something you should listen to and think about," she replied sharply. "You're a young man, twenty years old, and nothing to show for it. No job, just jumping around like your pants were on fire. Anybody would think you were taking some kinda drugs."

I was leaving. "Don't be ridiculous, Mother."

She called after me. "You be careful out there, now."

It was still light outside, just the golden shades of the late twilight. The elves in the garden watched me as I made my way past them to the barn, where I found some lengths of sacking twine. I put the twine under the front seat and drove toward town. As I passed the old Walters ranch down the lane, I saw a dilapidated bus parked there. Several long-haired people about my age were sitting on the porch, smoking and passing a butt back and forth. Marijuana. Hippies. That would infuriate old man Cahill, in the place across the lane, just a stone's throw from our house. He hated hippies. He used to yell at me to get a haircut, but my hair really isn't long, not like theirs. I hoped one of the hippies would pitch a rock through Cahill's window.

I drove aimlessly, letting the car guide itself. All those pistons and valves and camshafts, powered by batteries, alternators, and gasoline! Just like brain waves and body fluids. It is something come alive. So I let the bug-car do its own thing. It took me by the bowling alley, but that didn't look very attractive. But the bug-car stopped, then made a U-turn, pulled up in front, and said, "This is the place." It had a very metallic voice, like the taste of pennies. I was a little surprised, because for all the faith I had in my car, it had never talked to me before.

"Wait right here," I told bug-car as I got out.

"What?"

"I said wait here," I repeated, and patted his hood.

"I thought you were talking to me."

"I was."

"No. To me. Not your car."

I turned, and there was a dark-haired girl watching me, a quizzical smile on her face. She took a drag from her cigarette and waited as I walked toward the entrance.

"Do you always talk to your car?"

"Only when I think he isn't listening." She laughed at this, and I opened the door for her and we went in together. It seemed so natural. There was never any question about us being together.

"My bug told me to come here. He must have known you were here," I told her.

She didn't look at me; her eyes kept darting over the dozen alleys. All were full. "I was supposed to meet some of my friends here tonight, but maybe they couldn't make it. Their parents probably locked them up." She giggled.

We went into the restaurant part, where we could still watch the games. It was crowded, but we found a booth in back. She sat facing the restaurant to look for her friends. I bought us each a root beer. I studied her as she drank. She kept looking out at the alleys. Strands of long hair fell forward around her face, around her dark eyes with long dark lashes. She was a Chicano girl, maybe Indian, with smooth olive skin, no makeup, not even lipstick. She wore a tight blue T-shirt with a red fist on it, and no bra underneath. Her jeans were new and clinging. She looked about eighteen, but some Chicano girls can fool you, and I bet myself she was only fifteen or sixteen.

"What's your name," I asked.

"Jeannie." She was about to ask mine, but she looked at my eyes and became distracted. Her pursed lips, strawberry ripe, poised about an inch above her straw. She forgot to suck as she looked at my eyes and smiled, a wide, gleaming smile with large white teeth.

"Hey, I really like your eyes. How come you've got an extra dot in one?" She wasn't shy.

"That's an extra pupil. It gives me insight into your insides. That's my insight sight."

"What?" She frowned at me. Her luminous eyes and tawny skin made me think of a South American jaguar.

"Nothing. It's just an extra dot, I can't see out of it." Then I whispered hoarsely: "But it gives me special powers. Lets me read your mind." She laughed at this and licked her lips.

"Okay. Go ahead. Read my mind." She stared at me.

I stared back, and I could feel the synapses clicking in my body, the current moving along in syncopated jerks. I could see her mind begin to unfold like a ripe flower.

"You are tired of this place. You're tired of your life. You would like to do something, go somewhere where there's action, where the fun is."

She smiled, large teeth again. "Right on."

"Guess what?" I gave her my very engaging smile. "I know where there's a party tonight. Some people who have it together, you know what I mean? A little grass, uppers if you want them. Want to go?"

She grinned and her eyes sparkled. "Sure. Only one thing. You have to get me home by midnight, okay?" Her eyes darkened. "I told my old man I was going to a girlfriend's house, and if I'm not back on time he'll beat me. I mean really beat me. Once I had to go to the hospital. You know?"

She finished her drink, and I looked at her fingers curled around the glass. I had not noticed before how long her fingernails were, or that they were painted red.

Outside, the bug-car laughed at me as I held the door for Jeannie. It was a laugh full of clanks and gurgles, but what else could I expect from a machine?

I didn't know which way to go. I thought of going back down where the hippies lived, even though I didn't know them, but the VW knew that wouldn't work. The car swung onto the freeway and we sped north through the night. The oncoming lights winked and smirked at me.

"Where are we going?" Jeannie asked.

"Oh, my cousin has a place up near Potterville, real isolated. Good for parties."

We rode in silence until I asked her how old she was. She said "Eighteen" with no hesitation.

I gave her one of my nicest smiles and said, "You look and act eighteen, but I thought you might be a little younger. Not that I care, but I'm into numerology. If you give me your real birthdate I can tell you something of yourself."

"Like reading my mind?"

"Sort of."

"You really do have special powers, huh?" She was a very trusting girl.

"Yes, I do have special powers. I am among the blessed. Now, when were you really born?"

"October twelfth, 1960. That's my real birthday. I'm only sixteen but I don't look it, do I?" She curled her legs up in a feminine fashion, like a cat curling up. Like Roberta Thomas did.

"October is the tenth month, added to the twelfth day, added to 1960 totals 1982." I was calculating out loud. "Add 1982 together and it makes twenty. Two and zero is two. You are a two." My mental gears whirred and whined at the thought. She was a two, the devil woman. This was the gray lioness! Again! Far down the road ahead of me, very distant but still distinct, came some laughter. It floated toward me as if riding a distant wave. It was happy laughter and I knew it was telling me I had the gray lioness.

"What does two mean?"

"What?" Her voice waves slid into my ear like the hollow tones of kids talking to each other through a hose.

"Does that two mean something about me? Like the stars?"

"Yes. Yes. Two means you are . . ." Did I dare tell her? The cat inside her young tawny body would hear me and put her on guard.

"Quite right. Be very careful." It was the voice talking to me now. "And when you are ready to act, be swift and firm. Take no chances."

"Well, two is a good number. It means you are a balanced person."

She seemed to be thinking this over, thinking that it didn't tell her very much. We were now on Canyon Road and there was no traffic around us. Everything would be all right. The bug-car knew its own moves and swung up the rough track to the mine shaft of its own accord. At the top I drove across the rocky tailings to park beside the mine shaft. No sense in carrying her a long way.

"What's this place?" She was peering into the dark through the window after I cut the lights. "What's going on?" She was looking at me. My eyes had adjusted to the dim light of the half-moon and I could see her staring at me. The lioness was watching. I would have to be very careful, for the night is her natural element.

"It's all right. My cousin's cabin is up behind this old mine shaft. They saw our lights. Someone will come down in a minute with a flashlight to guide us."

"It's kind of spooky up here." Her voice was hushed, the brazen quality gone. The night had silenced itself on our arrival, but then one tree frog began a solo sonata. He was joined by others, until the nocturnal chorale was in full voice. Their music swelled into a crescendo of natural Beethoven, louder and louder until my ears rang.

"It's time. What are you waiting for?" I could hear someone speaking to me from well beyond the frog chorus.

"I know it is, but we have to be careful."

"What?" Jeannie was looking at me strangely. Her voice boomed inside a steel drum.

"Let's go. We can walk up the trail. There's enough light." I got out of the car and walked around to her side. She had the door open and her legs out but remained sitting.

"Maybe there's no one up there. I mean, I don't hear anyone. I can't see any lights. You sure you got the right place?"

"Sure. He lives up a trail so no one will bother him. Come on." Synapses were racing between neurons up and down my legs. I could barely control them. I held out my hand and she allowed me to pull her to her feet. We started walking, still holding hands, and I could feel her next to me in the dark, her breast brushing my arm.

"Well?" The clear question came on the night wind. It made my heart hammer.

"Just a minute," I said. I released her hand and stepped behind her. She was starting to turn when I moved. It was surprisingly easy. I whipped my right arm around her neck and snapped it back while at the same time grasping her left wrist. Her feet came off the ground and there was a gurgle in her throat. She was catatonic for a second, like the sheep had been, and then she began flailing back at me with her feet, but she had no leverage and was helpless. Her right hand, which I couldn't control, raked at the back of my neck. I buried my head in her long hair, but still her nails flashed at me. She had a grip on my hair and jerked and jerked and jerked, but I only squeezed harder. I felt my flexed muscles bite into her neck arteries, my own power growing and hers rapidly diminishing. Now her fingers were on my arm, pulling desperately, but I was steel and she was fiber. She bent under my grip until she stopped altogether and hung limply from my arm. It only took a few seconds.

I lowered her to the ground and knelt over her, my breath coming in gasps. She lay on her back, arms and legs akimbo, with her raven hair glistening in the faint moonlight. Her breasts heaved beneath her T-shirt; she was merely unconscious. I had purposely achieved this by putting pressure on the carotid arteries. I needed her alive for now. I needed to talk to her, to make her admit she was the gray lioness in the guise of a woman. This time I would be certain. I pulled the two pieces of cord from beneath the car seat, shoved them in my pocket, and pulled her into a sitting position. She was too heavy to lift so I got behind her, slid my arms under her breasts, and dragged her across the rocky flat to where the bushes began growing beside the mine entrance. She was making noises and moving her arms by the time I got there. I tied a cord around each wrist and the other end to a bush, pulling each one tight so she couldn't move her arms. I sat down beside her and waited for her to return to full consciousness. Her head rolled on the ground, her eyes fluttered, then widened as she saw me in the pale moonlight. She struggled to sit up but could do no more than raise her head.

"Madre, Madre." Tears filled her eyes.

I leaned over and grasped the finger of one bound wrist. They were cold. I took her index finger and bent it up. "Look at this," I said. She kept on rocking her head back and forth until I pulled the finger sharply up, and she cried out. "Look at this finger. Why are your nails so long? Why are your nails painted red? Because they are claws and they have been dipped in blood. Isn't that right?" I leaned over very close to her face now, and I could smell the cat scent flowing from her pores. "Let me hear you admit it, you bitch. You want to castrate me and other men, don't you? Don't you?" I could hear myself screaming at her.

"Now," I said hoarsely. "We know you are the lioness. I know it and you know it. But why are you trying to kill me? Why do you want to snap my balls off? Why?"

Her mouth worked as she stared at me, but nothing came out. "You know what you are?" I leaned close to her face again, drinking in her powerful scent, stealing away her breath. "You are a succubus. That's what it's called. That means you are the devil in female form. You came in the night and forced me to have intercourse with you. Many times. You were trying to drain me and steal my power away. You are a succubus. Your numbers tell me. Your skin and nails tell me. You are a succubus and you are the gray lioness." I sneered at her and bared my teeth. "But no more. No, you will not steal away my powers in the night. You will not take my balls, like you did my dad's. Now our worlds are reversed. I am going to take you."

Her head was rocking back and forth again. *"Madre, Madre, Madre de Dios."*

She would not talk, but she had to be punished and made to understand.

I straddled her and slid her shirt up to expose her breasts in the pale light. I filled each hand with a breast and squeezed hard, fingers biting deep, until she cried out. "No more will you suckle your young with these breasts! No more suckle, succubus. Sucklebus."

Suddenly she bucked under me, trying to throw me to one side, and her mood changed from fear to hatred. "Get off me, you son of a bitch. Leave me alone. My father will cut your cock off for this." She spat at me and lunged with her head, trying to bite my hands.

"See, now the lioness in you comes out! Come on, bitch, fight! Fight with me. I like it! I like it!" I slid down her legs, keeping my weight on her knees. She was powerless as I unbuttoned her jeans. They opened to reveal lace panties underneath. I pulled them both down to her knees, then to her ankles and completely off. The moment her legs were free she lashed out with one foot, fast as a striking cat, and caught me in the chest. The blow sent me sprawling on the rocks.

"Fight, you lioness, you lying-ess," I hissed as I warily approached her. She swung her legs again, trying to strike me, but I anticipated her and caught them in my arms and fell upon her. Her smooth stomach was before my eyes now, and I bit her where hip curved to loin. She screamed and I stopped.

"See, you bite and tear and rip away at me, but when it comes back to you it doesn't feel good, does it? Does it?" I slid upward over her body, pressing down heavily upon her, forcing my knees between hers, forcing her legs apart, wider and wider, because she was now going to pay.

"I am going to burn you," I said, and though I kept my face out of striking distance of her gleaming teeth, I could see she had changed again, was growing weaker. But it was a trick. "I am going to burn you, and you are going to be in agony. It is justice."

She was writhing again, bucking and twisting in a vain attempt to avoid me, but it was no use, I was inside her and I knew she was burning, because she was crying out now, making piercing cries. With each thrust I felt my heated weapon grow from red to orange to white, a flaming sword that would destroy her wickedness. She would not stop screaming, and my hands closed around her slim neck. My fingers tangled in her hair, but my thumbs locked over her windpipe and then closed hard and fast, pressing down into the darkness. She surged beneath me, trying to throw me off. I clamped my fingers tighter and felt myself rising inside her, burning away her sins and then exploding within, blowing away forever the gray lioness, forever, forever, ever.

I lay exhausted upon her, my face close to her still features, and waited for the strength she had stolen from me to return. My fingers loosened and I could feel the blood begin to flow back into my brain. Slowly, energy coursed through me again and I rose and straightened my clothes. The lioness, her fur tawny in the moonlight, lay with teeth bared in a final snarl, her sightless eyes cold with fury at her loss.

I untied her hands and then pulled the T-shirt over her head. I took her sandals and all the clothing and cords back to the car. I removed the flashlight from the glove compartment and returned to the lioness. It would not do to leave her so exposed. She could go where Roberta went; the mine shaft made a good animal burial ground. In my weakened state I could not carry her, so I dragged her by the arms. Her head struck rocks as we moved, but it wouldn't matter now. In the back of the shaft, where the rocks were black and glistening beneath my light, I threw her on her back beside the rivulet of clear water, the only thing pure in the chamber. I turned to leave, then remembered her jewelry. I removed her thin gold ring and two hoop earrings. As an afterthought I placed one earring on her breast. Something for her to remember me by.

"You want some more coffee?" The waitress gave Deputy Larry Blanken a smile and he straightened up so his stomach would not hang over his gun belt.

"No. I better go out and serve justice and protect peace. But I'll be back later on. You gonna be here?" He looked at her nameplate above her breast. "Helen." She was new, and not bad-looking. Something to work on.

"Every evening from three to eleven." She moved on with the pot of coffee. But she had smiled, and Blanken knew he was on his way with her.

He rose and went outside, where the heat came down like a velvet hammer. He got in his patrol Blazer and headed up the river. Despite the open windows he could feel his pores opening and the perspiration oozing out. Maybe if I lost twenty pounds it wouldn't be so bad, he thought, and then pushed that aside. It wasn't worth it to give up beer. Blanken made a swing through several picnic areas to show the flag and got the usual mixture of smiles and jeers. At Canyon Creek

Road he turned along its twisting and shadowed turns, enjoying the cool serenity of the stream. There were few cars on the road, mostly older tourists making the circle drive through vineyards between San Miguel and Potterville. He passed the narrow road that led up to the old Turpin mine and recalled the good feeling of being first on the scene, doing a thorough job. It could have meant a promotion, he thought. Only one problem: nothing ever happened on that. Homicide had not made a crack in that case. If I were handling that case, he thought, it would be settled by now; just dog every lead until you come up with something. There was a clue that would unravel the whole mess. Homicide just couldn't find it.

Two miles beyond the Turpin mine, on a hunch, Blanken made a U-turn and drove back to the mine. He had not been up there since Roberta Thomas' body was discovered, but it was a quiet place to go and maybe catch a nap. He parked on the flat tailings area. Cicadas buzzed in the trees and there was the chatter of some sparrows in the bushes near the mine. All other animal life seemed snuffed by the heat. Blanken's eyes skimmed the area. Nothing new. Nothing out of order, just the usual beer cans left by the last couple that came up here to hump. He listened to the radio chatter and wished he could find a couple whanging away up here some afternoon.

He wished he had a beer. Just a little ice-cold six-pack that would fit under the seat. The job wouldn't be half bad then. A few beers, a few chicks to talk to, like that new waitress, Helen. She had possibilities. Not much up front, but she came on friendly. That was worth something. He sighed, reached for the keys, and was about to start up when he decided to have a look in the mine. Maybe there was something the dicks had overlooked. Hell, Eriksen wasn't God; he could make mistakes. And if Blanken found something, it would mean a good write-up on his records. It could even get him into the detective section. The September sun burned his back as he walked swiftly to the mine, where it was cool and damp. He walked carefully trying to avoid the drops from the ceiling and the small stream of clear, icy water that ran along the floor of the mine. He made his way slowly, not needing his flashlight, not with all the light being reflected from the wet floor. Even when he turned the corner and started back into the farthest reaches, there was enough bouncing light to reveal something that made him leap backward with a curse and unsnap his revolver.

Blanken stared, unbelieving, and felt his heart begin pumping. Jesus, it couldn't be! He started forward again, cautiously, but now his bulky body was blocking the outside light and it was too hard to see. He turned and ran back to the truck for his five-cell flashlight. Maybe it was just a mannequin. Maybe some punk kids playing a trick. He turned and walked swiftly back toward the mine. Even if it were a dead body, it was too hot to run. The beam of light filled the back of the mine, making the girl seem to float on the black rocks. She lay on her back, legs spread, hair fanned beneath her, and one hand trailing in the icy little stream. Blanken looked for footprints but knew he would see none on the rocks. He moved closer. The girl had probably been good-looking once, but she looked grotesque in death. Like everybody does. Every body. Her eyes were open but absolutely vacant. Blanken was always surprised how the eyes more than anything revealed that life had fled. Her mouth was open too, revealing small teeth bared in agony. He could see the bruises around her neck, and more bruises around her breasts and wrists. The son of a bitch had worked this poor girl over. He backed out and returned to the truck. Somebody, he knew, was going to be highly pissed off about this latest 187.

5

"Goddamn, Eriksen." Nye leaned forward over Eriksen's desk, his stomach hanging loose. "*Another* one. Same MO. Exactly. And he even dumps her in the exact same spot. And what have we got on it? Nothing. Not one damned thing."

Eriksen leaned back in his chair and studied the chief of detectives with an impassive eye. He had spent a long day on this latest death and was short on humor, especially with Nye.

"That's right, Harry. Very little to go on. But we've got something. The killer left a small hoop earring again on the body. ID also got some fingernail scrapings that showed she had taken some hide off the attacker. And two strands of hair not her own. Plus teeth marks."

Nye slumped back into a chair across from Eriksen. "What the hell is that going to get us? Any prints? No. Nothing."

"But why did he leave the earring? That bothers me. It was almost certainly left on purpose. He placed it over the nipple of her left breast, just like he did with Thomas."

"So what?" Nye was not impressed.

"So why did he do that? If we knew, it might tell us something about this asshole," Eriksen replied.

"Somebody better tell us something. The sheriff is fucking berserk over this one. The first murder was just cooling down, and people were thinking maybe it was done by some guy from somewhere else out trolling for chicks on the ramps. But now they know he's right here in town." Nye chewed his cigar a moment. "So what do we know about this latest one?"

Eriksen pulled a sheaf of notes from his file. "Her name is Jeannie Maria Chavez, born in San Miguel. DOB 12 October 1960. She lived on the south side of town with her father and two brothers. Her old man works in the vineyards. She was easy to ID. She was a runaway last year, picked up for shoplifting, put on probation, and returned to school."

"What was she doing the night she bought it?" Nye asked.

Eriksen lit a Camel and blew smoke across the desk at Nye as he bent over his notes.

"She told her father she was going over to a girlfriend's house to study. The other girl was supposed to say the same thing and they were going to meet at the

Sun Bowl. Only the other girl, one Carla Montoya, was refused permission to go out at the last minute. Both girls used to hang around the Sun Bowl, meet some guys, smoke some pot, play a little kissy-feely in a car, and go home. But it looks like the only regular there two nights ago when it happened was Jeannie. Nobody remembers her or a guy she might have been with."

"She was in a goddamn crowded bowling alley and nobody remembers her?" Nye looked incredulous.

"*Because* it was so crowded nobody remembers her." Eriksen flicked his cigarette ash impatiently.

"Did you go over there and check those people out?" Nye asked.

"Look, Harry. We got back from the mine two hours ago and back from her old man's place thirty minutes ago. I just sent Darby to the bowling alley."

"Well, you go over too. We need to talk to every damned person who was there that evening. You check them out real good, Eriksen."

"Just what I had in mind," he said, and it was hard to cover the sarcasm. It was after six before he finished taping his report and left the cassette on Nancy Hall's desk for her to transcribe. He walked toward the front exit and he knew he should have gone out the side door, because filling the hallway, talking to Harry Nye, was Sheriff Conrad. Eriksen did not feel like taking any more flak.

"Dan, you've got another one." It wasn't a question from the sheriff, it was an accusation.

Eriksen eyed Conrad without speaking, and the sheriff said, "I've been fighting off the press all afternoon. See me in the morning. We've got to talk about it."

As Eriksen walked on. Nye yelled after him: "If you need any help tonight, let me know. I'll be available."

Eriksen turned. "Sure, Harry." You bet, Harry, sure thing. Only one problem, Harry. You've forgotten what it is to be a cop. You've been sitting behind your desk shuffling papers too long.

Still seething about Nye, he decided to swing by the Hilton first for a drink. He took a seat at the end of the bar and waited for his eyes to adjust. After ordering a Jack Daniels, he turned to scan the room. Waitresses in miniskirts and black net stockings moved briskly among the full tables. Eriksen nursed his drink, moving his eyes from table to table, automatically registering faces. And then he saw Nancy, sitting near the rear with two other women and a man. She was looking directly at him and she smiled slightly when his eyes reached hers. He raised his glass to her and swept idly through the rest of the faces before coming back to her. She was still watching him.

He ordered another drink and when he turned back to the room she was coming toward him. He watched her easy walk, black hair swaying as she moved. Men pulled their chairs closer to the table to let her past and then followed her with their eyes. He rose to give her his seat at the crowded bar and then stood close to her.

"Preserving peace and tranquillity here?" she asked with a smile.

He considered a lewd rejoinder, then skipped it. He ordered her a drink and then remembered something. "I've got to make a phone call. Don't go away."

"I won't." She smiled.

He found a telephone on the corner near the door and dialed his wife.

"Look, Cynthia, I forgot to call you earlier. But I'm going to be tied up tonight," he said when she answered.

"Where are you? Sounds like a party," she said.

"I'm at the Hilton. Just stopped for a drink."

"What happened? Why are you going to be late?" Her voice was flat.

"Another girl was found today, murdered. Same place, same MO. I've got to check some people out."

"Oh, God. I heard something about another girl killed. Was this one raped too?"

"I haven't seen the coroner's final report yet, but it appears so."

"Well, what time will you be home?" Her voice was flat again.

"I'm not sure. Probably around ten. See you." He

hung up and found Nancy chatting with the man next to her. Eriksen looked at him, a rising junior-executive type, and shoved his thick body between the two. The junior executive leaned forward on the bar, peering around Eriksen's shoulder, to continue his sentence, but Eriksen gave him his level gray stare and the young man decided he didn't want to talk to Nancy after all. Eriksen looked for a table, but they were all still full. He ordered another Jack and another martini.

"What brings you here?" she asked. He could feel her legs pressed against his beneath the bar.

"I have to work late tonight and I heard this was a pretty good watering hole. Do you come here often?"

"Oh, two or three times a week."

"Maybe I'll come more often."

"You should, Dan," she said, with her eyes smiling over the rim of her glass. "You need a change." It was a cat-and-mouse game, he knew, but he wasn't sure who was catching whom.

He finished his drink and asked if he could drop her somewhere.

"No, I've got my car. But don't rush off. Let me buy you a drink."

"Is that because you're liberated? I like that kind of liberation."

"I thought you would." She smiled again at him, holding his eyes. She recrossed her legs and he could feel her thigh run over the front of his pants. He backed away slightly, afraid he would have to walk out of the bar with his pants in a triangular configuration.

"I'd like to stay, Nancy, but duty calls. A few more Jacks on an empty stomach and I won't hear any call." He started to move away, but still she held his arm.

"When you finish, come over to my place. I'll fix you something to eat." The invitation was forthright, without coyness.

"I might be late." He realized he wasn't turning her down, just making polite noises that sounded like yes.

"Never mind. I'm a night owl. Just come when you're ready." He looked at her, and she held his gaze, eyes wide and calm. "If you want to, that is."

"I want to." He pressed her arm and left. At the doorway he looked back. The guy next to her was trying to smooth in again.

It was almost dark when he parked in front of the Sun Bowl. He lit another cigarette and looked the bowling alley over. It was a square concrete building topped by an animated neon light that showed a bowling ball knocking down pins. It was located in the Sun Plaza, a shopping center that had once been fashionable but now was only rows of cut-rate dress shops, budget furniture, liquor stores, and two porn shops. Eriksen mused about why everything that starts out looking so nice finally goes downhill. He flicked his ashes out the window. Who cares?

Only half the alleys were in use, but business was picking up. He had to wait several minutes until the tired-faced woman with red-tinted hair behind the counter finished handing out bowling shoes. Eriksen showed her his wallet with badge and identification card.

"Yeah," she said. "Another one of you guys was just here asking about that girl. That's what you want, isn't it?" She stopped chewing her gum while she awaited his answer.

"That's right." Eriksen pulled out a picture of the girl. It was a mug shot, taken when she had been booked in juvenile hall for shoplifting. "Did you see this girl here two nights ago?"

The woman ran roughened hands through her red hair and glanced at the picture. "No. I didn't see her. I told that other guy the same thing. Don't you ever talk to your partner?" She cackled at this.

Eriksen gave her his card. "If you remember anything, please call me."

He walked to the restaurant area. From the end of the counter, he ordered coffee from the waitress, a heavyset girl in her early twenties with a bad complexion. When she brought the coffee he showed her his badge. Her eyes turned cautious. Eriksen saw from the corner of his eye that a middle-aged man in a T-shirt, two stools away, was watching.

"I'm trying to find out something about this girl." He produced a picture and the waitress took it and studied it. "She was in here two nights ago. Did you see her?"

"Is this the girl that was just killed? I seen her on TV tonight."

"That's the one." Eriksen didn't know the story had been on already. "What time do you come to work?"

"Six. Six to midnight, when we close." She looked at the picture again. "She looks familiar. I seen her before, I think. But I don't remember when it was."

"Think carefully. Two nights ago. She might have been in here. Ordered something to eat or drink."

The waitress scratched her head. "Two nights ago was league night, you know? We was really busy. I hardly even got a chance to look at people. I'm sorry. I don't remember seeing her." Customers were filling up stools down the counter, and she looked from them to Eriksen. "Can I go now?"

"Yeah." He rose and went behind the counter to the cook, a thin man in a dirty T-shirt. He hadn't seen anything. Eriksen went back to the bowling counter to talk to the little red hen.

"Two nights ago was league night. You got a list of all the people that were bowling that night?" He hated to ask, because he knew she had the list and they would all have to be questioned. That would be a task for Darby.

"You can get it from the manager, but he ain't here now. He won't be back for a couple of hours."

Eriksen then started to one end of the bowling alley, showing the picture to each bowler and asking if anybody had seen her two nights ago. It was tiresome, slogging work, but he was used to it. And he was used to the negative shakes of heads. No one had seen her. He finished and went back into the counter to order another coffee. The middle-aged man in the T-shirt, with a beer belly hanging over his pants, was still nursing a Coors. The man signaled to Eriksen and pointed at the stool next to himself. Eriksen sat.

"You the fuzz?"

"That's me," Eriksen said. He ordered a coffee, and the man waited until it had been served and the girl had moved on.

"You looking for that girl that just bought it?"

"I want to find what she was doing here that night."

"How do you know she was here?" The man sucked on the bottle while he waited for Eriksen to reply.

"We talked to someone who was supposed to meet her here and then didn't show." Eriksen was growing impatient. "Do you know anything about her?"

The man sucked on the bottle again before turning his unshaven face toward Eriksen. "Yeah, I've seen her before. I'll tell you something about it, but I don't want to get involved. You know? I'm a married man."

"What's your name?" Eriksen asked.

"I don't want to get involved. You can just call me Joe. You don't need my name. But I can tell you something."

"I'm all ears, Joe."

Joe cradled the bottle in one hand and looked at Eriksen with red-rimmed eyes. "She made a play for me one night, see? Two or three weeks ago. She got real friendly, but I backed off. She was too young and a guy can go to jail for fooling around with that stuff. You know?" He paused and signaled the waitress for another beer.

"Well, I seen her a time or two since then, and I watched her. She kinda got on my mind, see? But I never tried nothing."

"What about two nights ago. Were you here?"

Joe pulled on the Coors, belched, and continued. "Yeah. I come here most every night. Gotta get a break from the old lady and the kids."

"Did you see the girl?" Eriksen had the distinct feeling that he was going to get the first lead in the case.

"Yeah. I seen her. She was sitting in the booth over there. I remember her because she had on a T-shirt with a red fist on it, and you could almost see her tits through that shirt. You know what I mean?"

The only picture that came to Eriksen's mind was that of Jeannie Maria Chavez, age sixteen, lying on her back on the stainless-steel autopsy table, her flattened breasts ringed by bruise marks.

"Well, that's all. I seen her."

"Who was she with?"

"Some guy. But I never got a look at him. They was sitting in the back booth over there. She was facing me but she didn't notice me. He had his back to me, so I never seen him. Anyway, I just kept looking at her boobs. You know what I mean?"

Eriksen questioned him further but could elicit no information on the man. No ideas of age, height, clothes, or hair color. Joe had looked at nothing except Jeannie's bouncy young breasts. Eriksen gave him his card and told him to call if he could remember something else.

"Now, what's your name, Joe? I might need to come back to you."

"I told you, I don't want to get involved. I'm just trying to help out."

"But you are involved, Joe." Eriksen's voice turned raspy. "You want to tell me your name here or go down to my office? How do I know you didn't take off with Jeannie?"

Joe's eyes widened. "Shit. I was just trying to help you out." He was frowning at his beer now. "All right. The name's Perrin. Joe Perrin. But if my old lady hears that I was looking at that broad, she's gonna kill me. You know what I mean? And you ask Judy there." He pointed at the waitress. "She'll tell you I was here all night, and you can check the league records."

"All right, Joe. Now, let me see your driver's license." Joe handed it over with more frowns, and Eriksen jotted down his address and license number. "Thanks, Joe. Your wife won't hear anything about this." He rose and was walking away when he heard Joe yell. He turned, and Joe was waving him back.

"I was going to tell you something else, but I don't know if I will now. You kinda leaned on me."

"No problem, Joe. We're square. What else were you going to say?"

Joe pulled on the beer again before answering. "They was in a Volkswagen. They got in a VW and drove away. I saw them through the window. Right from here." Eriksen could see the parking lot through the windows, but the cars were only dim shapes.

"That's all I can tell you. It was a VW. I don't know what year or nothing. Can't tell them apart anyways. But it was white. That's all."

"Did you see the license plate? Remember any letter or number?"

Joe turned angry. "I didn't see nothing more than that. That's all. I just seen her get in it."

It was after nine when Eriksen caught the manager coming in and got the list of league players who had been bowling the night Jeannie was killed. It was late and he debated going home, but swung by Nancy's apartment first. If there was a light on he would go up. There was a light. She met him at the door in a floor-length white caftan.

"Come on. I've got some stew on the stove." He followed her, noticing how the caftan swayed in and out against the curves of her body as she walked. She mixed him a Jack Daniels and water. Eriksen looked at the drink.

"I thought you drank martinis," he said.

"I do. But somebody I know has good taste in bourbon. So I had some on hand." She eyed him. "Always the detective, eh?"

He ate the stew, surprised at how hungry he was.

"How did it go?" she asked when they returned to the small living room. She sat near him on the sofa, her legs curled beneath her.

"I think we have a break. Just a little break, Nancy. I found a guy at the Sun Bowl who recalls seeing Jeannie the night she disappeared. She was with some guy who he didn't see, but he recalls they drove away in a white VW."

"Oh, good," she said with sarcasm. "There can't be more than ten thousand white Volkswagens in Socorro County. But it is a start. I'm glad for you, Dan." She put her hand in his and he closed his fingers around hers.

"I'm going to need some kind of a start when I see the sheriff tomorrow. According to Nye, the sheriff is hopping over this. He's afraid it will blow his re-election chances." He finished his drink and looked at Nancy.

"Seems like all we do is talk shop," he said. "I wish I could stay and talk about something else, but I better go. I'm keeping you up."

He rose to his feet, but she kept a hold on his hand. "You're not keeping me up." She looked up at him, her eyes serious. "Will you come back again when you can spend some more time?"

"I'd like that. Thanks for inviting me this time." He leaned down and kissed her lips, which were moist and warm. He felt a mild electric tingle run through them both.

"May I ask you a question?" he said, still standing close to her.

"That depends."

"How old are you?"

"Twenty-four. Why? Is that important?"

"Not really. It's just that I don't know much about you. And I'm not really sure why I'm here."

"You looked like you could use a drink and a hot meal. That's all," she said with a smile that said more.

"I'm a married man, you know," Eriksen said.

Her eyes widened. "Do tell. Is there something illicit about you having a drink here?" Her face was all innocence.

"Of course not, honey chile." He grinned. "May I come back?"

"If you're good."

"Good at what?"

"You better go play detective some more," she said, and gave him a light kiss on the cheek. He could feel her breasts on his arm through her thin caftan.

"Do you have any jealous boyfriends that are going to beat me up?" he asked.

She looked at him seriously for a moment. "Did you ever make the rounds of singles bars in this town? They're full of insurance salesmen and kids just out of the fields. All very dull. Detectives are much more interesting. That's why I got a job with the sheriff's office."

He left, wondering what she was getting at.

I sat very still as the television hissed at me. I wondered if the television circuitry could trigger my own electrical system. Or possibly short-circuit it. Certainly our electrical fields could intermingle and establish antimagnetic fields that would disrupt the entire room. So I sat still. Mother didn't even notice I was here, she was so engrossed in the six-o'clock news.

"Another one." My mother's voice was full of feedback wails, which proved the countermagnetic fields were disrupting the room.

"Another what?" I asked.

"Another girl found murdered and raped. And in the same place! What's the world coming to?"

I stared at the set, but the words came in waves, shifting from whispers to roars.

"That's him again," Mother said.

"Who?" I really didn't have to listen to the TV. Mother could interpret everything for me.

"That detective. Don't you listen?" She sipped her wine and then turned glistening eyes on me. "That's the detective who is trying to solve this thing. Detective Dan Eriksen with the sheriff's department. You should keep up with the news."

By concentrating this time, I could see a man walking about on rocks with the mine behind him. The mine! Then they did find Jeannie. Or was it a rerun on Roberta? It could be the same thing. But there was a picture of Jeannie, her face filling the whole screen. That was the gray lioness, coming into thousands of homes. She was dead now, but no one cared that I had saved the men in this town. Then Jeannie was gone and two women were walking toward me, kicking and laughing. I could see them, but the words would not enter my ear properly.

"Who's that?" I asked.

"Don't you ever listen?" my mother said angrily. "That's the detective's wife and daughter."

The women walked right toward me. One was round, but not as round as Mother, with reddish hair and large teeth. Next to her was another woman who was smaller and wore a short skirt with knee socks and walked with springy steps that made her tawny-colored hair swirl about her face. They kept marching at me and I heard their laughter ringing about the room, bouncing off the walls and plunging into my head. Such terrible noises!

"For heaven's sake, Sonny, get off the floor. Get up! If you're so tired, go to bed. You act like a child, the way you carry on sometimes."

I collected myself and sat in silence for long minutes. I would force her to speak first.

"I've been thinking, Sonny," Mother boomed. "Maybe we ought to sell the ranch and move into town. My social-security and welfare payments don't hardly even pay the taxes anymore. We can't live here much longer, unless you get a job, but I know how hard it is for you. You're just not designed to be a worker. You're what they call a lover and not a fighter, aren't you, Sonny? Sonny, my lover boy."

There was a rush of wind, which I took to be laughter. Mother watched me, and I knew she was waiting for me to speak, trying to draw me out.

"There is no sundown when there is work."

"What is that supposed to mean, Sonny?"

"It . . . I mean when the sun is down, it is time to play. Not to work, see?"

Mother said nothing, and I continued. "We can't sell this place. It's all we have." I was surprised. She had never talked this way before.

"It may be all we have, but it isn't enough. The price of everything has gone up. Food, feed for the sheep, taxes, gasoline, electricity. What I have coming in just doesn't cover it anymore. I didn't want to worry you before, because you seemed to have so many other worries. But unless you get a job again and can help pay to keep this place going, I just think we'll have to sell it. Move to an apartment in town." My mother looked down, and I could feel her vibrations of sorrow.

"I'll get a job. I will, Mother. I am going to really try." I rose from the couch. "I'm going out now. Talk to some people about a job."

Mother looked up. "Nothing's open now. No sense in going out now."

"But I have to. I have to." I turned and left. Once outside, I almost went back in; maybe I had left her too abruptly. She needed a little help these days. I was about to turn back when I heard angry gurgles from my bug-car. He was anxious to go. Anywhere. We set out in the warm night. The summer kept hanging around, clinging to the leaves, but winter-white death was coming. Coming soon. Winter-white.

The bug-car and I wound through downtown San Miguel; it seemed strangely quiet. I was either too early or too late. In a limbo. We drifted north for a while, my little white VW a life raft alone on an asphalt sea, just sliding with the currents and the wind. I wondered if the bug-car would have any thoughts on this situation, but it was silent. Probably afraid I would short out its whole system.

My mind turned back to my mother, who demanded that I find another job. She was right. Do something. I turned down a side street that led up to the freeway and sped north. I knew what to do. Headlights winked at me, but I ignored them. I would see Helen. She would know where there was work. She might even find me a job in the kitchen. As an outlet. Yes, they could just plug all their appliances into me and I would light up the entire restaurant. What was that place . . . the Blarney Stone, just off the freeway north, and there it was, a truck-stop restaurant with a green leprechaun on top. He had one green leg in the air as if he wanted to crush that restaurant beneath his feet. I was concerned he might bring that Irish foot down while I was in there, but I went in anyway.

It was crowded with truckers and people traveling to or from the City. No one permanent. I stood inside the door looking for Helen. Several girls moved among the full tables. Helen, dressed like the others in a ruffled black skirt so short you could almost see the cheeks of her fanny, worked behind the counter. I took a seat near the end. She brought me a glass of water and stood with pencil poised over her order pad, not even looking at me. When I didn't speak, she finally swung her black eyes away from the truckers at the other end.

"What are you doing here?" she asked in surprise.

"I just came to visit you." I didn't know what else to say.

"You did, huh." She was chewing gum, something I didn't recall seeing her do before, and she cracked it as she watched me.

"Well, you want to order something?"

"A cup of love."

"What?"

"A couple of gloves."

"Oh, come on, Sonny." She looked down at me, the vicar's wife looking down at the neighborhood boy she had just caught masturbating. Sparks leaped the synapses inside me, and my hair crackled with electricity.

I carefully held myself in check. "I'll just have some coffee, if it isn't too much trouble." She returned and set the cup and saucer in front of me, spilling a little into the saucer. Very careless. She cares less. She took the pot and started down the counter, pouring for others, ignoring me.

When she replaced the pot on the burner, I spoke to her, but she didn't hear. I spoke again, louder, and the man four stools down from me turned and gave me an idle glance, then inserted his great long lip again into the coffeecup. Helen came over to me.

"I came out here because I need a job. I thought you could help me. Maybe they need some help here."

"They got all the waiters and busboys they can use." She softened a little. "You've been looking for a job for a long time, Sonny, but never any luck. Maybe you go at it wrong."

"Maybe they need a dishwasher, or floor sweeper. It would be fun to work here with you. We could talk over old times, like when we were in school."

Her gum cracked again as she looked down the counter. It was like she hoped I would not be there when she looked back. "You can ask the manager, but I don't think there's anything open." She straightened up suddenly and a smile lit up her face, and I turned to see a large man, almost fat but not really, come toward us along the stools. He sat down between me and the trucker with the lipstraw. He was two stools away but he seemed to overflow my space. I felt my air being slowly drawn out of the room. And from him came the smells of showers and after-shave lotions. Helen moved toward him with a steaming cup of coffee. She was still smiling, and I could hear the buzz of voices, bees among the honey, but the words were broken and indecipherable when they reached my ear.

"Helen!" I called loudly to override the growing buzz, and I saw the smile shatter on her face. The large man, in a white poplin windbreaker and electric-blue slacks, also turned his heavy face toward me. His mouth moved at Helen and I knew he was asking who I was.

Helen came over to me. "What?" It was a bark, a little feisty dog bark.

"I want a job. I want you to help me, that's all. Is that so much? Is it?" The cook was watching me now from behind the counter.

Helen ripped my coffee order from her pad and put it in front of me. "You better not make any trouble for me here, Sonny." She swung her head toward the great white seal two stools down. "That man is a deputy sheriff, so I wouldn't start anything."

I looked at the check. A quarter for a cup of coffee. I found one in my pocket and put it down. "Don't touch that money, it's still hot. It will burn you." As I rose from my stool I turned toward the seal, who sat poised, nose in air, and gave two short seal barks at him. I saw him begin to rise from the stool, a white iceberg rising out of the sea, but then Helen was beside him, and her voice was coming in little yelps. I barked again and walked past him, headed for the gray curtain that had come down between me and the door. At the end of the counter, I turned, and they were all watching me, eyes expectant, hoping I would leap at them, or bound across the counter and ravish Helen before their very eyes. Instead I merely snarled at them, a deep roaring sound, as if the gray lioness herself were in the room. Then in the quiet that came over the restaurant, I distinctly heard the white seal and Helen talking.

Seal: That jerk is spaced.

Helen: No, he just acts that way sometimes. Let him go, Larry.

Seal (barking): Some friend you got.

I turned and found my way through the gray curtain and out into the velvet night to my car. As I started it, the bug-car clanked a warning and I looked up to see the seal standing by the doorway, pencil in hand, writing something down. He probably had my license number, but everyone knows seals can't read. So what good would it do him?

Eriksen was applying lather to his face in the morning when Cynthia slipped into the bathroom.

"We have to talk a little, Dan."

"Right now? I'm already running late."

"I know, but you got in so late last night I didn't get a chance to talk to you."

"About what?" He couldn't imagine that she knew he had visited with Nancy last night.

"Well, I'm worried."

"About what?" There was impatience in his voice.

"About these girls being kidnapped and raped and murdered. A lot of women are calling me and asking what is going on. Irene Donato spent nearly an hour on the phone with me yesterday. She wants to know if it's safe for Cheri to even go to school."

"For Christ's sake, Cynthia. It's terrible, I agree, but it's not like this killer was stalking up and down the streets just waiting to grab the first girl he sees. He's some kind of psycho who—"

"Dan, you may not think of him as stalking the streets, but the mothers do. Every day the papers, the radio, and the television are filled with the killings. It's all we hear."

"And it's all I hear at the office too. I don't like it any better than you do." He nicked himself on the chin and cursed.

Cynthia was silent for a moment, then asked, "Did you see the news last night on KSM?"

"No. Why?"

"Denice and I were featured on it."

Eriksen stopped shaving and turned toward her. "What do you mean?"

"Their reporter, Fred somebody, came to the house yesterday afternoon and took pictures of Denice and me in the backyard without us knowing about it. Then they came around to the front door and tried to interview us. They had film of us telling them to leave. There were some other reporters around earlier, but I wouldn't talk to them either."

Eriksen felt his anger rise. "Those sonsabitches. Next time they come around, call the office and ask for a patrol car to swing by. And I'll see Thomas personally about this."

"It's awful, Dan. I'm afraid to go anywhere now. I just know somebody is out there waiting to take our picture or ask what we think about these murders, and what is my husband doing about it, and why isn't he doing more? There were some calls last night too, some crank calls. One lady yelled that all those girls deserved to die and you shouldn't try to catch whoever did it. It's getting worse, Dan, and I don't want Denice to hear those calls." Her voice was rising as Dan washed his face and tried to maintain his composure.

"If you were home last night, you could have taken those calls and maybe done something about it," Cynthia said heatedly.

"Jesus, Cynthia, I've got a job to do. I want to be home as much as anybody, but right now I've got to work almost around the clock. And I'll be doing this until we find the nut."

"You had time to go to the Hilton for a drink," she replied accusingly. "You're not even supposed to be drinking while you're on duty."

"Let's not get into that again," he said quietly.

"Well, you could come home and drink here just as well. And a lot cheaper. How much does a drink down there cost? Two dollars? So why don't you come home instead?"

Eriksen dried his face and left her in the bathroom. She followed him into the bedroom. "I'm home every day and night while you're out having a fine time running around."

He turned on her angrily. "Oh, sure, just a great time. Nothing I like better than interviewing a bunch of creeps in a bowling alley or sitting half the night in front of my desk trying to figure out some pattern to this mess." He pointed his finger at her. "I've got enough problems at work without all of this, Cynthia. Just see if you can hold up this end. Do something useful like getting Denice off to school on time."

"Dan! You don't even understand what I'm saying! You're not listening. You tell me to stay home and be a good mother. There's nothing in this house to mother. What am I supposed to do all day, sit here and wait for you and Denice to come home so I can cook dinner? Wonderful, just wonderful," she said bitterly. "All right, go to work. Do your thing, I'll do mine."

He left at that and drove to work still fuming. He parked and started in the front entrance to the sheriff's department when he saw Fred Thomas and several other newsmen on the steps. Cameras started clicking and rolling as he crossed the sidewalk and started up the stairs. Thomas, with microphone in hand, blocked Eriksen's path.

"Sergeant, as you well know, there's been two girls raped and strangled in less than a week's time. Can we expect a solution to this anytime soon?"

Eriksen felt something snap in the back of his head as he faced Thomas. "You're supposed to be such a hot-shot investigative reporter, why don't you get off your ass and find who did it? Why sit around here bugging people with stupid questions?"

"Finding killers is not my line of work," Thomas replied smoothly. "My job is to find out how well you're doing yours, and—"

Eriksen suddenly grabbed Thomas by his tie and jerked him close. Thomas gave a little yelp and dropped the microphone as Eriksen shoved his face close and snarled, "Listen, you little asshole, if you ever come around my house and take pictures of my family again I'm going to stick that microphone down your throat. Sideways." He shook him once, and the reporter's head bobbled. "Understand?" Eriksen shoved him away and pushed through the crowd of newsmen.

As he strode through the reception area he heard his name barked and he turned to see Sheriff Conrad standing in his office doorway. From that vantage point he had seen everything. "Come here, Eriksen." Conrad's beefy face was red. He closed the door behind Eriksen and stood with hands on hips.

"Just what the fuck you think you're doing out there, boy? You don't go around punching reporters."

"That asshole was sneaking around my house yesterday taking pictures of my wife and daughter without their permission. He's just lucky I *didn't* punch his lights out. Next time I will."

"Next time, hell! You do and I'll throw your ass right out of this department. Those reporters are riding me enough as it is without you getting in it. You seem to forget, Eriksen, that this is an election year, and I don't intend to let someone like you ruin it just because they took pictures of your wife. Hell's bells, Dan, I saw it last night. It wasn't all that bad. It showed you out working hard while your little ladies were home trying to make the best of it. That story had a personal touch that made this department look good. Now you come in and really fuck up the works."

Eriksen contemplated telling the sheriff what he could do with his election but held his tongue. There were other ways to deal with Conrad. Besides, he knew that in less than two months Conrad might be gone anyway.

"So what's the matter, Dan? You shouldn't lose your cool like that. If you feel you're overworked and need a break, then just say the word. Darby is doing fine work, and what's-his-name from burglary who's been helping out, Slater, both those boys could probably handle this alone if you want to take off."

"You mean you don't want to risk having me embarrass you again?"

"See what I mean? You're edgy, Dan." Conrad sat his big frame in his leather chair behind his desk and put his yellow boots up. He was placating now. "A few days off just might do you good."

"I don't need any time off. I need six more hours in the day. I need more men. I've got Darby up at the state mental hospital today going through their records. That's going to take a day or two at least. We need to talk to a psychiatrist and see if he can give us a lead on this thing. We need—"

"Hold on, Eriksen." The sheriff put his feet down again. "Why would we need a psychiatrist?"

"He can look at all our evidence and perhaps find a behavior pattern. Maybe he can tell us something about the kind of person we should be looking for. It's something to consider, Sheriff, and I happen to know of a good psychiatrist here in San Miguel. He used to work in the City but came up here to get away from the rat race. He did quite a bit of work for the City police."

"We don't need a shrink messing around in this," Conrad said sharply. "First thing you know, the press would find out about it, then all our information would be leaked and we would blow the whole case. Just think what a field day the press would have interviewing a shrink. Christ, they'd probably say I was seeing him too. And who's going to vote for a sheriff who spends time with a psychiatrist? Hell's bells, the voters would think their sheriff was crazy. My opponent would play that up big. So let's just leave off on the shrink, okay?" Conrad started looking at some papers on his desk, and Eriksen knew he was dismissed. As he turned to the door, Conrad spoke once more.

"Remember now, if you want some time off, just say so."

Eriksen went to his office and closed the door. Lighting a Camel, he leaned back in his chair and studied the wall beside him where he had pinned up notes and photos of the two girls. Two girls. Both young. Both stripped of clothing and all jewelry except one earring. Both had pierced ears. Both girls had long hair parted in the middle. Both had been raped. Both had been manually strangled. Somewhere, he knew, there was a pattern in this, and he had better find it soon. He sat staring at the wall, so engrossed in his thoughts he barely looked up when Nancy brought him a fresh cup of coffee and made a weak attempt at small talk before realizing his mind was elsewhere. She was halfway out the door when he said, "We need a psychiatrist."

"Just because of last night?" she asked.

Eriksen came back to earth and rose for his coat. "Not for that, although I may ask the shrink why I didn't stay longer. I'm going to talk to a psychiatrist about this case, but don't tell the sheriff or Nye, or anyone."

He took a file containing fifty pages in which he had condensed every known aspect of the girls' deaths and Xeroxed them in the ID section. Harris sat nearby eating a thick sandwich.

"We got all kinds of good little items of evidence if you would just bring in a suspect we can pin it all on," he said through a mouthful of chicken.

Eriksen looked at him and ran off the copies in silence. He was tired of the jibes.

He drove slowly across town with the windows of his car down, but still the heat left him sweating heavily when he pulled up in front of a redwood-faced office. A carved wooden sign out front said "Benjamin A. Friedland, M.D., Psychiatrist." Inside, a matronly receptionist gave him a noncommittal "May I help you?"

"Yeah, I'm Sergeant Eriksen, sheriff's department." He paused and added heavily, "From homicide." He watched her eyes widen slightly and then said, "I need to talk to Dr. Friedland."

She thumbed quickly through a calendar in front of her. "I'm afraid he's tied up for several weeks. I can give you—"

"I don't want an appointment. I want to talk to him. Now." Eriksen felt his patience draining away.

"I am sorry, Sergeant," the receptionist said as she adjusted her glasses on her nose. "Dr. Friedland has just finished with a patient and is expecting his next one right now. If you would like to wait—"

"I don't want to wait," he said loudly. As he anticipated, Dr. Friedland emerged from a door marked "Private."

"What's the problem, Mrs. Thornton?" Friedland

was much younger than Eriksen had expected. He was in his early thirties, but the shock of red hair and a bushy red mustache made him appear even younger.

"This is Sergeant Eriksen from the sheriff's department. He insists on seeing you."

Friedland gave him an easy smile and told him to come into his office. After closing the door, Eriksen handed him the thick sheaf of notes.

"Your reputation precedes you, Doctor. Lieutenant Stallsworth with the City P.D. is a friend of mine. He told me some time ago that you had done some work for him. Here is just about everything we know about the deaths of Roberta Thomas and Jeannie Chavez."

"And?" asked Friedland with a quizzical look.

"I'm asking you to read through it all and see if you can't come up with something for me. Some pattern. Or at least tell me what this guy is like, what is driving him. Why is he killing young girls, and why these in particular." Eriksen sat down and dug a Camel out of the pack in his shirt pocket. Friedland watched in silence as he lit up and slowly exhaled.

"May I have one of those?" he finally asked. "I'm trying to give it up, but I'm not having much success. Instead of quitting, I find myself bumming more and enjoying less. A classic quandary."

Friedland puffed in obvious delight as he skimmed the notes. "Most interesting. I've been following the case, of course. Can't get away from it, in fact. It seems to be all the news there is. But this is much more detailed and accurate. So you want a profile of this person, eh?"

"I'll take whatever you can give me," Eriksen said. "Only one thing. I can't pay you."

Friedland looked up and pulled on his mustache. "Why not?"

"Because the sheriff won't authorize a psychiatrist. He's afraid it will result in bad publicity for him. So I'm asking you to do this out of the goodness of your heart. And keep it secret."

"Good-heartedness never paid a bill," Friedland said.

"I'll give you free cigarettes."

Friedland grinned. "All right. Besides, I can't resist

playing detective. The weekend is upon us, so check with me Monday and I'll see what I can do."

6

Eriksen opened his eyes, then slowly flexed the muscles in each leg and pushed his toes to the bottom of the bed. He turned his head and glanced at the clock on the nightstand. Just after seven, and the sunlight was only now reaching the window they always left uncurtained to catch the morning light. The days were definitely getting shorter, he thought. Daylight is running out. Everything seems to be running out.

Cynthia stirred beside him, and he turned toward her. She lay with the tip of her slightly freckled nose touching his shoulder and her auburn hair curling over one exposed shoulder. He kissed her ear, and she snuggled closer to him, eyes still closed. He rolled toward her and slid his hand over the full breasts encased in her silken nightgown. She stirred. One warm leg slid over his, and he could feel her nipples rise as he ran his fingers lightly over her breasts. Cynthia had put on weight in the past few years, which had given her a broad butt and a second chin, but Eriksen figured she still had the greatest knockers in town. Bigger than ever, now. The kind you want to put your face in and roll around on. She responded by kissing his neck, and for a while to Eriksen it was like old times. Like in the first few years of their marriage, when they had been lovers and enjoyed making love anytime, anywhere. For the moment he forgot the strangeness that had grown between them, forgot his job and the tenseness that he brought home each night. He forgot about her frustrations, how she felt about staying home all day with nothing but housework, cleaning, gardening, and television to entertain her mind. All this was put aside for a few minutes as he and Cynthia came together again in a passion play that was slow and leisurely. They lay locked together for nearly a half-hour afterward, until Eriksen began to stir.

"I better get going. Work to do." He pushed out of bed and went into the bathroom off their bedroom. Cynthia called to him from the bed.

"It's Sunday, Dan. You're not going to work today, are you?"

"I better. We just aren't coming up with any leads. Nothing. The sheriff is pissed at me, and so is Nye. So I'm going to reread, for the thousandth time, every report that we have on the girls. Maybe there is something in there that I have just overlooked. Something obvious."

"You know there isn't, Dan. You've done everything you or anybody else could. Why not put it out of your mind awhile?" He could hear her sitting up now. "You know what? It's such a beautiful day, why don't we go to the coast and go clamming? You and I and Denice. Make a whole day out of it and just forget the department for a day."

Eriksen looked at himself in the mirror. When he was in high school, another boy had taunted him that his face had caught on fire and someone had beaten it out with a track shoe. Dan had punched the boy senseless, one of the few fights he had ever been in as a kid. Nobody had talked about his face after that. But he had to admit that his face did look like it had been beaten with a track shoe. And the lines were deepening around his eyes, long tracks of time. The beach, he thought. Why not? The hell with Conrad. A few hours at the beach wouldn't hurt anything. Besides, he owed it to Cynthia and to Denice. He stuck his head out of the bathroom.

"Well, you better get up and get your britches on and get Denice up, because it's time to go clamming."

Cynthia laughed in delight. "It's about time, Mr. Detective."

Denice, who would sleep to noon on Sundays if ever given a chance, roused herself quickly at the prospect of going to the beach.

It was a clear and cool day, the first hint of fall. Eriksen put his arm around his wife as they drove, something he hadn't done in years, and Denice told them she thought they were ridiculous.

"Why? How about when you go out on dates? Don't the boys put their arms around you?" he asked.

"Daddy! It's not the same anyway. That's all right for kids, but not when you get old."

"Old! My daughter calls me old." Cynthia laughed. "Not yet forty and consigned to an old folks' home."

Eriksen stopped at a bait shop along the river before they hit the coast and bought a six-pack of beer. Today was a day to party, and they were going to enjoy it. At the coast he turned down a narrow road between two pasture fences that led to the sea. Dairy cows grazed on the bluffs above the breakers. The beach was deserted, and Eriksen felt like whooping as they clambered down to the rocky beach. There was a light offshore wind, just enough to catch the tops of the waves creaming toward the beach and spin the salt froth into a fine mist. Gulls wheeled in the bright blue sky overhead, and Eriksen eyed them suspiciously.

"If one of you craps on me, you better move out fast," he yelled, and patted the .357 on his hip beneath his windbreaker. Cynthia laughed, and Eriksen was struck by the fact that it seemed years since he had seen his wife so carefree. She was almost childlike in her delight to be on the beach with her family. He went over to her and put his arms around her, engulfing her in a bear hug. He slid his hand up under her sweater, cupping her breast in his hand. Cynthia yelped and pulled away.

"Dan! Not here. Denice is right here." She straightened her sweater and glanced around, brushing back an auburn lock. Denice was prancing down the beach, doing high kicks and twirls from her cheerleader routine. Eriksen turned back to his wife.

"She's gone. Let's slip behind that big dune over there for a quickie. How about it?" He moved toward her, but she ran squealing after Denice. Eriksen picked up the shovel and followed. The tide was out, just barely a minus tide, but enough to expose the small and delicious butter clams. He called the girls back and began digging.

He quickly uncovered more than a dozen of the cream-colored shells and took a two-inch ring from his pocket. Any shell that slipped through, he put back in the hole. While Cynthia and Denice went down the beach to gather some driftwood for a fire, Eriksen rinsed the clams in his small tin pot and went back to where they had left their supplies. Opening another beer, he lay back in the warm sun and allowed himself the luxury of imagining how he would catch the killer of Roberta Thomas and Jeannie Chavez. He saw himself pulling up at the Turpin mine just as another young girl was being dragged from the car by the killer. The girl was fighting and kicking but could not break free of the killer's powerful grip. The killer did not hear Eriksen until the last minute, when he whirled and dropped the girl. Eriksen reached for the killer and then stood paralyzed as he looked down at the girl choking and crying before him. He couldn't make out her face, but it seemed he should know her. As he bent to help her, the killer danced away, laughing and kicking his heels. He sat up with a start. Denice and Cynthia were staring at him.

"You sure were thrashing about, Daddy." There was a worried look on her face.

"You started talking and twitching just as we walked up," Cynthia added. "You were having a bad dream. I was going to wake you, but I was afraid you would jump up and attack me."

Eriksen shook his head to clear his mind. "Let's get this fire started."

"What were you dreaming about?" Cynthia asked, watching him carefully.

"Nothing. Something, but I can't remember," he said as he piled the kindling.

After the fire settled into a bank of coals, he covered the clams in white wine and put the pot on the fire. He let them cook until the clams opened their shells, then used a large spoon to set them on a plate. Eriksen popped a beer for himself while Cynthia poured another glass of white wine.

"Why don't we do this more often, Dad?" Denice asked.

"I can't give you any reasons against it. The question is, why weren't we doing it all summer?"

"Because you were so locked up in your job. You were being Sherlock Holmes at work and at home. You couldn't forget your job, even for one hour. This is the first time I have seen you relax in months." Cynthia was on her third glass of wine.

"I know it. I'm truly sorry, fair ladies. I shall try to do better by you. We will plan more family outings, and to heck with the job. All right?"

Denice smiled at him, but Cynthia poured another glass of wine and said quietly, "We've heard that before." A silence followed her statement, and Eriksen pushed himself to his feet.

"Time for another dozen clams. Want to help me dig?" He spoke to both, but only Denice jumped to her feet.

"I will, Dad. Let's go. Race you to the water." She darted away, and Eriksen watched his wife draw aimless patterns in the sand with her finger. She didn't say anything.

He walked toward the water's edge, where Denice was already shoveling back the surf-rounded rocks. She dug for only a few minutes before opening up another rich bed of the honey-colored clams. They squatted together and swirled their hands about in the cold ocean water, pulling out and sizing the shells.

"Can we just take a whole bucketful back, Dad?" Denice asked. "You know how much Mom and I love them."

"A dozen apiece is the limit."

"Who is going to know out here? We just eat them and then throw the shells back in the ocean. There's so much that if we eat an extra dozen or so no one will notice."

"But it's not right. It's a fair law and we should abide by it."

Denice was quiet for a moment as she ran her fingers around the pool for some more clams. "I hope it stays a nice day. I don't want you and Mom to get mad."

"I don't either." He didn't want to talk about it

anymore. "You run back and put a little wood on the fire while I wash these out." He watched her walk slowly back to where Cynthia sat having another glass of wine. Denice's earlier prance of a filly had given way to a dejected walk. She can sense our tensions and fears better than we can ourselves, Eriksen thought. He washed the clams in the surf and strode back to the fire, determined not to have the day spoiled. As he cooked the clams, Cynthia chattered brightly with Denice about how pretty the beach was, and Eriksen knew she was trying to smooth their moment of bitterness.

They ate the clams, then relaxed in the sun while he finished his six-pack and Cynthia downed the remainder of the wine. Eriksen said little as Cynthia began to tell Denice how she first met Dan, a story she retold every time she got a little high.

". . . and he looked so handsome in his deputy's uniform. He came into City Hall, where I was working, to ask about a robbery that had occurred the night before in my dad's store. They never did find that person, either. Well, there he was, so big and handsome and thin."

Eriksen sat up, abruptly bored by it all. "Let's go."

Cynthia, cut short in mid-sentence, turned toward him in annoyance. "We just got here. Can't we relax a minute? I suppose you want to rush right back to your precious little office."

"No, I don't want to do that at all." He kept his voice purposefully relaxed. "I want to drive down to Benton's Harbor. We can watch the fishing boats, and get some fresh crab. And buy a rock cod or two to take home. Make a real feast of today."

Denice jumped up in delight. "That's a great idea, Dad. You're not at all an old grouch, are you?" She laughed. Cynthia followed slowly as they returned to the car.

Eriksen picked up another six-pack for the drive along the wild and rocky coast south to Benton's Harbor, a small fishing village built around a narrow cove that people from the City had declared picturesque. On weekends it was filled with old men in sandals and straw hats, women with blue-veined legs bulging out of shorts, and scores of long-haired youths. The fishing boats, fresh crab, and braless girls made it attractive to Eriksen.

The harbor was jammed, and they had to park on the hill above the quays and make their way down the narrow main street lined with weathered houses and shops catering to the tourists. Eriksen viewed the crowd with mixed emotions. He liked to watch people, found their faces and mannerisms endlessly fascinating. But he could recall how it was just five years ago when Benton's Harbor had not yet been "discovered" by the City escapees. Then he knew several fishermen by name, and old Brittsan, who owned the Hook, Line, and Sinker Grill and Saloon, had time to lean across the polished redwood bar and spin him yarns about how hard it was to work the big fishing trawlers. Now Brittsan was gone, sold out to a City man who wasn't interested in idle talk. He would rather you drank and ate in a hurry so the people standing in line could unload their money.

There was a crowd around the sheds near the jetty. Two trawlers had arrived, not loaded with tons of their own catch, but with a crowd of Sunday fishermen. It was just as profitable to take the tourists out for a few hours, let them catch a few rock cod or flounders, then return for another load. More fishermen were standing in line to have their catch cleaned. They could have done it themselves, but that would mean getting their hands messy, Eriksen guessed. For just another dollar or two, the fishermen's wives would do it. The knives flashed as the women opened the fish bellies, spilled the innards into a barrel, and filleted one side in a long sweeping cut. Then the fish, with white bone exposed on one side, were flipped, and the other fillet removed in a single slice. Fish after fish.

With his big hand around a beer and his lungs full of the salt air, Eriksen led Cynthia and Denice around to a small store near the quay, where they bought two large crabs that had just been pulled from a drum of boiling water. At the end of the quay, away from the crowds, he cracked the crabs to get at the succulent white meat. Eriksen had a crab, and juice smeared all over his face.

"Why wasn't I a fisherman?" he asked no one in particular.

"Because you would be bored stiff in a week doing this. No chase, no challenge, nobody to catch." Cynthia was just nibbling at the crab.

Resentment flared in Eriksen. "Look, let's not get bitchy. All right? Let's just enjoy the air and the sun."

Denice threw the shells of her crab into the sea that swirled around the pilings below and rose to her feet. "I want to walk around for awhile, okay?" She was already moving away.

"Don't go too far," Eriksen yelled after her. He turned back to Cynthia, who was staring out to sea. "Don't ruin the day, all right, Cynthia? Let's try to keep it a little brighter, if only for Denice's sake."

"For Denice, Denice, Denice. How about for my sake? I'm your wife, you know! How about something for my sake?"

"Like what?"

"Like a little attention. Like a night out on the town sometime. Like you coming home for dinner, staying with us on weekends. That's what like." Her voice rose as long-suppressed anger filled her throat.

"Cynthia, we've been married fifteen years, and I've been a cop all that time. You knew I was a cop before we got married. I've been away night and weekends for much of my career. And there were years when I didn't even get overtime for the extra hours. Do you think you could have your nice clothes, a new car every other year, and new furniture or appliances when you need them on my regular salary? Overtime makes a big difference."

"But I didn't marry you to get a new car or a new stove. I married you because I loved you and wanted to be with you." Cynthia had her head down, staring at the curling waves below, trying to hide her tears. "I just want you home more, spending some time with me, caring what I think about, what I do during the day. That's all."

Eriksen opened a can of beer he had tucked in

the pocket of his windbreaker and offered her a drink. "Here. It will make you feel better."

She shook her head. "I've had too much already."

Eriksen drank in silence, watching the gulls wheel about the trawler that was preparing to take another noisy group of Sunday fishermen out to the point.

"We better be getting back. We've got to find Denice."

Cynthia flashed at him. "Damn it, Denice can take care of herself. She's not a baby, you know. What about us? What are you going to do? You haven't said anything. You just drink your damned beer."

"What the hell do you want me to say? That I'm going to quit my job and stay home all day? Or that I'm going to tell Nye and the sheriff that I can't spend any extra time on cases because my wife wants me to come home and hold her hand? What can I say? What the hell can I do? I've got a job to do and it happens to be a job I like. At least I don't get bitching and crying from people in the office." He stood up, angry now and aware of the rasping bite of his voice as he spoke to her. "Let's go." He turned and walked away, leaving Cynthia alone on the end of the quay.

I lay in the sea grass on the bluff overlooking the small beach where they played, and wished I had my sunglasses. I had to remain constantly on guard. It was the painful lightbarbs that danced toward me off the waves that I worried about, not them seeing me. They hadn't noticed me on the drive from San Miguel to the beach, even though at one time I parked only three cars away from them when he stopped to buy beer. Now they were drinking again and cooking clams and would never see me. The girl with the mane of hair might look up, but she was not my concern. I wanted to know more about this man who was chasing me without knowing who I was. So far it had been easy to watch him without being seen. Even this morning as I waited down the street, just waiting and watching their house on the chance he might go somewhere, it had been so easy. I thought they were going to church when they all drove off, but here we are on the beach.

Now I was the cat and they were the mice, and I could play with them all day. It was so simple! The detective even had his name and address in the telephone book. I thought the police had unlisted numbers, but not Eriksen. So now it was just a matter of watching and waiting. Finally, after nearly two hours, Eriksen put out the fire and collected their garbage, indicating he was about to leave. I turned and ran down the slope back to the road. By jogging all the way I easily made it back to my car before they appeared. They turned the other way, not toward town but on toward Benton's Harbor, so I let them pull out of sight before I turned to follow.

When we reached the hill above the harbor, I found the glitter from the water to be quite painful; the light-shards from the waves were unusually threatening. A lightspear in the eye can hurt sharply, and moreover, from the eye it can penetrate the body's system and do extensive damage. I rummaged about in my glove compartment and found my sunglasses. At least my eyes would be protected; that is most important. The eyes are not only vulnerable but revealing, often giving away information that the brain wants to be kept secret. But eyes are essentially feminine and thus more vulnerable, more open to damage. I believe that is an accepted medical fact.

The Eriksens were making their way down the hill as I parked, and I soon lost them in the crowd, but I wasn't concerned because, again, they were trapped in this little bay. As I was getting out of the car, I distinctly felt a neuron crackle in my left knee as it leaped a synapse. I paused, concerned that there would be more, but my system coordinator was quiet now. I walked down the steep hill that led to the harbor and the fishing boats crowded along the jetties. I was conscious of increasing movement around me. The colors were tending to blur, and I knew my eye filters were opening wider than they should, but the dark glasses would help. I wandered about with my hands stuffed in my blue jeans like everyone else until I picked up the scent of the Eriksens again. I saw the girl first, coming down the jetty toward me; her parents were still sitting at the other end. I followed her at a distance, watching the way her blond ponytail swung as she walked, how her low-cut jeans clung to the curve of her hip, and how her blouse was tied in front, exposing a smooth expanse of skin. I closed the gap on her, trying to ignore the stares from other girls passing by. Several laughed as they walked, and while they didn't do it to my face, I knew they were laughing at me. They usually did. It was something I had faced all my life. It got worse after I finished high school. I sought refuge in the library, in my wonderful world of books. But even there I wasn't safe. The smiles and whispers were always around me, but I wouldn't let them destroy me right now. I put them out of my head, no easy task when you have a racing mind like mine, and eased up beside the girl, who was watching the women clean the fish. There were many people standing around, some fishermen, but mostly the tourists, who stood with a horrible fascination watching the bright knife wink as it slid smoothly into the anus of the fish and then easily to the gills, exposing the coils of intestine, the large stomach, and the red heart. The women wore bloody rubber gloves. Their rubber aprons and rubber boots were also spattered with blood and innards and water. I looked at the faces around me, impassive men and women with their mouths slightly parted as they watched the knives slide in so easily—in-and-out-and-blood, in-and-out-and-blood. From the safety of my dark glasses I studied the expression on the Eriksen girl. Her small pink tongue came out slowly to wet her lips, her eyes were wide with the thrill of butchery. But as she saw the innards of a particularly large rock cod burst from the stomach onto the wooden table, her nose wrinkled. "Yeccchh," she said. It was my opening.

"It's not bad when you get used to it. My mother did it for years for a living."

She turned toward me now, and her eyes were bluer than the sea, bright with light. "Really?" She made a face.

"Yes," I said easily with a smile that I knew revealed my very even and white teeth. "I grew up here.

My father was a fisherman and I was going to be one to. But then . . ." I looked down at the wet concrete floor and kicked my toe a little. "Well, he was killed, and so that was that."

She was listening now, and so were others around. I just wanted to talk with her, so I touched her arm and said, "Come out here and I'll show you the boat he used to own." She hesitated. "Come on," I said with a smile. In the bright and warm sun on the jetty I pointed at a particularly large trawler halfway down. "That was it. It used to be called the *Sea Witch*. Maybe it wasn't a good name, didn't have the right vibes, because it was a sea witch that killed my dad."

"A sea witch?" I could see she was incredulous.

"Yes. Oh, everyone said he just got washed overboard in a sudden squall. But my mother and I knew it wasn't true. It was the sea witch who reached from the green waters, an arm of white froth, and pulled him from the ship. She wanted him then, and when the sea witch wants you, there is nothing you can do, nowhere you can hide. And she knows it, because a fisherman will always return to the sea. And she will always be waiting."

She was looking up at me, and I could see a dusting of freckles across her short nose. Her mouth was parted, lips bright pink without the need of lipstick, teeth small and even. Then she laughed. "You're just putting me on."

I gave her a small, sad smile, one that would evoke sympathy. "Well, I lost my father, and my mother had to go to work there in the sheds cleaning fish. When I was small I used to help clean up so she could get home earlier and take care of us kids." I didn't want to come on too heavy, so I said cheerfully, "Come on, I'll show you where I used to play. And I know which shop makes the best ice cream. I haven't been back here in years, and I want to look around. Do you come to Benton's Harbor often?"

"No, just sometimes during the summer. I came down with my folks today. It's only the second time we came down this year." I saw her turn and look toward the end of the jetty, where her two parents still sat alone. "That's them out there. They're having a fight. Again." She made a face of disappointment.

"Well, come on. We'll have some ice cream and leave them to work out their problem. Let's not get ourselves involved."

She shrugged and followed. I wasn't sure how old she was, somewhere, I guessed, between sixteen and eighteen. Maybe younger, but she was tall, about five-feet-four, and her young breasts pushed at the fabric of her thin white blouse. I could see the outline of her low-cut bra through the blouse.

"My name is Jerry," I said as we walked through the crowd toward the shops. I don't know why I told her a phony name, maybe because I had already woven a pattern of deceit and I wanted to continue it. Besides, it was important to know her before she knew me.

"Mine's Denice," she said, and added, "If you don't live here now, where do you live?"

"In San Miguel, going to the junior college."

"That's where we live too. My daddy is a detective for the sheriff's department."

"Oh," I said, and let it go at that. I bought us each a double-decker chocolate cone and we just walked, idly looking at the shells, necklaces and bracelets, and clothes for sale in the small shops. A synapse popped once more in my knee, a reminder that the current was still strong within me but just not switched on at the moment. I found myself relaxed with Denice. There seemed to be no threatening vibrations from her, which was unusual. Most girls I knew held deep hatreds against me, and I was always aware of their hatreds, which were really fears. But not so with Denice, and—

"I think my Dad is looking for me," Denice said. From where we were standing, about halfway up the hill, I could see her father come slowly out of the shed, his head turning, eyes pivoting, like a bird dog tracking a pheasant. He was looking for her, all right.

"The detective is trailing you." I smiled.

"I think he wants to go home now. Either that or he has left Mom to find some more beer. I guess I better go down and see him." She turned toward me, not looking at me, but waiting for me to tell her to stay with me.

"I guess you better," I said, and there was a perceptible sag to her shoulders.

"Come on down and meet him. You'll like him," She took my hand in hers and gently pulled me down the hill. I resisted, and she stopped and turned toward me.

"I can't right now." I looked at my watch. "I'm late. Lot of studies to catch up on. You go on down and I'll see you again sometime . . . okay?"

"Okay." She wasn't smiling now, just looking at the ground. She looked up at me. "I'm a cheerleader, and so if you ever go to any of the old high-school games, maybe I'll see you there." There was a question in her voice, and I said I would like that. Then she smiled and said, "Good-bye, Jerry."

I raised my glasses for the first time, and I saw her eyes study mine, switching back to the one with the second pupil. " 'Bye, Denice. Take care now." I turned and began climbing the hill toward my car. When I neared the top, I paused to catch my breath, and turned to see her making her way slowly down. She was near the bottom now, and her father had spotted her and was gesturing at her to follow him.

"I've been looking all over for you. I told you not to go too far." Eriksen felt angry at everything. The day seemed spoiled, even the sunshine didn't seem as bright, and he looked up to confirm it. A high thin layer of clouds had moved in and veiled the sun. "Where have you been?"

"Just walking around looking in the shops and watching the boats. This is such a pretty place, Daddy." She took his arm as they walked back toward the jetty. "And I met a nice boy. He bought me an ice-cream cone. And you know what? He must have thought I'm a lot older than I am." She grinned impishly at her dad.

"Who was he?" Eriksen asked.

"His name is Jerry."

"Jerry what?"

"People don't give their last names anymore, Dad. You only need one name."

"How did you meet him?"

"What is this? Sounds like the third degree!" Denice said mockingly.

"Oh, honey, I just don't like the idea of a strange boy being friendly with you." He paused then asked again, "How did he approach you?"

Denice couldn't resist. "I was watching them clean the fish, and we just started talking. He used to live here. His dad was a fisherman who got killed by the sea witch."

"The what?"

Denice giggled. "That's what he said. A sea witch got his father at sea and he drowned. Then his mother had to work at cleaning fish to support them. Now he goes to school in San Miguel, at the junior college. He must have been nineteen or twenty, Dad."

"You, young lady, are still too young to be going around with boys that old."

"Why?"

Her question disconcerted Eriksen momentarily. How to tell your daughter that a guy is dating you for only one reason, to get into your pants. "Well, because older boys are more experienced. You should learn experience at your own pace, with boys your own age. With older boys, you might go too fast."

"That's what they invented the pill for, Daddy." She grinned at him, but Eriksen felt stunned. No girl ever talked like that to her parents when he was growing up. But then, he reasoned, they didn't have the pill, either.

"Run out to the end of the jetty and tell your mother to come on. Time to be getting home." He was glad he didn't have to carry the conversation any further. He wasn't ready for it yet. Cynthia chatted with Denice as they came toward him, and he knew she was trying to keep up a bright front, but he could see her eyes were red and puffy from crying. Denice knew it too, but she was carrying on as if nothing had happened, telling her mother about the super boy she had met and how there were so many boys around here and they should come every weekend.

"Mom, if he asked me to a dance at the college, could I go with him?"

"Let's worry about that when it happens," she said in a manner that ended the discussion.

7

Eriksen swung into the parking space in front of Friedland's office and wondered how it could be so hot before noon. His shirt stuck to his back as he walked to the office door, and he considered leaving his coat off, but then that old bag of a receptionist would see the .357 on his hip and have a heart attack.

This time there was no flak from Mrs. Thornton. "Go right in, Mr. Eriksen. Dr. Friedland is expecting you."

Friedland's greeting was to the point. "You have some problems, Sergeant."

Eriksen did not find that an auspicious opening. He sat down with a sigh. "I know you're going to tell me more than that." He lit a Camel and blew a thin stream of smoke at the floor as he watched Friedland return to his desk and shuffle through his notes. He considered offering a cigarette to the psychiatrist but then decided that would not help him quit the habit.

"I've got everything written down—or rather I should say, my secretary is transcribing my scrawl for you now. But I'll give you my impressions of this man. He is what we searchers of the mind, in all our professional majesty, call a real loony." Friedland flashed a boyish grin and went on. "My overall feeling—just a gut reaction—is that he is a paranoid schizophrenic and not a sociopath. I'll explain this eventually. As a schizophrenic, he suffers from a gross distortion of reality. His thought is disorganized and fragmented much of the time. At times he can be quite normal, and then he slips away from reality. It's as if the protective screen that shields our mind from too much input simultaneously is removed and all his senses begin bombarding the brain. The brain can't, and won't, take it. The most inane sound, such as someone coughing, may cause him to believe he is being followed and that the person is out to kill him. He will strike back again and again until stopped, because he cannot control himself. Could I have one of your cigarettes, please?" Friedland found his own match and lit the cigarette Eriksen gave him. He inhaled with pleasure.

"I go a week or so and then I smoke a couple times and go another week. No willpower at all. Sometimes I think my mind is dissolving." He looked down at his papers again and went on. He seemed to need no reaction from Eriksen.

"This man we are looking for believes he is being persecuted by someone or something and he must strike back. There will be more detail and explanation in my final report. I'll go on to the person himself now. First, we can assume it was a man, because both girls were raped and semen was found in their vaginas. Also, considerable strength was used in overpowering and strangling these girls. Now, how would he approach these girls? I would imagine he is quite normal, even pleasing, in appearance. He has a manner that puts the girls at ease. He is, I am sure, older than they are, but he can still relate to these young teenagers." Friedland appeared totally absorbed in his notes.

"He knows the area well, as I'm sure you already deduced. 'Deduced' is a good word for police work, isn't it? Conjures up images of Sherlock Holmes solving crimes by deduction." Friedland stubbed out the cigarette in nervous little pile-driving motions and went on. "Well, why does he take the clothing off in all instances? Probably a fetish need on his part. He associates the clothing with his victims. It probably gives him a continued feeling of superiority over them. He still has them in his control. He may even keep this clothing somewhere, like a hunter would hang trophies of his kills on the wall. If any of your deputies should come across a room full of young women's clothing, they should become very alert." Friedland flashed another grin and continued.

"Now. He takes most of the jewelry but leaves one earring behind. Why would he do this?" Friedland stared at Eriksen as if expecting an answer. Eriksen slowly drew another cigarette from his pocket and lit it, noting that the psychiatrist's eyes dropped and followed the measured ritual of smoking. Friedland abruptly turned back to his papers.

"He leaves a piece of jewelry, I believe, because he is deliberately challenging the police to catch him. That reflects guilt, and that is why I suspect he is schizophrenic, not a sociopath. Leaving the earring may be a subconscious move on his part. Such actions are not at all uncommon. But this man is very cunning, very careful. He also probably works alone, and talks to no one about his crimes. So, Sergeant Eriksen, I think you are going to have a very difficult time with this man."

"That I am already very much aware of. Can you tell me more about him as a person?"

"As I mentioned, he is almost certainly pleasant-looking and has an easy manner when he wants to approach his victims. I suspect there is something in common about them, some reason that makes him think they must die. It could be a Messiah complex on his part, he being imbued with religion and out to save the world by ridding it of certain evil women. It could also be he is acting out his subconscious hatred of his mother. He may find something in these girls that reminds him of his mother and that sets him off."

"But what about him, anything about his physical characteristics?"

"He is most likely Caucasian. Why, you ask? Because the greatest percentage of rape-murders are done by Caucasians. He is a young man—because of the rapes involved—and we can assume he is somewhere in his late teens to early twenties because of his ability to approach and gain the confidences of these young women.

"I want to go back to another point." He paused and

looked at Eriksen. "May I have another cigarette, please? One is never enough." He lit it and drew the smoke deeply into his lungs. "Blessed nicotine. Where was I? Oh, yes. I believe that in general he distrusts women, even hates them. Again, possibly acting out his maternal hatreds. He feels great contempt for women in general, and this contempt becomes so great in certain cases that he takes their lives. And by destroying those lives he receives certain gratification at the time, to later be replaced by feelings of guilt and some remorse."

Eriksen allowed himself a crooked grin as he stood up. "So if I find some punk haranguing his mother and then picking fights with young girls, I've got my man?"

"That's it. See? Simple. Once again psychiatry strikes a blow for justice. Wouldn't it be nice if it were so simple?" He shook hands with Eriksen at the door. "I am very much interested in this case now. Keep me posted on any new developments, will you?" Eriksen assured him he would and turned to go, but Friedland continued talking.

"One other thing. It's in the report, but I want to emphasize it now. This killer isn't going to just stop his actions, heal himself, or go away. He will continue killing girls until you find him and stop him. That is the nature of his illness."

Eriksen's pale eyes swept over the slender psychiatrist, "You really know how to make a guy feel good."

He headed back to his office and found himself thinking about yesterday on the beach. Why hadn't they gone more this summer instead of just letting everything slip by? He sighed and rubbed his neck. What a fucking mess this is, he thought. Why not just chuck it all and go live on the beach? Live off clams and beer. There were worse ways to go, he thought. Maybe things would look better if his fragile peace with Cynthia hadn't broken down. This morning she was halfway friendly again, as if a cautious truce had been declared, but both of them knew it was more for Denice than anything else. He wasn't sure how much longer it would last, or how long he wanted it to last. He couldn't help comparing how easy it seemed to talk to Nancy, and the pleasure he found in her company compared with the tense mood in his own house. He put the thoughts out of his mind as he pulled into his parking space.

He hung up his coat and was about to sit down when Bill Darby burst around the corner and dashed into his office.

"Dan, glad you're back. This will make you happy." Darby was hurriedly putting on his jacket. "Car 14 is rolling on a fight at the Ace of Spades. One dude reported down and dead."

"Son of a bitch! I'm going to kick Ace's black ass," Eriksen said. "He passes out Ripple to those dudes as fast as he can cash their welfare checks, then just stands back and lets them go at it."

He was still fuming as they sped toward the southern edge of town, where blacks, Chicanos, and Indians were jammed into row upon row of clapboard duplexes. "That's all we need is a whole rash of homicides now. But on the other hand, it would give the papers and television something else to talk about besides Thomas and Chavez."

"And that would be a break. You ought to hear my old lady get on me every time I go home," Darby said. "All she wants to know is when are we going to take that rapist off the streets. She says all the neighbors ask her the same thing, so she's just passing it on to me." At a stoplight, Darby removed his sunglasses long enough to wink at a redhead driving the adjoining car. As the light changed she yelled, "Turkey!" and laid rubber for thirty feet.

"Now, how could she say that to me," Darby groaned. "We ought to pull her ass over. She just doesn't understand who she was talking to."

"We've got a 187 laying on Ace's floor, remember?"

"Yeah, well, maybe Ace will at least give us some ribs. Man, he has the best barbecued ribs in town."

Two patrol cars with lights revolving blocked both entrances to the Ace of Spades parking lot. The restaurant was a small white frame building with a green asphalt shingle roof and a long sagging porch. About twenty black men and half a dozen women stood on the porch peering through the door and windows. As Eriksen mounted the wooden steps to the porch the crowd fell back. They didn't need to ask who he was.

"Come on, let the man through."

"Yeah, *po*-lice gonna check it all out."

Inside, where the light was dim and the air cool, the first thing Eriksen saw was a slender black youth, about twenty, lying on his back with a bone-handled knife protruding from his chest. Eriksen swung his eyes to the left, where Ace stood behind the linoleum-topped bar, massive arms folded across his chest. Ace was past sixty and gray-haired, but was still a huge and powerful man. Rumors, fed by Ace himself, said he had killed at least six men in years gone by. He looked enormously bored by the whole scene. One of the two deputies inside was taking notes as Ace gave his laconic description of what had happened. Eriksen went over, and Ace stepped forward to shake his hand.

"Hello, Sergeant Eriksen. Ain't seen you in a long time."

"Yeah, I go away for a few weeks, and look what happens. Another stiff on your floor, Ace. That's no way to do business."

"Shee-it, you telling me, man. Look at all them thirsty tongues out there on the porch, and can't serve a one of them till the *po*-lice leave. How about it, Sergeant, can you get that body out of here right now?"

"That depends, Ace. Suppose you give me a real good description of who did it."

"Aw, it happened so fast, Sergeant, I hardly seen anything. You know, I'm tending bar and serving ribs."

Eriksen turned and surveyed the body again. Darby was admiring the knife still in the chest. "That's a real pig-sticker, Dan."

"We might have to leave that body there half the night, right, Bill? We can't just hurry through this business."

Ace unfolded his arms. "Say, my man, you just trying to put a hurt on my business, ain't you?"

"You know we wouldn't do that, Ace," Eriksen said in an apologetic tone. "But we can't do much until we find out what happened here."

"Shee-it." Ace looked at the sea of faces pressed against the window, watching his moves. "No way I can tell the *po*-lice anything. I don't *know* nothing," he said loudly.

Darby stepped forward. "How about we just close this place up and you come down to our office to talk about it? How about that?"

"You want to bust me, go ahead, man," Ace said, loudly again, and grinned at the faces in the window. They grinned back.

Eriksen said nothing as Darby turned to get confirmation from him. Instead he walked to the far end of the bar and said, "You still making good ribs, Ace?"

"The best, you know that, Sergeant. You ate enough of them." Ace laughed and slowly walked away from the window to stand close to Eriksen. "Look here, man, you ain't going to really run my ass in, are you?"

"Come on, Ace, who did it? Was he a friend of yours?"

"Shee-it no, just one badass nigger who can't handle his wine," he said in a low voice. "His name's Selwyn Hopkins. Lives with his old lady in a jive-ass shack down the end of Russell Street. You know that place?"

"Yeah, I know it." He turned to leave. "Thanks, Ace."

"You won't tell nobody I tole you, will you?" Ace scowled down at Eriksen.

"Of course not."

Ace gave him a broad wink. "You the man, you got all the guns," he shouted, "you want to take Ace downtown, then put the cuffs on and let's go."

Eriksen ignored him. He went to the deputy guarding the door. "As soon as ID finishes the pictures, tell them to get the stiff out of here and let Ace open up again." He turned and signaled to Darby. "Come on."

Eriksen gunned the unmarked car south for two more blocks and swung down a narrow dirt road. "The guy who did it is named Selwyn Hopkins. He lives right down here. You take the back and I'll see if our friend happens to be in."

As soon as Darby leaped the small wire fence around the backyard, Eriksen knocked on the front door. There was no sound from within, but he saw the drawn window shade to the right of the porch move slightly as someone eyeballed him. He freed the .357 on his belt and knocked again.

A woman's voice close by the closed door said softly, "What you want?"

"I'm looking for Selwyn Hopkins."

"He ain't here."

"Open the door, ma'am, or we'll come in by ourselves. We have reason to believe he's in there."

The door latch turned, and he saw a glittering black eye stare at him through the slightly open door. "Say, Sergeant Eriksen. How come you askin' after Selwyn?" She opened the door wide and Eriksen saw it was Darlene, a girl who used to be a waitress for Ace.

"Is he here, Darlene?" he asked, and remained away from the door.

Darlene came out and looked cautiously up and down the street. "He was here just about fifteen minutes ago. That no-good nigger hit me upside the head! For no reason. What he do, anyway?"

"Somebody got knifed at Ace's. Dead. We want to talk to Selwyn about it."

Darlene, a pretty girl of twenty-two with a wild afro, stared at Eriksen. "Damn! He come runnin' into the house just cryin' because he was so afraid. He had blood all over the front of his pants. Said someone cut him. I tried to help him, tried to get his pants off, and that's when he up an' hit me. Then he took my car keys and just tore outta here."

Eriksen stepped inside as he listened, and made a quick search.

"I done tole you he ain't here. Whatsa matter, you don't believe me?" She was growing angry.

"I believe you, Darlene. Where'd he go?"

"I don't know. He just flat-ass tore outta here. Only about fifteen minutes ago. He was yelling about bleedin' to death. He had blood on the front of his pants, you know."

Eriksen called Darby and explained what he had learned as they drove.

"You want me to alert the highway patrol?" Darby asked, and reached for the mike.

"Yeah, he went off in a gray 1965 Mustang, license number ORN 311."

As Darby relayed the description, Eriksen drove at high speed toward General Hospital. "I'm going to play a hunch," he explained.

He wheeled into the emergency area and pushed through the glass doors, with Darby close behind. In the waiting area sat an old man with blood trickling from a scalp wound. A mother held a weeping young boy who was decidedly green about the face. There was no bleeding black man.

"Son of a bitch," Eriksen said. "I felt sure we would catch him here. If he's hurt, he's not going to drive too far."

"We could wait for him, or get a patrolman over here," Darby said.

"Yeah, maybe." Eriksen walked across the green-tiled floor to where a nurse behind a receiving desk sat watching him. He showed her his identification.

"Did a black kid, about twenty-five years old, come in here just a few minutes ago?"

"Yes. He said he had been stabbed in the groin. He's in room eight, just to your right. They just took him in there."

Eriksen grinned at Darby. "How's that for luck?" He opened the door, and the two detectives slipped in. Hopkins lay on a stainless-steel table covered with green sheets. He groaned and his head rocked back and forth as a doctor and nurse pulled down his blood-stained pants.

"Oh, man, it hurt! Be careful, man, I think that dude must've got me in a nut."

The doctor looked up inquiringly at Eriksen, who silently showed his badge and signaled for the two to proceed. Hopkins lay with his head pointed at Eriksen and could not see him.

"You say you were knifed?" the doctor said as he cut away the blood-soaked underpants.

"Yeah, this guy just stabbed me for no reason. Just got me where it could do the most damage."

The doctor looked up with a slight grin at Eriksen and then asked Hopkins: "Where did you get cut?"

"Can't you see it? All that blood, man, he must have cut an artery. Felt like it must be the nut, or somewhere down there."

"Thought you might bleed to death?" the doctor asked.

"Hey, man, I don't need all the questions. Just fix me up."

"There's nothing to fix up."

Selwyn propped himself up on his elbows. "Say what?" He looked down at himself and then up at the doctor. "Look at all that blood. What you mean I ain't cut?"

"All that blood is from somebody else," the doctor said.

Selwyn grabbed his pants and slid off the table. "Shee-it. I gotta get outta here." He had his pants halfway up when he turned and saw Eriksen and Darby watching him.

Eriksen wagged a finger at him. "You've been a very naughty boy, Selwyn."

Hopkins' eyes bugged, and he sagged back against the steel table. "Oh, man, the pigs got me already. This is the worst day of my life."

"Get your britches up, Selwyn, or I'll have to bust you for indecent exposure too," Eriksen said, and pulled out his handcuffs. "Let's go."

By the time he finished booking Hopkins and taping his report, it was nearly six. Where the hell did the day go? He looked up as Nancy came in with a sheaf of papers. She wore a straight green plaid skirt and a clinging soft jersey top.

"Too bad about that murder today, Dan. That's just going to mean more time in court and more paperwork."

"That's what I'm paid for. At least it wasn't another girl."

She looked through the partially open door into the adjoining office, where Darby was still bent over his paperwork. "I'm going now," she said, and added softly, "Are you going to be able to get away? Meet for a short one at the Hilton?"

Eriksen waved at the stack of paper on his desk. "I'll be lucky if I get out of here tonight at all."

"Well, if you need a cup of soup later tonight, I'll be home," she said quietly.

"I'd love that, Nancy, but there's a freshman football game tonight, and I promised my daughter I'd watch her be a cheerleader. This is her first game, and she's been working on routines with the other girls for weeks."

"All right, another night." Nancy gave him a quick smile and walked away to get her coat.

"I'd still like to crawl in bed with her," Darby said. He was leaning against the door, watching her in frank admiration.

"Ever ask her?"

"No, I'm waiting for just the right moment. Timing is everything with a girl like that."

"Well, rots of ruck," Eriksen said noncommittally, and wondered if Darby had overheard them. He asked, "Did you ever come up with anything from the nut house?"

"*Nada.* Not one thing. They didn't have any released sex offenders that we hadn't already checked out. It was another bust."

Eriksen lit a Camel and leaned back in his chair to study for the thousandth time the photographs of Roberta Thomas and Jeannie Chavez on the wall beside his desk. "We've checked nearly two hundred possibles and eliminated them all. We're still up shit creek without a paddle."

"Something will break pretty soon."

"Yeah. That's what I'm afraid of. The wrong kind of a break." He turned back to his paperwork. "Take off, Bill, I've got to watch Denice be cheerleader tonight, so I'm going to work until game time and then head over there. See you in the morning."

At eight P.M. Eriksen locked his office and drove

across town to the school football field. Halfway, he turned toward Nancy's apartment. He had a little time. If he got there before the end of the game, it would be all right. He parked and ran lightly up to the second floor where she lived. He felt younger tonight than he had in weeks, and he knew it was all in anticipation of things to come with Nancy. She met him at the door, wearing a gray silk robe that resembled a kimono. Sliding her arms around him, she gave him a light kiss and said, "Take that big gun off. It's in our way."

"I've got another big gun that'll be just right." He grinned.

"Don't be lewd."

"That's my natural self. And the law says two consenting adults can be lewd in the privacy of their own home." He followed her across the small carpeted living room to the kitchenette, where she poured him a long shot of Jack Daniels.

"Tell me about today," she said as they sat on the couch.

"Didn't you type my report?"

"Yes, but I want to hear it from you," she said, eyes bright with excitement.

"Nothing special. A black kid ended up with a shiv in his chest. The dude who stuck him thought he was cut, and we found him at the hospital. Why this interest?"

"I like police work. That's why I took a job at the department. I thought I could be close to the action." She leaned toward him, and he could smell her hair. "Could I ride with you some night when things will be happening?"

"I don't think Sheriff Conrad would be too wild about that idea," Eriksen said. He leaned over to nuzzle her neck.

"I suppose your wife wouldn't be either," Nancy said, and moved back. She placed a slender fingertip against the slight indentation in his jaw. "What would she think if she knew you were here right now?"

"I don't know. I'll ask, if you wish."

Nancy laughed. "You do that and you'll be investigating my murder next."

Eriksen sipped his bourbon and eyed her over the rim of the glass. "Since you brought up my wife, why are you sitting here with a married man?"

"Now you're getting personal again, Dan."

"Just curious."

"Well, I have quite a few dates, but most of them are either dull or just want to get married. I'm not ready for that. There's got to be more to life than just working or having babies, don't you think?" She watched him with wide blue eyes.

"Like what?" he asked cautiously.

"Oh, I don't know. But something. Some wild fling, some wild gamble. Like we're gambling with each other, aren't we? You being here puts you in a compromising position. If Conrad found out, he might even fire you. And if your wife found out, who knows what would happen?" She leaned against him and put an arm around his neck. "But I don't care. That's what's wild and fun."

He kissed her, long and deep. "I like your kind of gambling," he said when they parted.

"But someone always has to lose in gambling. Right? Everyone can't be a winner," she said, and ran a finger down the crease in his pants.

"Well, let's not worry about that right now," Eriksen said, and pulled her close again. She resisted.

"Who's going to be the winner in this round?" she asked, and gave him a level look.

He leaned back, feeling the moment slip away. "You're getting too philosophical for me, Nancy. Philosophers only confuse everybody by raising questions with multiple answers. Choose whichever suits you best."

She pulled the robe tighter about her and picked at an invisible piece of lint that lay on the curve of her breast. "I don't have any answers, I'm just curious to know where you think we're headed."

"How about to bed?" he said.

"We'll see," she said without smiling.

Eriksen knew the moment had definitely gone. He stood up and clipped his holster back on his belt.

"Don't go," she said.

"I've got to. I promised to see Denice at the game, and it must already be the fourth quarter." He kissed the corner of her mouth and she held his arm until he gently pulled away and let himself out.

There were less than five minutes to play when he arrived at the stadium. Fewer than one hundred people sat on the wooden benches, mostly parents and students. Denice was in the middle of a routine with the four other girls, and he watched her graceful movements with pride. Her blond hair swirled and glinted in the stadium lights and her dance steps were quick and sure. He clapped loudly when the little band wheezed to a stop, and found he was the only one in the crowd clapping. It was then he saw that the home team was trailing by fourteen points. When the gun sounded he joined other parents and kids who milled about on the grass in front of the seats. He lost sight of Denice in the crowd and had to stand on a bench to find her again. She and Cheri were talking with a boy who had his back to Eriksen. Someone trying to line up a date with Denice, he thought to himself, and started toward her. When he broke out of the crowd of parents and players and saw her again, the boy was on his way out of the stadium and Denice and Cheri were giggling and hugging each other.

"You don't seem particularly upset at watching the San Miguel frosh get shellacked," he said.

"Hi, Daddy. Did you get to see much of the game? Did you see Cheri and me do our thing? We're the real stars out here, you know," Denice said, and they both burst out laughing again. Then she grabbed his arm and tilted her blue eyes up at him in a look of mock seduction. He knew a curve ball was coming.

"Daddy, the team and the other cheerleaders, and lots of kids, are all going over to the Pizza Palace to celebrate."

"To celebrate what, a fourteen-point loss?"

"No, just to celebrate. It's what they always do after night games. Can I go?" She held on tighter. "Please?"

"Tomorrow's a schoolday, Denice. It's late enough as it is."

"Please, Daddy!" She bit her lip.

"Not tonight, honey." He looked at Cheri. "Do you want to ride home with us?"

Cheri's brown curls swung as she shook her head. "No thanks, Dan. My folks said I could go to the Pizza Palace, and then I'll ride my bike home from there. It's not very far."

"All right. But be careful," he said. Denice gave Cheri a mournful look and followed after Eriksen. They walked in silence toward his car, and then she brightened.

"Guess what?"

"What?"

"You know that boy I met at Benton's Harbor? The one who was going to the junior college? Well, he was here tonight." She gave a little dance of excitement. "He came here, and I know he came here just to see me. Isn't that something? I saw him about the last quarter, sitting down near the front. He is really cute, Dad."

"What was his name again?" Eriksen didn't like the thought of a strange boy zeroing in on Denice.

"Jerry."

"Jerry what?"

"I told you, Daddy, we don't worry about last names. That's not important. It's what kind of a person you are that counts."

"What did he want?"

"Oh, we just talked a few minutes after the game. He said he remembered I was a cheerleader and he was passing by so he came in."

"Did he ask you out?"

"Yes. Just for a Coke. I told him I could meet him at the Pizza Palace."

There was still hope in her voice.

"No," Eriksen said.

"Why?" Anguish.

"I told you. He's too old. I don't know anything about him, I've never met him."

"Just because you're a detective, you don't have to investigate every guy who wants to talk to me," she said with a pout.

Eriksen could think of no reply as they drove home.

The stadium lights drew me like a moth to a flame. Even Bug-car wanted to go there after prowling the streets with growing frustration. We knew she was out there in the night, but where? She wasn't gone; just waiting. I knew I would have to be very careful, for she could attack me in the bright lights as well as the dark. But in the light I could see her too, and so we went, Bug-car and me, to the stadium. As I entered the brightly lit stadium I felt an explosive ripple run through every joint in my right foot and I knew positively then that I had to be on guard.

Ignoring the stares that I always drew, I took a seat halfway up, not far from a man and his wife who were nipping steadily from a silver flask. He pointed angrily at the signboard, and I followed with my eyes: Hampton 14; San Miguel Frosh 0. There was an audible crackle from my left foot as the electrical neurons raced through every nerve synapse there, and I glanced around to make sure no one heard. The electricity was running now, and I knew why the lights had drawn me here. I had read about the game, and my subconscious mind led me here where I could see Denice Eriksen. She told me she was a cheerleader; she practically begged me to come see her. Now I was here.

The crowd noise swelled as some play unfolded on the field, and the voice—I could almost recognize it!—said quite distinctly over the roar: "Be careful." I shook my head and concentrated on the girls in white dancing before me, and I could clearly see Denice with her slim legs pumping and her pleated skirt flaring to reveal her ruffled underpants. The small band cranked to a disjointed stop and the girls ran to sit on the bench directly below me. I saw Denice sweep the crowd with those ice-blue eyes, seeing all and seeing none, until they slid across my face. Her mouth dropped and then she smiled and waved and hugged the girl next to her, a girl not as tall, more filled out, and with long brown hair that hung in ringlets down her back. I could see Denice nodding toward me and talking in her ear, and the girl swept the people around me, searching with bright brown eyes until she settled on me because I was the only one looking back at her. I smiled and gave a small wave to the girls and they sat down giggling on the bench. Throughout the remainder of the game I could see they were trying to ignore me but their eyes always darted toward mine for a moment to make sure I was watching. And I was always watching.

I remember nothing of the game; the sounds of the crowd rolled over me like breakers on the beach. The sounds bothered me but I did my best to ignore them. It is important that I show strength, internal strength, and resist the pressures that are always within me. Energy always seeks the exits, in much the same manner that electricity in a closed area will always find the weakest point and disperse itself. I needed that energy, and I would not let it disperse. But the pressure built and I felt the synapses click in anger, and currents pulsed through my fingers, making my fingernails into small neon lights. I put my hands in the pocket of my blue nylon windbreaker so they would not attract the attention of people around me, people who were already covertly looking at me and whispering among themselves. I turned quickly once and saw almost all the people in the crowd whispering and looking at me, nodding in a knowing manner. I only did that once, and then I kept my mind on Denice and her friend. I would not even acknowledge these idiots. The game ended, and not too soon for me. It was as if a breeze that had been gusting all day suddenly calmed itself. The silence was soothing. I joined the parents and kids down on the field after the game to offer congratulations and condolences. Denice came toward me, pulling at the arm of the girl with the brown ringlets.

"Hi," she said. "Hi, Jerry."

"You mean Sonny," I said. Why did she call me Jerry? I must have frowned, for I saw them both pause with slight consternation in their faces.

"Oh, I thought you told me it was Jerry at Benton's Harbor. I'm sure you said Jerry," Denice said, and I could see her eyes carefully watching mine. Nothing was revealed in those ice caves. And then I remembered I had said Jerry. Why had I done that?

"Oh, yes, well it is Jerry, but everyone calls me Sonny. I guess I was being formal that day." I smiled. "We must be formal on first meetings, right?"

Denice laughed now, relieved, and pulled her friend forward again. "This is Cheri, my best friend. I told her I met you yesterday at the beach," and she and Cheri both giggled at a secret they shared.

Cheri swept her hair back from her eyes, smoothed it over her shoulder with a languid hand, then calmly studied my face. I could see her eyes come back to my right eye, the one with the second pupil. Both girls giggled again in the small silence between us, and then Cheri asked what I thought of the game.

"I liked the dolphins at play. The sea was especially beautiful tonight, so green and calm."

Both looked at me, and then Cheri asked, "Are you studying to be a poet?"

"No. Poetry is just around us at all times. It is up to each of us individually to interpret the poetry that nature provides, to see beauty in anything."

They nodded, not sure what to say to that, and then Denice spoke. "We're all going over to the Pizza Palace now. It's what we always do after the night games. At least, I hope I'm going, I'll have to ask my dad first. But can you come? Could you?"

I looked at Denice but could see nothing in her eyes. They were like reflections, just fathomless blue ice caves. Cheri's were different; there was heat in those brown eyes, and they watched me with the quiet tension of a cat.

"I don't know," I said. "I've really got a lot of studying to do. I was just taking a break, driving around, when I came over here. I remembered you said you were a cheerleader for the freshman team, and I thought I might run into you." I was suddenly edgy, and I could feel electrodes popping inside the breaker switches on the back of my neck. I started backing away, my feet light and sure in the sneakers I wore with my faded blue jeans. "I don't know. I'll try to make it. If I do, I'll buy you both a Coke," I said. I gave them a smile that said I had to leave but really didn't want to. I turned and ran past the bleachers to the parking lot.

Most of the cars were gone, and the bug-car sat alone. Vulnerable. Thinking it might be a trap, I approached cautiously and kicked the bumper hard to startle the lioness. There was no sign of her, but still I checked the back seat carefully before I got in.

"The lioness is not going to be sitting here waiting for you!" the voice said. It came easily out of the dark, such cultured tones, and suddenly I knew who it was! Francis Macomber! Of course, it had to be. Who knew the evils of the lioness better than he? And that's why he was protecting me.

"You must find her, search her out," Francis said in words that surrounded me.

The words echoed in the recesses of my mind as I drove the four blocks to the Pizza Palace and parked at the far corner of the lot. The dolphin boys arrived shortly, hair still wet from showers, and laughing girls followed. I saw Cheri go in, her white uniform a beacon in the night, but Denice was not there.

"Where is she?" Francis hissed. "Is she hiding from you? She invited you and then didn't come herself. A typical feminine trick."

Angry at this deceit, I still chose to wait. Besides, it was Cheri who had those watchful, feline eyes. Why had she watched me so closely? Did she know something? I would wait and find out. Rummaging in my glove compartment, I found a box of jujubes and chewed slowly to pass the time. The sticky substance sucked at my teeth and pulled small fragments of my nostril lining loose as I worked my jaws. I had nearly finished the box when the kids began leaving, most with parents. I saw a boy talking to Cheri, who laughingly shook her head and then pedaled her bicycle down the brightly lit street. I watched her grow smaller, winking in and out of the streetlights until she disappeared.

"Get going," Francis said.

I started bug-car and drove swiftly after her, turning where I thought she had turned. When I had gone two blocks without seeing her I worried that I had turned on the wrong street. Then, there she was, just ahead, pedaling with unbroken rhythm. It was hard to see her, because the residential street was not well lit and the trees, still bristling with foliage, blocked much of the light. I drove past her for half a block and then pumped the gas pedal hard, making the car buck and snort. With the engine still running, I pulled over to the curb and opened the rear end. Cheri pedaled toward me, but slower now, and I knew she was nervous. As she was about to swing wide around me, I stepped into the lamplight.

"Hi, Cheri," I said easily.

She coasted, still unable to clearly see my face. "Cheri, it's me, Sonny," I said again, and gave a relaxed chuckle. She turned back and braked to a stop beside me.

"God, you scared me. I didn't know what you were doing." Streaks of waterlight ran down her hair and shadows encased her eyes, but I knew she was watching me carefully.

"It's lucky I saw you. I made a wrong turn and I think I'm lost. Then my car started acting up."

She relaxed at this. "I just live about three blocks from here. My dad knows a lot about cars. You want me to go ask him to help you?"

"Oh, I don't want to bother him. If you could do one little thing for me, I think I could fix it. It'll just take a minute, Would you mind?" As she laid her bike on its side, I looked around the street. Lights shone from houses on both sides, but they were lights behind drawn curtains, so the people would not have to look out at the real world.

I stood behind the car and peered at the engine while Cheri waited expectantly beside me. "Get behind the wheel, and when I tell you to, push on the accelerator, okay?" I asked.

Once she was inside, I closed the hood and opened my pocketknife. Two steps and I was beside her, the blade at her throat. "Move over to the other side and don't make a sound," I hissed at her.

"What . . . ?" Her eyes widened as she saw the knife. "What are you doing?" Her tiny voice drowned in fear.

"Get over!" I whispered again, and pushed her toward the other seat. She whimpered as her legs tangled in the stick shift. I held the blade before her eyes. "If you make a wrong move, I'll cut your face."

There was a crunching sound as we drove away, but I didn't stop. My skin prickled, and I wanted to race down the street, but I didn't dare attract any attention.

"Well done, my boy," Francis said. "You've got her."

"This time I've got to be sure," I said aloud. There was no answer from the night, and I turned toward Cheri. She sat pressed against the door, unblinking eyes fixed straight ahead. Tears streaked her cheeks.

"Why aren't you looking at me?" I asked angrily. "Everyone wants to stare at me. You were watching me at the game, watching all the time. Why not now?"

She turned and looked at me from her dark eyes. "Please, don't hurt me."

I waved my knife at her. "Are you the gray lioness?"

She stared uncomprehendingly. "What do you mean? I don't know. Please let me go. I won't tell anyone, I promise."

"Let you go so you can destroy more men? So you can teach other women how to put men down, how to hurt them and ruin them?" I sneered.

"I'm not a lioness. I don't know what you mean," she wailed.

"Don't lie to me! I'll find out who you are in a few minutes. So don't tell me any more lies. Don't even talk to me unless you want to get cut," I said, and brandished the knife again.

The elves leered at me as I swung around the gravel driveway and stopped beside the pumphouse. There was only one light in the house, and I knew it would be Mother watching television. Across the field I saw a light in old man Cahill's place, and I figured he was watching TV too.

"Get out this side," I said, and pushed her toward the darkened doorway into the pumphouse. "The ladder is to your right. You go first, and don't forget I'm right behind you with a knife."

She started up, and I followed close behind, my head

to one side of her feet so she could not kick me. I felt her skirt swirling just over my head, and her scent was strong. At the trapdoor she stopped.

"I can't lift it," she said tearfully. "It's too heavy."

"Move over." I climbed up beside her and pushed on the door. I was halfway into the loft when she suddenly began scrambling down the ladder.

"Stop," I cried, but down she raced, disappearing into the darkness. As I started after her, the trapdoor fell and struck my head. I clung to the ladder as red flares flashed in my skull, and I knew I had dropped the knife. I started after her again, taking two rungs at a time, then dropped the last ten feet. I caught her just as she cleared the door and careened off the side of the Volkswagen. I grabbed a handful of hair and snapped her head back. She tried to cry out, but I clapped my other hand over her mouth. Quick as a cat she bit me, and I felt blood run through my fingers. I released her hair and whipped my arm around her neck, pulling back hard until I felt her convulse as I threatened to crush her windpipe. Still fighting, she drove an elbow into my stomach, and nausea swept me. I pulled back harder and shifted the angle of pressure slightly to cut off the blood flow in her carotid arteries. Abruptly, as she was kicking my shins, she sagged and went limp as her blood-starved brain fogged over.

After resting a moment to catch my breath, I draped Cheri over one shoulder and struggled up the ladder into the loft. I thought my arms would break before I made it. I wanted to lie beside her and rest—I was so tired—but she began moaning and writhing as she returned to consciousness. I had to hurry. Flicking on the lights, I dragged her across the old carpeting to the north wall. I was still untangling a piece of cord to bind her wrists when she opened her eyes and screamed. Her shriek exploded in my head as I flung myself on top of her and seized her by the throat.

"You yell one more time and I'll squeeze the life right out of you," I whispered. Her lips were open, and terror flooded her eyes. She coughed and turned on her side as I quickly tied her arms behind her. I sat back for a moment, then crossed the loft to turn on my tape recorder. Instantly the flowing sounds of Beethoven's Fifth filled the loft, drowning out all other noises. I turned back to Cheri, who lay without looking at me, a small figure lying in the glare of the single overhead bulb.

"She's not the gray lioness," Francis said. His smooth tones slid right through the windowpane.

"How do you know?" I cried. "If she's not, then why did you make me bring her here?"

"She will tell you everything you need to know." Francis sighed.

As I knelt beside Cheri, she spoke in a wavering voice. "Are you going to kill me?"

"Are you going to help me?" I countered. At this she swung her dark eyes up to mine.

"What do you want?" I detected a note of hope.

"What do you think I want?" I laughed. "I want to be done with all this, that's what." I felt neurons crackle across my spine. "I want the gray lioness!"

Cheri stared at me. Winding her thick hair in my fingers, I jerked her head from the floor. Pain flashed across her face, but I knew it would take more pain before she revealed her secret. "I don't know what you mean," she cried, and tears burst from her eyes.

"I want that lioness," I said, with my face close to hers. She must understand me. "If you're not the lioness, then you better tell me who is. I know you're hiding her from me."

"Force her to tell you," Francis said from a corner. "You know the way, like you did the others."

"Yes," I shouted, and ripped off her white boots, then flung up her short pleated skirt and pulled at her satin shorts. Her eyes widened in fear, and she drew her legs up.

"No, please don't hurt me. I don't know what you want to know."

"Who is the lioness?" I shouted.

She turned her face away at this, and tears streaked her face. "I don't know what you mean," she wailed.

"You bitch." I tore at her satin pants, and she struggled desperately to get away from me, but it was impossible. In a moment I was on her, thrusting and hurting her while the crescendos of Beethoven smothered her screams. The bright light above us sizzled and washed all color from the room, all color from Cheri's face and hair. My head swam, and I was lighter than air, rising above her but holding to her neck, tighter and tighter, until she lay white and motionless beneath me. Finally I collapsed beside her, my breath tearing at my throat and my eyes wet with tears.

"Why wouldn't she tell me?" I cried aloud.

"Because she is evil," Francis whispered. "You must search again."

"Oh, God, I'm so tired. Let me rest. Go away," I said, and lay with my face buried in my arms. In the silence, his unspoken words told me I could not rest.

The music stopped and the room was silent as I rose and wearily stripped Cheri of her clothes and laid them out beside those of Roberta and Jeannie.

Someone's laughter slid down a long tube into my ear. "All right! I'll find her!" I said angrily, and the laughter grew louder.

Eriksen stirred reluctantly as the telephone beside his bed whirred. He looked at the alarm clock's luminous dial—12:40. The call would be bad news. At this hour, he thought, anything is bad news. He picked up the receiver and grunted.

"Dan, this is Anna Donnato." Eriksen came fully awake as he heard the distress in her voice. "I'm so sorry to bother you at this hour, but Cheri isn't here. Could she possibly be with Denice?"

"No, I brought Denice home right after the game. Cheri told us she was going to the Pizza Palace and then on home."

"Where could she be? We just got in from a dinner party about ten minutes ago and I checked on Cheri but she wasn't there. Her bed was not even mussed."

"How about some of the other cheerleaders?"

"It just isn't like her to go off without telling us first. She never has. And she knew where we were tonight in case she needed to call." She lowered her voice. "Dan, I'm very worried, and Phil is almost frantic.

He's searched the entire house and the yard. Her bike isn't here either."

Eriksen swung out of bed. "I'll be right over. Meanwhile, you call the other girls and anybody else she might have gone home with."

He began dressing in the dark, but Cynthia rose to one elbow and turned on her bedside lamp. "What's the matter? Was that Anna?"

"Yes. Cheri didn't come home after the game. I'm going over there to see what's up."

"Oh, my God," Cynthia said, and started to get out of bed. "I'll go with you."

"No, things are going to be confused enough."

"Dan!" Cynthia said indignantly. "Anna is going to need a friend around at a time like this. I think I should be there. After all—"

"Please stay here. We can't leave Denice, and I don't want her awake all night worrying about this. There may be nothing to it. Cheri may just be out with a boyfriend, since she knew her parents wouldn't be in until late."

She sank back on her pillow. "All right. But will you call me and let me know what's going on?"

"Sure." He knelt across the bed and gave her a light kiss. Suddenly Cynthia's arms were tight around his neck.

"I have a bad feeling about this, Dan. Do you think the person who got the other two girls could have . . . ?"

"Let's not worry until we find something concrete. Okay?" As he drove away, he saw the bedroom lamp still on, and he knew Cynthia would be lying there, eyes staring at the ceiling as she tried to puzzle it out.

Three blocks from the Donnatos' his headlights picked out a bicycle lying in the gutter with a crushed front wheel. He stopped and briefly checked the area but saw no signs of blood or a struggle. Still, Cheri had been riding a bike, this was a girl's bike, and just three blocks from her home. He grabbed the radio mike: "Five-twelve; San Miguel."

"San Miguel," the dispatcher instantly replied.

"Send a patrol car to see me at 3741 Larkspur. A

possible missing person. Also advise P.D., since we are in city limits, but tell them this may be related to the other girls found murdered and that we will handle."

Every light in the Donnato house was on when he pulled into the driveway. Anna met him at the door, her thin face drawn and her eyes veiled with concern.

"Thank you for coming so quickly, Dan. It's like a nightmare here," she said. They went into the living room, where Phil Donnato sat on the sofa with his head in his hands.

"I feel so terrible," he murmured. "We should have been waiting here for Cheri, not at some party. We should have met her at the game and driven her home like you did. We should—"

Eriksen interrupted gently. "Did you call the other girls?"

"Yes. They all saw her leave the Pizza Palace on her bicycle. They all left at eleven sharp because the Palace closed up then. So where could she be?" Anna asked.

"What kind of bike did she have?" he asked.

"It was blue and white, from Sears. And it had reflective tape all over it, even on the handlebars."

Eriksen nodded, recalling how easily he had seen it beside the street. "There's a girl's bike just three blocks down the street." He didn't know how to make it easy for them other than get right to the point. "It looks like it was run over. Phil, come with me and see if you can identify it as Cheri's. Anna, write a list of everyone who was with Cheri tonight."

Anna was crying as they left the house.

"It's hers, no question," Donnato said as they stood beside the bicycle. "I wrapped the handlebars with that reflective tape myself." He was trembling as he turned to Eriksen. "Do you think the guy that killed those other girls has Cheri? I mean, here's her bike, all run over, and she's gone, just disap—"

"Phil!" Eriksen said sharply. "Don't get worked up. We don't know what it is. Maybe someone accidently hit her and took her to a hospital." He didn't want to think the obvious.

A sheriff's patrol car swung up behind them, and

Eriksen quickly outlined the situation. "Have the dispatcher get an identification team out here immediately, and then you start checking every hospital or clinic in a fifty-mile radius," he said.

Inside the house he asked Anna for a recent photograph of Cheri; she came up with a picture of the girl in her white cheerleader's costume. Eriksen looked at the picture: bright smile, bright eyes, silky hair. A face eager to take on anything life could offer; a face that never even considered death.

"I'm going back to the office now. We'll put out an all-points bulletin on her. And we've got to start checking everyone who saw her tonight. I'll call you as soon as anything turns up."

As he pulled away from the house he saw them standing together in the doorway, desperately alone.

8

Eriksen let himself in the rear entrance of the department and told the dispatcher he would be in his office if any calls came in. He turned on all the lights in the detective section, then made a quick call to Cynthia. She lifted the receiver before the first ring was completed.

"I'm afraid it doesn't look so good," he said without preliminaries. "I found her bicycle about three blocks from the house. It had been run over."

"Well, what do you think happened?" she said carefully.

"I'm not sure yet. It may have been a hit and run, and the driver took her with him. Maybe to a hospital, but that hasn't turned up anything yet."

"It could be the killer, couldn't it?" she said, and Eriksen could hear her voice turning brittle.

"It could, but we don't know. I'll call you if we get anything."

He started to hang up, but she broke in quickly.

"Dan, this is happening in our neighborhood! This is just down the street. Denice's best friend just disappears! I mean, what is happening? What's going on?" Her voice grew louder. "Pretty soon it's not going to be safe for any of us to walk out the door."

"Come on, Cynthia," he said angrily. "It's not like this guy is out there every night stalking pretty little girls."

"You're not going to convince any mother of that! It's terrible, Dan, and I'm frightened. And so worried about Cheri. I don't like to think where she might be right now. Do you think I should call Anna?"

"Yes. Do that, but get a hold of yourself first."

He called Darby and told him what had happened. "Get down here as soon as you can, Bill. I've got a long list of kids to check out. We'll call everyone tonight."

He had completed four calls to angry and then disturbed parents of children who had gone to the Pizza Palace when Sergeant Coleman from the ID section entered his office.

"We tested for blood all around the bike but got no positive benzidine reaction," he said. "We've got the bike here now and are starting to go over it. If we come up with something, we'll let you know."

"Did you see any signs of a fight on the grass around there?"

"No."

"And no fibers from her dress where she might have fallen, or some skin at least?"

"Nothing, Dan. Sorry. I understand she was a friend of the family."

"Yeah." Eriksen ignored Coleman's use of the past tense.

It was seven when he and Darby finished contacting those who had been with Cheri at the Pizza Palace. Their story was all the same: they left at eleven o'clock; Cheri talked briefly with Eddy Pokorny, a football player who asked her to go to a movie next Friday; she was last seen riding down Wilson Boulevard toward home.

"We had Deputy Donsing check every house on the

block where her bike was found, but nobody heard anything," Eriksen said to Darby. He rose and put on his coat. "I'm going home to get some breakfast. And I've got to talk to my daughter. See you in about an hour."

When he arrived home, Cynthia was sitting at the kitchen table with a cigarette and a cup of black coffee. She rose and lightly caressed his face. "How do you feel? Did you sleep at all?"

"No, but a few strong coffees will keep me rolling." He sank down at the table and lit a Camel. "Did you tell Denice yet?"

"No, I was hoping you would come home. I don't think I could do it."

As if on cue, Denice bounced into the kitchen. "Good morning, everyone," she said, and turned on the wall radio. Hard rock filled the room, and Eriksen had to yell as Denice shimmied around the table.

"Denice! Turn that thing down."

She gave a little pout and said, "You need a little noise in the morning to get you going. It's good for you, Dad."

"I don't need that. I've been up all night."

"I'm starved, Mom. Are you fixing pancakes?"

Cynthia set a bowl of cereal before her. "There isn't time this morning. And your father wants to talk to you."

Denice looked up with a mouthful of Cheerios. "About what?"

Eriksen rubbed his lined and unshaven face. "Cheri didn't come home last night after the game. She's missing."

Denice stared, a second spoonful frozen halfway to her parted lips. "Where is she?"

"We don't know where she is. I found her bike near her house, run over. We thought it might be a hit and run, but that didn't turn up anything. She's not in any hospital."

"When did you find all this out?"

"Early this morning."

"Well, why didn't you tell me?"

"Because you came home with me and would have

had no way of knowing what might have happened. And I didn't want to worry you."

"But she's my best friend," Denice wailed. "If I had gone to the Pizza Palace with her and we had come home together, she would be all right."

"Denice," Eriksen said sharply. "Nothing you might have done would make any difference. So please don't cry. I want you to think a minute. Do you know any boy that would want to hurt Cheri?"

Denice's eyes widened. "No. Everyone really likes her. She's probably the most popular girl in school."

"Who are her boyfriends?"

"No one, really. She thinks Eddy Pokorny is cute, but he wouldn't do anything like that."

"We've checked almost every boy on that football team, and none of them sounds like a possible. What about boys outside of school? Did she know any older boys?"

"Not that I know of." She pushed at her cereal without tasting it. "I introduced her to Jerry after the game, but we just talked for a minute."

"Who is Jerry?" Eriksen was attentive.

"He's that boy that I met at Benton's Harbor last Sunday. Remember?"

The incident clicked in Eriksen's mind. "Right. And he was at the game last night?"

"Yes, he said he was tired of studying and wanted a break. He remembered me telling him I was a cheerleader and he came over to watch, that's all."

"What's his last name?"

"I told you, Daddy, he didn't tell me, and I didn't tell him mine. Just Jerry."

"And he told you he went to the junior college?"

"Yes."

"Studying what?"

"I don't know."

"Is he from San Miguel?" Eriksen stubbed out his cigarette impatiently.

"I guess he lives here now. But he used to live at Benton's Harbor. His father was a fisherman who drowned, and his mother used to clean fish. But, Daddy, I don't think he would have anything to do with Cheri. He didn't even know her."

"Didn't you tell him you wanted to go to the Pizza Palace after the game? And Cheri was going?"

"Yes, but . . ." Denice stopped suddenly and stared at her father. "Oh, wow, I asked him to meet us over there, and he said he would try. So he knew we were going over there. You mean he could have waited there and then followed Cheri home . . . ?"

"It's possible," Eriksen said, and lit another cigarette. Suddenly he felt something was beginning to develop. "First, we've got to find this Jerry, which shouldn't be too hard. You will have to miss school today. I'm going to need your help." He crossed the kitchen to the phone and dialed the office. "Hello, Nancy. You're in early. . . . Oh, thanks. I'll explain to you later. . . . Yeah, let me talk to Bill." He quickly told Darby what he knew. "You drive over to Benton's Harbor right now and see what you can come up with on this kid. I'll go to the junior college. Right. See you."

He picked up his coat. "Come on, Denice. We'll go to the office, and we'll see if we can put together a picture of this Jerry. Then we'll go to the j.c."

At the office he led Denice through the detective section and into the ID lab, where he pulled the Identikit from the shelf. They sat at the table and Eriksen showed her how it worked. "All right, we'll begin with the shape of his face. Round? Square? Long? Then we'll get the eyebrows, eyes, and so on. I'll keep laying different parts of the face across here until we come up with him."

Forty minutes later Denice said the picture looked "pretty much like him." Eriksen knew she wasn't too enthusiastic. He made several Xerox copies of it and studied the thin face of a boy in his late teens or early twenties with soft brown hair swept low across his forehead. He had a straight nose and thin lips that curved up pleasantly. It was the eyes that struck Eriksen; they were lidded and flat, not open and relaxed like the rest of the face. Denice said the eyes were not exactly right but it was as close as she could come.

"Now we'll see how many Jerrys the j.c. has," he said.

At 1:30, while he and Denice were still plowing through hundreds of photographs, Darby reached him by telephone.

"Dan, I think Benton's Harbor is a false lead. I've talked to almost every fishing family here, and none of them has ever heard of a Jerry whose father drowned at sea."

"It's looking like a dead end here too. We've matched every Jerry, or Gerald, or Geraldo with the composite, and none of them are even close. Now we're going through every picture." He sighed. "You might as well head back."

One hour later he dialed the sheriff. "We've got some dead ends. Darby got nothing at Benton's Harbor and we've got nothing here."

"But he's not even a good suspect," Conrad grumbled.

"But he's better than anything else we've got, which is nothing. Are you going to release the picture to the press?" Eriksen asked.

"I don't know," Conrad mused. "It might drive him underground."

"But it might flush him out. Remember, we've got another witness, Joe Perrin, who saw him drive away from the bowling alley in a white VW. So if we could come up with this Jerry, and he owned a white VW, we—"

"And do you know what my opponent and the newspapers would say if we just went out and arrested everybody named Jerry who owned a white Volkswagen? They'd tear me to pieces. So I'm going to think awhile before I release any composite picture of this guy." He hung up.

Eriksen dropped Denice at home and drove on to the office. He felt dejected. Everything about this Jerry looked good, but every lead fizzled. And Conrad had his head up his ass over this election, he thought. So we're back to square one.

As he walked into the detective section Nancy was on the phone. She signaled for him to pick it up.

"Detective Erskine? This here's Ernie Cahill. Now,

listen, boy, I want something done about a buncha damn hippies livin' across the road from me."

Eriksen groaned audibly. "Mr. Cahill, I—"

"Now, I ain't gonna be put off. Them long-haired no-good punks was playing their long-hair music half the night, and the women was screamin' and carryin' on so bad I couldn't hardly sleep, and my hens wouldn't lay this mornin'. Now, I want you to come out here—"

"Mr. Cahill, I can't come. We'll send a patrol car out there to take your complaint." He hung up before the old man could grab him with his voice, then dialed the dispatcher. "Send someone out to Hawkins Lane. There's an old man named Cahill out there complaining about hippies."

He looked at his watch. Three o'clock. His eyes burned from lack of sleep. He poured himself a cup of coffee and started for his office, when Nye rounded the corner.

"The sheriff wants us to meet him in his office at four. The press is going berserk over this latest missing girl. He wants us to come up with some hard answers, so get it together, Eriksen. You and Darby." He rolled the black cigar across his lower lip and left.

Deputy Larry Blanken parked near the river where some of the college girls often took an afternoon swim. He felt sure he would get something lined up with them. It was just a matter of time. His thoughts drifted across images of girls peeling off wet bikinis, to Helen in her short little waitress dress. He considered going code seven for coffee at the Blarney Stone, even though she wouldn't be there yet. He just needed some coffee to stay awake. His mind jerked when the dispatcher radioed him.

"Car 22, a 415 reported at Hawkins Lane. See a Mr. Ernie Cahill."

He started the Blazer and followed Hermosa Drive until he could cut away from the river through the old prune orchards to Hawkins Lane. A disturbance at Cahill's place didn't sound right, Blanken mused. What could that old fart do to make a disturbance? He pulled over beside the picket fence and made his way up the broken concrete walkway to where Cahill sat waiting for him on his porch.

"Took you long enough," Cahill said.

"What's the problem, Mr. Cahill?" Blanken asked with one foot resting on the porch.

"It's them damned hippies," the old man said. He paused to pull a round box of Copenhagen from his pocket, tapped the lid to settle it, then placed a pinch on his tongue and expertly slid it between his teeth and lower lip. He spit once and turned back to Blanken. "Chew?"

Blanken shook his head. "What hippies?"

"Aw, them long-haired snot-nosed kids that moved in over there in the Walker ranch. They's always making a racket, runnin' around half-nekked." He paused to spit again, and staggered a marigold beside the porch. "Last night they was playin' music all night. And girls yellin'. Couldn't hardly sleep. Long-hair music, and real loud. Damn chickens didn't even lay this mornin'. Ain't there a law agin that?" he asked, and fixed Blanken with a beady stare.

"Disturbing the peace. Do you want to file a complaint against them?" Blanken asked.

"No. Don't want that. But I would like you to go over there and talk to them. If I go, I'm going to take my twelve-gauge. They's a woman over there that swings a mean ax. I seen her once, splittin' wood better'n a man."

Blanken stubbed out his cigarette. "You stay here, and keep your twelve-gauge in the closet. I'll go talk to them. You're sure it was them playing the music?"

"Well, who else? Just them and the Sills ranch over there down this end of the road. And nothing happens at the Sillses. Ain't seen the old lady in years, and the boy, he's always gone somewhere."

Blanken sighed as he drove the fifty yards farther on down the road to the Walker place. As he braked to avoid an arrogant chicken that wouldn't move, he saw a tall woman splitting wood with rhythmic ease. Blanken's interest grew visibly as she stopped and turned toward him. She was wearing a T-shirt and no bra and her breasts were large and jutting. She came toward him, ax swinging loosely in her hand, and Blanken couldn't decide whether to watch the ax or the sensual bounce of her breasts. He got out and stood behind the door, hand on his gun butt.

"Hi, Deputy." Her smile was broad and white. She was tall and seemed friendly. Stepping from behind the door, he introduced himself, and she gripped his hand hard and said her name was Jane.

"We have a complaint that there was loud music being played here last night. It disturbed some of your neighbors."

Her eyes widened. "Us? Not us. It was over there at the Sills ranch. But it was Beethoven. Beautiful. We sat on the porch and listened. I guess that kid who lives over there was having a party."

"Mr. Cahill said he thought the music came from here." Blanken's eyes roved up and down Wonder Woman's body.

"Oh, that cranky old bastard. He just doesn't like us. He thinks we're a bunch of hippies. Which maybe we are, but we're fixing the place up. Isn't our garden great?" she asked, and half-turned to wave at the corn. Blanken didn't look at the corn. He could see only that jutting breast.

"Mr. Cahill said he heard some girls yelling and carrying on too. That's why he particularly thought it was from here," Blanken said.

"Oh, we heard a girl once before the music started. Sounded like she was having a wild time, you know what I mean?" Jane said.

"I thought just some woman and her son lived there."

"Yeah, Mrs. Sills and her boy. So I guess he was having a party. Any law against that?"

"Not really." Blanken didn't believe her, but neither did he want to offend her. She was friendly, and that made her a real possible. He knew he would be back. He gave her his card. "Thanks for your help, Jane. If you need anything, just call me, okay? My phone number is on there too, so don't hesitate to call if you need something." He got back in his Blazer and eyed her again. "You need anything now?"

"No, but you'll be the first to know when I do," she said, and flashed him a bright smile.

He drove out of the yard wondering how he could line up Wonder Woman. She was ready. But so was Helen. Helen had already told him she lived a too-sheltered life and was looking for a new life. All right! So get Helen first, and then move in on Wonder Woman. Don't complicate matters.

He drove another fifty yards to the end of Hawkins Lane and pulled into the Sillses' yard. Faded and chipped statues of elves grinned at nothing as he swung around the drive past a Volkswagen parked beside the old pumphouse. Funny ranch, Blanken thought. There was no sign of life. No dogs, no cats, no chickens or pigs or anything else associated with a farm. He could see into the open barn, but the cavernous building was empty. No hay, no equipment. He walked beside the garden toward the long, dark porch that was totally screened in. His footsteps in the gravel seemed unnaturally loud. Blanken looked for a doorbell on the porch, saw none, and gave a couple of raps on the screen door. Hearing no movement, he entered the porch and knocked on the main door with his knuckles. There was still no sound from within, and he rapped hard with his nightstick. He was about to leave when the heavy oaken door silently opened. A short woman with hair loose about her shoulders appeared. Her eyes were puffed, and her unnaturally white face was splotched. Veins like red lace covered her cheeks.

"What do you want?" Her voice was throaty.

"Mrs. Sills?"

"Yes?"

"I'm Deputy Blanken, Socorro County Sheriff's Department. We had a report there was some music being played loudly here last night. Some of the neighbors complained." He said it like a question.

"I didn't hear no music." She opened the door a little wider, and he could see she was in a blue robe with fluffy pink slippers on her feet. "I was watching television. I watch it most of the night because I don't sleep so good, you know?"

"Do you have a son?"

"Yes, but I didn't see him last night. I guess he was out with some girl," she said, and gave a laugh that resembled a cough.

"Is he here now?"

"No, I don't think so. I sleep most of the day, you know, so I don't see him then."

"There's a VW over by the pumphouse. Is that yours?"

"No, that's my son's. He usually don't go nowhere without that car. But he could be out hunting, or with a friend."

Blanken felt he was getting nowhere. All this talk for a goddamn 415 that doesn't amount to anything. "All right, ma'am. If you see your son, would you ask him just to keep the music down at night?"

"Whoever complained must have made a mistake," she said.

"All right, ma'am. Sorry to have bothered you."

Blanken stepped out into the sunlight and took a deep breath. He started to walk back to his Blazer, then, on a hunch, turned and walked toward the pumphouse for a closer look at the VW. It rang a bell, but he couldn't place it.

I lay on the floor of the loft, my heart hammering at my throat. Why was that sheriff's car here? They couldn't have found out anything. Could they? Why were they here? Oh, shit. It had been so close. I couldn't believe it. I was at the bottom of the ladder with Cheri's body on my shoulder, all wrapped in a blanket. I was right there, ready to put it in the back of the bug-car when that truck with the sheriff's star on the side pulled in. I went back up the ladder as fast as I could with Cheri and thought my lungs would burst. I let the trapdoor down quietly and then watched him through a crack in the wall while he went into the house. Mother must have told him I was here. He'll be coming to find me now. Maybe I should go down and meet him, just act natural. But maybe he knows something and he'll grab me, or just shoot me. I better stay just where I am. Maybe he's not even here to see me. But now he's coming this way. Oh, shit ohshitohshit! I lay down on the floor, paralyzed. What if he comes up into the loft, what'll I do? He'll hear me breathing, or he'll hear my heart pounding, it must be shaking this whole pumphouse. I can hear him now. He's walking around the bug-car. He's stopped, he must be looking in one of the windows. Is there anything in there that might give me away? Anything of Cheri's? No, I got it all out. I did, I know I did. Now what's he doing? His feet are large and heavy. He's on this side of the car, right by the pumphouse door, and I can hear him step over the threshold, on the old boards around the covered well; he must be right beside the ladder. I'll bet he's looking at the ladder, looking up at the trapdoor. But he can't see the door. It's too dark inside, but he knows that ladder has to go somewhere. Sweat ran down my face, dripping into my eyes, and it burned. I blinked them, but it got worse. I wanted to rub them clear, but the slightest movement might give me away. It is so quiet down there. What's he doing? Sneaking up the ladder. Maybe he's going to throw that trapdoor open and shove his fucking gun up my nostril. No! There's his feet outside again in the gravel driveway. He's stopped; now he's going away again.

I listened to the steps fade and let a thin stream of air slide from my lungs. Rising cautiously to my knees, I looked through the crack again. He was getting back in his truck, talking on the radio. Maybe he found something. He's calling reinforcements! They're going to surround me. But as I watched, he backed out into the road and left. He was in no hurry. It must have been routine. What was it? Why did he come? Why did he leave?

I scuttled down the ladder and hurried over to the house. Mother was just coming out of the bathroom, headed back toward her bedroom, when I came down the dim hallway.

"Sonny. Where were you?"

"I was out in the back field. I thought I saw a sheriff's car here. What did he want?"

"He said someone had been playing music so loud last night that it disturbed the neighbors. I bet old Cahill is the one that complained. He probably heard some music from over there at the hippies' place and thought it was you. It wasn't you, was it?" Mother fixed me with one of her looks.

"I was playing some music, but not loud. They wouldn't have heard me." I looked at the floor and pushed at a piece of worn rug with my toe. When I looked up, Mother was still watching me from behind her puffy eyelids. Why were her eyes so puffy during the day and not at night? She made me think of a cat with eyes fixed on a mouse, motionless, just waiting for the mouse to make a move, and then it would pounce. So I outwaited her, just looked back at her from behind a brick wall that I built in my mind. She couldn't look through that.

She eyed me for a few moments, then turned and went down the hall to her bedroom in her slow shuffling walk. Why had she looked at me like that? It was as if she was trying to force a confession out of me. She never looked at me like that before. What was she trying to do? I stood there a moment, puzzling, until Francis Macomber's voice slid up from the floor and surrounded my ears.

"Time to move on, old boy. There's much to do."

I returned to the loft and pushed the trapdoor open, then froze with my head at floor level. The old army blanket around Cheri's body had fallen back to reveal her face and torso. Her eyes were open and staring accusingly at me. One arm lay flung forward with the fingers half-curled, as if reaching toward me. God knows how long I might have stayed there if the voice had not spoken to me, close and urgent in my ear. "Get on with it, man."

I pulled the blanket tight around her again without closing her eyes. I didn't want to touch the body. I knew it would feel cold, like marble, or like a snake, and just imagining what the skin would feel like made my spine shudder. I slung her limp body over my shoulder and once more made my way down the stairs. Doing this in broad daylight seemed insane, but I had to. Francis ordered me to. I peered carefully out the door over the top of the bug-car, but there was nothing out there, no sound except the hum of bees looking for a last bit of pollen before winter set in. The sun was so bright it washed all the color out of the landscape, except from the roof tiles, and they flickered redly, as if burning. I opened the bug-car door and thought I heard the machine protest with a small squeal what I was about to do. And what if the deputy returned now? Sweat streamed down my face as I tried to support Cheri's body with one arm and flip the seat-release lever with the other, the lever that never worked right. As I strained to move the seat, Cheri slid slowly off my shoulder and hit the ground with a thud. Once more the blanket fell back, and she was looking straight at me again—staring right at me with those blank dark eyes, empty but accusing. I threw the blanket back over her face, then savagely pushed the seat forward and stuffed her unceremoniously behind the seats. She didn't fit well, and I had to bend her legs up at the knees. I went to the barn to gather some feed sacks and cardboard boxes to better hide her in case I got stopped for something. Maybe the deputy was waiting for me. The thought of talking to a cop with Cheri lying back there, eyes open and watching me, made my stomach churn. But I couldn't stop now. Francis said I must go.

As I drove toward the main road, the tall hippie girl that was always working in the garden or chopping wood waved at me and smiled, but I barely saw her. My mind was concentrating on where to go. Not the mine. Somebody might be up there, or the deputies waiting. What if I went in that mine with the body on my shoulder, my flashlight searching the darkness, and as I rounded the corner there was Eriksen and that big deputy waiting for me, grinning? My stomach lurched. No, I would take Cheri far away, where she would not be found right away. They must find her someday, for she would be a warning to the gray lioness that I was closing in for the kill. She would hear about

Cheri and know her time had come. It would give me a psychological advantage for Cheri's body to be found. Bug-car wanted to return to the mine, but I turned him away and we headed down Hermosa Drive, beneath the freeway and southwest toward the ocean. I knew I didn't have to go far because five miles beyond the freeway Hermosa Drive wound along close to the Rio Hermoso and houses gave way to widely separated farms. Willows and alders grew thick along the riverbanks, and small dirt lanes cut through them toward the river where lovers hid, where college kids came to drink their beer and swim and play with girls. I chose a lane at random, and the thick growth immediately surrounded me. Within thirty yards the car emerged into a small clearing beside the bank. The river angled into the bank at this point, cutting it away and creating a sheer drop of about ten feet. Perfect. Pulling Cheri from the rear of the car, I laid her on the ground and unwrapped her, but this time her head was turned away, as if she no longer wanted to see me. I tried to lift her, but now I felt so weak that even dragging her to the edge of the bank was exhausting. I laid her out at the edge and then from a sitting position pushed her hard to keep her clear of the bank. She splashed loudly, then floated facedown, her body turning in the eddies as the current gradually caught her outflung arms and pulled her away. I drove out of the glen and parked on the paved shoulder of Hermosa Drive, then walked back to the river. I broke two branches from an alder tree and then, walking backward, I carefully wiped out every tire print and footprint I had left in the soft dirt. I put the branches in the car and drove away with a sense of relief. It was almost over now! At last I knew for sure who the lioness was, and I would trap her and destroy her, so that she would never again come after me. She would never destroy me, or bend me to her will, or bend and break any other men.

At four P.M. Eriksen poured another cup of coffee, despite protests from his stomach, and headed down the hall to Conrad's office. He hoped Dr. Friedland would be there. When he had called at three, the psychiatrist complained that he was a busy man and he would have to cancel appointments. Eriksen then dryly promised him lots of cigarettes and Friedland said he could make it.

Friedland rose from a bench beyond the receptionist when he saw Eriksen. "I don't know that I can offer much more than what's in my report, but let's have a go at it."

"Yeah," Eriksen said. He felt clammy and shaky and knew that coffee nerves were getting him. "Look, the sheriff doesn't know that you're coming to this meeting, or even that I asked your help. He might turn green, but just let me handle it."

Friedland gave him a quizzical look, and then they were in Conrad's office.

"If you're a reporter, I won't have anything for several hours," Conrad said from behind his desk. Nye and Darby were already there.

"This is Dr. Ben Friedland, a psychiatrist. I've asked his assistance," Eriksen said.

"What the *hell?*" Conrad said, and put his yellow boots down.

Eriksen was in no mood to make excuses. "I know you didn't want one brought into this case, but I felt he could help us. So I arranged it—at no cost to you—and if you want to make an issue of it, we'll do it after this meeting." He and Friedland sat down under the sheriff's stony stare.

"All right," he said finally. "We've got a real fucking mess on our hands. Two known dead and one missing. Most likely dead, don't you think, Eriksen?" The detective nodded, and Conrad continued. "And all by the same man?"

Eriksen lit a Camel and felt the smoke bite his raw throat. "That seems likely. Dr. Friedland has analyzed all the available evidence"—he saw Conrad's eyebrows go up at this—"and his preliminary diagnosis is that this man is a paranoid schizophrenic. The bottom line is that he cannot help himself and will keep doing it again and again until we catch him."

"Holy Jesus," Conrad said. "That is one line I don't

want the press to get. And that reminds me. I don't want to see either you or the shrink here talking to the press, understand, Eriksen? And I don't want to see any more pictures of my detectives manhandling reporters. Now, what else do we know?"

"This Jerry that I told you about on the phone, Sheriff, is a leading contender. We have established him as a common link between my daughter and Cheri Donnato. Denice introduced him to Cheri the night Cheri was killed."

"But we haven't the faintest idea who this Jerry is, do we? Did either of you turn up a lead at the coast or the junior college?"

"No, but that doesn't disqualify him. It just means he's one clever son of a bitch," Eriksen replied. "Are you going to release the picture of him?"

Conrad pulled at his lower lip and looked out the window. "I don't know."

"Sheriff," Eriksen said impatiently, "if we put that picture out, somebody is bound to recognize him and call us. This is a major break."

"On the other hand, you don't know who he is. You just *think* his name is Jerry. No facts. Can't trace him anywhere. We could end up with every nut in the county telling us they know who it is, and then we'll have a bunch of false arrests on our hands. And probably drive the real killer completely underground."

"He couldn't be much deeper underground than he is now," Eriksen said angrily.

"Gentlemen," Friedland interrupted, "I have been idly sitting here doodling with the birthdates while I listened to you, and one little thing has appeared which I find quite fascinating." He paused, enjoying the eyes coming to rest on him. "Have any of you heard of numerology?" The detectives shrugged, and Friedland continued. "It is a means of analyzing an individual by determining what his number is, and then assigning to him all the characteristics of that number. Much like one is supposed to accumulate all the signs of Scorpio because you happen to be born under that sign. Numerology has many complexities, but a simple beginning is to use birthdates to find your number.

Now, curiously, two of these girls—the first two—have the same number. Two. Roberta Ann Thomas, born the second month, third day, 1959. Put that in a column and it totals 1964. Add 1964 in a linear fashion and you get twenty. Eliminate the zero and you have a two. A two, in numerology, can be a devil woman. In its worst form, it is a succubus who seeks to destroy men."

Friedland paused at this point to take another cigarette from Eriksen's pack, which lay on the chair separating them. He lit up, and sheer enjoyment illuminated his cheerful face. "This is most curious, because I believe the killer to be a woman-hater. He may have discovered these girls had a numerical sign of two and killed them because of that, or he may have sought them out because he knew in advance they were a two. Only one thing upsets this whole business. Cheri Lee Donnato was not a two."

Conrad made notes but did not appear impressed. Nye spoke up, coming back to the boyfriend theory. "You've checked every boyfriend, right? No possible chance that you overlooked one who knew all the girls? That, I think, has got to be the link. Find that lover boy and we've got it wrapped up." He looked at Conrad for confirmation, but Conrad was contemplating the ceiling.

Eriksen, curious about the new game, wrote down Denice's birthday. She was born January 1, 1962, and was six months older than her best friend, Cheri. He added the numbers: 1964. He felt his heart skip a little, and his breathing quickened. Someone was talking, but he heard nothing. The number two stared up from the page at him. He drew a circle around it, darker and darker as his pen coursed around the number. And then carefully and bitterly he drew a fine cross hair. The sight seemed lined up on the breast of the number two.

Roger Kirk drifted lazily in the river, concentrating only on the sensation of the current pulling at his body, tiny fingers probing every indentation on his 230-pound frame. His mind turned from the sense of the water to the happy guilt of skipping classes at Socorro Junior College to go swimming. The late-afternoon sun was yellow and warm. Fall was coming slowly to the valley. Before long the water would turn cold, and then there would be no more swimming. He had argued this point with Tenley Wilson, a righteous-looking redhead in his Western Civ course. He had dated her after the first home game of the season, where he had played with honors as right guard, and he knew she was going to be all right. When he had stopped at the water's edge, she told him to go in first while she changed and she would be right with him. He turned on his stomach and looked toward the shore and wished for the thousandth time that he had good vision. She might be changing right over there, just for his benefit, but he could see nothing except a green blur of vegetation. He began swimming upstream, enjoying the strength in his arms as they pulled against the current. He was almost up to where he had entered the water, and he expected Tenley to be stroking out beside him, but he still couldn't make out any movement on the shore. She must be playing some kind of game, he thought. He took a deep breath and began swimming underwater, the clear green river water caressing his face as he pulled and lunged still more upstream. He was about to surface when he saw Tenley floating above him. She was motionless, and he knew she must be watching him, waiting for him to come up beneath her and hold her. He let himself drift a little to keep her just overhead, and then began rising toward her, wishing he had a face mask on so he could better see the long smooth lines of her body. Underwater with a mask he could see fairly well. Everything was magnified. But without the mask his vision was worse than ever. He closed slowly toward the motionless Tenley, rising like a seal with arms at his side, face extended to cut the water. Now just a few feet away, he slowed and smiled in the water, for he could see her bared breasts jutting at him and the dark island of pubic hair farther away. So that was why she had taken so long! She wanted to enter the water unseen, to surprise him with her smooth, unclothed body. She was ready, and he was ready. He put his hands forward now and kicked twice to close the last foot, taking both breasts in his hands as he surfaced beside her. He pushed her up, lifting her clear of the water with a laugh that turned into a choke and then a scream of shock. His face was inches from the staring eyes and sagging mouth of Cheri Donnato before he realized something was terribly wrong, that this wasn't Tenley Wilson, it wasn't anybody he knew, and it wasn't even alive. He backpedaled in the water furiously and began shouting.

"Tenley! Goddammit, where are you? Son of a bitch! Come here, hurry! Help me. Jesus, there's a dead girl out here. Tenley, I thought it was you." He stayed with the floating body but didn't touch it, and then Tenley was beside him, her red hair sleek against her face, which had gone chalky white as she watched the body turn beside her. Together they dragged it to shore, and Tenley drove off to call the sheriff's office while Roger Kirk stayed behind, but only after angrily shouting for Tenley to bring him his goddamn glasses before she abandoned him here in the jungle with this dead body.

The sheriff's office door opened and his secretary stuck her head inside.

"We've just got a report that the body of a young girl has been found. It is nude, no jewelry, and possibly strangled. I thought you would want to know immediately, Sheriff." She closed the door.

Conrad said "Son of a bitch" and hammered out his cigarette as the others hurriedly left the room.

Outside, Eriksen took Friedland's arm and waited for the others to pass by. Friedland looked at him expectantly.

"I was thinking about what you said in there, about numberology."

"Numerology," Friedland said.

"Yeah. Well, I didn't say anything in there, but I figured out my daughter's number. It's a two. And she is fourteen years old, and she was Cheri Donnato's best friend."

Friedland's eyes, Eriksen noticed, had a curious ability to express his whole face, and his eyes were now filled with both dismay and concern. "And you have established that this Jerry knew both Cheri and your daughter?"

Eriksen nodded.

"Well, I agree there is cause for alarm. It is too coincidental, the number two and being Cheri's best friend. You know better than I do, but I think your daughter had better be carefully guarded."

"I do too. I just wanted to hear someone intelligent say the same thing," Eriksen said. He offered Friedland another cigarette but the psychiatrist declined.

Eriksen saw Bill Darby waiting impatiently for him at the side-entrance door and waved at him. "One sec. I've got to make a call."

"Cynthia. Is Denice there?"

"No. Why, what's wrong?" Cynthia's voice came back immediately with an echo of the alarm in his own voice.

"Well, where is she?"

"She went for a ride on her bike with some other girls, some of the other cheerleaders. She said she—"

"Do you know where she was going?" he cut in.

"Dan. What's the matter?" He could hear the strain in her voice.

"I just don't want any chances taken. They've found a body and it sounds like it might be Cheri. I want Denice watched every minute now."

"Oh, God."

"I've got to go now. Go find Denice and keep her home. Okay?" She agreed, and he rang off and headed for the door with jacket in hand.

The ID technicians already had the area roped off and were measuring and photographing when Eriksen and Darby pulled in. From a distance he could see the body where it had been dragged clear of the river. It lay on its side, with arms bent up near the face as if in prayer, and Eriksen walked over near the bank to get a look at the face. Strands of her brown hair fell across the chalk-white face, but there was no mistaking the pug nose and the wide brown eyes, still innocent in death. Eriksen stared at the girl's face. How many dead people had he seen? he wondered. Hundreds, from battle lines in Korea to eighteen years in police work. So why should another body worry him? It didn't, he told himself, it's just another body. Don't get yourself involved in it just because you knew her. But he couldn't stop thinking that but for the grace of God this could be Denice lying here. Cheri was dead now, but Denice was going to stay alive. *And when I catch this son-of-a-fucking-bitch bastard I'm going to cut his balls off and stuff them down his throat while he looks at me and screams, while he tries to stop the river of blood flowing down his legs.* Eriksen's vision clouded briefly as white-hot rage flooded his mind, and it took him a long second to realize someone was calling him. He swung his head toward the car, where Darby was waving while talking into the mike.

"San Miguel. Five-twelve. Go to Channel two." He flicked to the second channel, which would not tie up the main airwave. "Five-twelve. Go."

The dispatcher responded immediately. "Five-twelve, your wife just called and said she could not locate your daughter. She has driven all over the neighborhood. Two other girls with her are out too, and now the other parents are looking. Your wife said you should be advised of this immediately."

"Ten-four. Five-twelve clear." Eriksen's voice was calm but his heart was speeding up as the adrenaline began to flow. He turned to Darby, who was about to continue interrogating the two college kids who had found Cheri.

"Bill, I've got to return home immediately." Darby gave him a quizzical look, and Eriksen went on. "Remember in that session this morning when Dr. Friedland was talking about numerology and how two of the girls had the number two? Well, Denice by that reckoning is a two. And she was a close friend of Cheri's. And that is definitely Cheri Donnato out there. So this business is getting too close to home. Denice was out bicycling with some other girls this morning, and I've got to find her and keep her home."

"Cheri was out bicycling when she was nailed," Darby said grimly.

"Yeah, and that doesn't make me feel any better. You catch a ride back with Harris or someone, all right? You handle this, okay?"

"No sweat. Good luck. If you need any help, let me know."

Eriksen drove home at eighty. A highway patrolman started off an overpass in pursuit, but Eriksen flashed the red light on top of his car and the CHP immediately broke contact. He radioed San Miguel again and shifted to Channel two. "If my wife calls back, advise her I will be home in less than fifteen minutes. Also, please alert P.D. and ask if they would put a patrol car into the area to assist in the search."

"Ten-four. Five-twelve. We've already put two deputies into the area and will ask P.D. for more backup."

Eriksen felt clammy at the thought that Denice might be in that asshole's car. He wrenched his mind away from the picture of her lying bound and gagged in the trunk or under a blanket on the back seat as he pulled into the driveway with a shriek of rubber. He got out and then had to go back and put the red light away. He saw Mrs. Dewitt watching with open mouth from across the street, where she was unloading groceries from the rear of her station wagon. Cynthia rushed at him as he burst through the door.

"I was just about to go out and look again. What is it, Dan? Why this terrible concern? Why doesn't someone tell me what the hell is going on?" She stood close, staring at his eyes and demanding an answer.

Eriksen pulled a cigarette from the nearly empty pack in his shirt and breathed deeply on the smoke before answering. "Listen carefully, and then I'm going out to look for her. There's this thing that mystics and witches—"

"Witches!" Cynthia shouted.

"Goddammit, be quiet and listen! There's this thing that spiritualists believe in, that everyone has a certain number, like a certain astrology sign. We figured out this morning that two of the three girls killed had the number two, which can mean they are a female devil. Cheri did not have that number, but—"

"You found her? It was Cheri you found?" Cynthia's hand came to her mouth, and she stared at Eriksen with wide eyes. "It was definitely her?"

"Yes, it was," Eriksen said softly, and tried to ease the hard lines in his face. "Now, listen. Denice has this number two also. You get it by figuring up their birthdates—"

"Oh, my God." Cynthia sank into a chair by the table, still staring at her husband.

"Denice has the number two, and she was a good friend of Cheri's. So I think that makes her a very likely target, and we've got to find her." He paused and added in a soft voice, "Before he does." He headed for the door. "I'll call you as soon as we get something. Then I've got to go over to the Donnatos' and break the word to them."

He drove slowly down the street, not knowing where to begin. It was late afternoon, and the sun blinded him as he peered down streets to the west. He felt panic rising in his chest. Where the hell would she go? How could three girls out riding bikes in a quiet neighborhood not be found by three or four police cars? He braked hard to narrowly avoid a pickup crossing the intersection ahead of him, and the curly-haired youth leaned out the window to yell something, but he didn't listen. Find her, find her! He drove for another ten minutes before he sighted a girl riding slowly toward him. He turned and sped toward her; then he saw it was an elderly woman with a basket full of groceries. Son of a bitch! This will take forever. On a hunch he swung over to Wilson Boulevard and raced toward the Pizza Palace. Why not? It was where Cheri had last been seen, and the girls might have been there. As he pulled to a hard stop, he saw three girl's bikes leaning against the wall. Maybe, just maybe, he thought, and burst into the pizza house. It took his eyes a moment to adjust to the dim interior light.

"Daddy! What are you doing here?"

He went outside and told the dispatcher to call off the search. Then he wound his way through the afternoon crowd and pulled up a chair with the girls. He waved away the waitress and looked at the other two girls. He knew they were cheerleaders, but he couldn't remember their names. He spoke directly to Denice.

"Honey, I hate to tell you this, but we found Cheri this morning. She was dead."

Denice and the others sat stunned, not breathing, not moving. Then Denice began sweeping up invisible crumbs and grains of salt from the table. Her hand kept going, and she looked down and Eriksen could see great tears coursing down her cheeks and dotting the white blouse she wore. The other girls put their hands to their faces and began crying. People at near-by tables were staring. Eriksen felt like kicking himself for telling them here.

"Let's go now, all right? I'll give you all a ride home."

"I can't," one girl said through sobs. "I've got my bike here."

"Me too," the other wailed in a voice that cut across the now silent and dumbfounded clientele. Eriksen confirmed from the slack-mouthed waitress that they had paid in advance and then herded the girls outside.

"I can't go with you," cried one girl. "Someone will steal my bike."

Eriksen saw the bikes were all chained. "Don't worry he said. "I'll tell your parents to come for them." He helped the girls into the car; all three sat in the rear, hugging each other and crying. As Eriksen told himself for the third time what an ass he had been, the sobbing girls directed him to their houses. He walked each to the door and explained to the astonished mothers what had happened.

The last mother pushed her daughter inside and then hissed through the screen door, "No girl is safe in this town, and you cops can't do a damn thing about it. Today I got a speeding ticket, and for no reason. Why wasn't that dumb cop out looking for this killer instead of hanging around highways? And now you bring my daughter home scared out of her mind." She slammed the door.

Back in the car, Eriksen lit a cigarette and sagged in

the seat. "Denice, honey, I wish we could say we know who this guy is and go out and pick him up. But we haven't got any hard leads and we don't know where to look. So it's going to take time until something breaks. But in the meantime, something came up today, and that's why we were so anxious to find you. You're going to have to be very careful from now on. You won't be able to go anywhere without prior approval from me or Mother. All right?"

Denice, ashen-faced, stared at the floor. "You make it sound like I'm going to be a prisoner."

"No, it's just that we will have to protect you at all times."

"Why?" she said, and looked up at him.

Eriksen gazed across the lawn to the big house where he had dropped the last girl. He saw the mother watching from the living-room window. He turned back to Denice.

"You see, honey, there's this stuff called numerology. It's like astrology, and—"

"I know," Denice said, and wiped her eyes with the back of her hand. "That Jerry told me about it. A little, anyway. He told me I was a two."

Eriksen almost dropped his cigarette. "He told you that? When?"

"When we were at Benton's Harbor."

"What did he say about it?"

"Nothing, just that it was a feminine number."

"Christ," Eriksen breathed. It could have happened that Sunday, he thought.

"What does that have to do with me?" she asked.

Eriksen hesitated. How much could she take? He decided to be open with her. "Honey, the first two girls killed were number twos. Cheri was not, and we haven't figured that out. But you are, so that makes you part of a pattern. At least, we can't take any chances."

Denice was biting her knuckles and trying to hold back the tears.

"Maybe I shouldn't have told you that, but I wanted you to know where you stood," he said.

"It's not that, Daddy, I was just thinking about Cheri again. How horrible it must have been. Was she . . . was she . . . you know, like the other girls?"

"Yes."

Denice turned into his arms and wept bitterly. He let her go until she collected herself. "Come on, we'll go home now."

He drove slowly, and when she was completely dry-eyed again and her hiccups had stopped, he asked, "Is there anything else—*anything*—you can think of about this Jerry? Something you overlooked?"

Denice stared out the window. "I've tried and tried, but I can't, Daddy. I'm not even sure about that drawing. There was something about it . . ." She turned toward him. "Oh, I just remembered. At the game he said his name was Sonny. When I said he told me it was Jerry at the coast, he laughed and said it was, but everyone called him Sonny. But I always thought of him as Jerry, and so I forgot the Sonny."

"But he said it was a nickname?"

"Well, he just said that's what people called him," she said with a shrug.

"I'll make a note of that," he said without enthusiasm.

They drove on in silence, and Eriksen found his mind weighted with the thought that they were so close to the killer but still miles away. He glanced repeatedly in the mirror and scanned the trailing cars for a white Volkswagen. He had the distinct feeling someone was watching him, or thinking of him. Oh, Christ, he told himself, don't get neurotic now. It could all be coincidence. After all, Cheri broke that number-two baloney. Still . . .

As they entered the house, Cynthia stood listening intently to the local television news: "And to recap the latest announcement from the sheriff's department, Sheriff Conrad says he now has a suspect and that more information will be made available. We'll try to have a filmed report of that for you at eleven tonight. Thank you and good night."

She clicked off the set and turned to him as Denice

ran up to her room. "Have you really got somebody?" Cynthia asked. "And why am I always the last to know?"

Eriksen poured himself three fingers of Jack Daniels and slumped in his chair. How long has it been since I slept? he wondered, then turned to Cynthia's question.

"We don't have anymore than what Denice told us. We only know about him, but we can't find him. No leads." He took a long swallow and felt the smooth sour mash light a fire in his stomach. He watched Cynthia make herself a gin and tonic.

"Remember what I said earlier, about Denice being a number two?" he asked. Cynthia put her mixing spoon down carefully and looked at him without saying anything. "That means we have to be extremely careful with Denice. We just can't take any chances."

"I agree, Dan," she said, and sat across from him. "Are you going to assign deputies to guard her and the house?"

"You know I can't do that. There hasn't been an explicit threat on her life, and the department doesn't have that kind of manpower anyway."

"Well, are you going to guard her?"

"Oh, Cynthia," he said in exasperation. "What I'm talking about is common sense. While in school she has to stay with the students and teachers. No going off the grounds alone. And we'll take her to school and bring her home."

"That means *I'll* be taking her and picking her up, doesn't it?" she asked. "You won't be here; you'll be working."

"I'll help wherever I can, but, yes, I *will* be working, Cynthia. That's what I'm paid to do."

"You're not paid to work twenty-four hours a day."

"That's how I collect all that overtime that keeps you and Denice in new clothes."

"Well, if you didn't have this job, we wouldn't be in this mess. Worrying about you was bad enough, but now I have to be worrying every minute if Denice is all right or if . . . if that killer that you or nobody else seems able to catch has got her."

"Let's not go through that routine again, Cynthia.

You knew what you were getting into when you married me. Look how many years I worked the swing shift as a patrolman."

"But then you were gone for eight hours and that was that. Now I never know if you're here or gone." Cynthia stared into her drink.

After a pause Eriksen said, "This isn't going to last forever."

"You hope."

Eriksen's temper flared. "If you've got any bright ideas on where this Jerry is, just let me know."

"I will," she snapped.

"Meanwhile, we both have jobs to do. Yours is to watch Denice."

"And what will you be doing?"

"I'm going back to the office in a few minutes."

"You're going only to the office?" she asked archly.

"I don't know exactly where I'll always be. If I have to leave the office and check on some people, I will," he replied angrily. "How the hell should I know where I'm going to be every minute? I've got a job to do."

Cynthia leaned back in her chair. "Yes, you do your job. Go out and see what you can get into, see what you can poke into. Get what you can while the getting's good, right?" She spoke with heavy sarcasm.

"What the hell is that supposed to mean?" he asked, but suddenly he knew damn well what she meant. How could she know? She hadn't been in the office three times in the past six months. She didn't know Nancy, or any of the other secretaries for that matter. Was she out tailing him? And if she really knew something, why didn't she come out and say it?"

"Nothing. Just do your job, Dan." She sighed and turned away.

"I will, and I don't need any goddamn snide remarks from you!" he flashed. He picked up his coat and went out the door. Sixteen years of marriage, he thought as he drove toward the office, and this is what it has come to. A stone wall. Robert Frost said something about building walls, but was he talking about making friendships over them or closing out other people? He couldn't remember. The hell with it, think about what's going down tonight.

He worked nearly two hours on the notes and charts that he had made on each death. He had a book from the library on numerology, which he skimmed through again in hopes of turning up a hidden clue that would unravel this mess. But he knew there was no clue to discover, just the killer. Just Jerry, or whoever he was; somehow, sometime, Jerry would slip, and Eriksen would pounce on him. But he knew he had to pounce before Jerry did.

He glanced at his watch. Nine o'clock sharp.

He threw down his pencil and rose to leave, when the telephone rang on his desk. It was Cynthia.

"I'm sorry I put you in such a bad mood tonight, dear." Her voice was muffled, and he knew she was still drinking. "I didn't mean to, I'm just so worried about us and Denice and everything." He sensed she was crying by the way she gulped as she talked.

"It's all right, it was nothing," he said. "Why don't you both go to bed right now, get a good night's rest."

"It's too early. And there's a good movie on TV now and I said Denice could stay up and watch it." There was a pause and he could hear the ice clink in her glass as it rose to her lips. "Will you be coming home soon?"

He paused. "I've still got some things to do and I want to check something out. Just a hunch."

"Check what out?"

Eriksen knew she was trying to pin him down. "I'm going back to the bowling alley where Jeannie Chavez was last seen. Maybe there's something there we missed before. I'm going to check that and then be home."

"You sure?" she said in a voice that hardened.

"Yes, I'm sure. I'll see you soon." He hung up without waiting for her reply. As he drove to the bowling alley, his mind drifted back to Nancy and the silkiness of her body. The alleys were half-empty and he saw it was not a league night. The same tired-looking waitress was behind the counter, but she did not recognize him. He glanced around thinking he might see Joe Perrin and ask him again what he saw that night, but Perrin was not there. Eriksen left and drove straight to Nancy's apartment. He knocked and heard her ask who it was before she opened the door.

"It's me, Dan," he said softly and the door opened and she stood in front of him, running her hand through her black hair and wearing only a red-and-white football jersey with a large number 87 on it.

"Going out for a pass?" he grinned as he slid inside the door.

"Depends on who the quarterback is," she answered, then moved languidly against him, sliding one arm around his neck and pulling his head down in a long kiss. He ran his hands down her sides, past her unencumbered breasts to her taut thighs. She was wearing no underpants.

"That pass was on the button," she said, and broke away from him. "Would you like a drink?" she asked, and poured him a double shot of Jack Daniels. She filled her glass with a cold white wine and then curled up in a chair next to the couch where he sat. Eriksen was about to ask why she was so far away when she said, "I didn't expect you tonight."

"I didn't expect to be here. I was checking out some things and all of a sudden I found myself here. I suppose I should have called."

"You know that isn't necessary," she said.

"Well, it could be embarrassing. What if I just arrived and you were here with another date?" He expected her to laugh and deny that she would do such a thing but she only gave him an ambivalent smile.

In the small silence that followed, Eriksen finally said, "I mean, you're not tied to me. I certainly can't say who you see and who you don't see."

"That's true, Dan," she said and continued to study the rim of her wineglass.

Eriksen put his own glass down and leaned toward her. "What happened? I came here and was greeted like I was Robert Redford, and now you've cooled down. What's going on?"

"I don't know, Dan." She looked up at him and her eyes were dark. "I have such mixed feelings about you. I was so happy to see you here. I was feeling alone, and your unexpected arrival made me so happy, but now I know you will be gone again in a few minutes or hours or whatever and then I'll be alone again." Her voice trailed off.

Eriksen suddenly felt uncomfortable at this serious talk. Things were taking a sudden and deeper turn. He knew what she was getting at and it surprised him. He ventured a counterploy. "Yes, but I'll be back again. It's not like we're separating and going our own ways for the rest of our lives."

"You'll come back only to go away again. You're leading your life but I'm leading yours too, not my own." She pulled her hand free and stood up to pour herself some more wine. "Oh, I don't know what I'm talking about. Everything has happened so fast between us. I don't know where it is all headed."

"Maybe it's not important for us to know. Just let it happen and we'll keep moving with the current."

"That's fine for you to say," she said, and sat next to him on the couch this time, leaning back as he slid his arm around her. "You've got your future cut out for you. Wife, kids, and work. But what have I got? A half-assed job. I'm twenty-four years old, Dan, and everything is passing me by."

"Well, I'm not passing by," he said with a grin, and kissed her lightly on the neck. "This conversation is getting awfully heavy. Are we going to philosophize all night or—"

"Or what?" she cut in.

"Or ball and enjoy ourselves."

"That's all you really want, isn't it?"

Oh, hell, Eriksen thought. I leave one drunken woman at home and come over here to find another one. Both pulling on me.

"That's a big part of it," he said.

When she didn't answer he pulled the hair back from the side of her face and he could see one tear welling from her closed eyes. He wiped it away by catching the glistening drop on the tip of his finger.

"You see, Dan, the problem is that I don't want to

get too involved." Her voice was tight with emotion. "That won't be good for you or for me."

"I thought you wanted to gamble. Maybe you need some lessons in how to be a liberated woman. Flitting from man to man, balling whenever you want with anybody you want." He tried to keep the conversation light but knew it wasn't working.

"You're probably right. I should start screwing other men and stop thinking about you." She spoke with some heat, and Eriksen took a cautious look at his wristwatch. He knew he would have to be going soon. So far the evening had been a bust. He cupped her breast and nuzzled her neck, trying to warm her up, but she lay inert in his arms, unresponsive. Then, without warning she rose from the couch and slowly pulled the jersey over her head and stood there in front of him, legs apart. The soft lamplight turned her body golden.

"Well?" she asked as Eriksen stared spellbound at her. "Are you just going to sit there? Let's get liberated."

He rose and carried her into the bedroom. Son of a bitch, I'm going to be late tonight, he thought, but there was no turning back now.

9

This morning I felt like I was rising from the ocean bottom past layers of darkness toward the silver ceiling of water overhead, and I knew I was getting closer and everything was clearer. Then I faded again. Bubbles came with me from the deep, following my dangling feet in long silvery trains, but as I slowed they quickened. Now they are about my head again, tiny charged bubbles that move with me, but I don't really know if they are a protective screen or a menacing envelopment. I really thought today I was going to rise into clear water. My head and my body felt fulfilled and light, but now the threat has returned. I could see the threat riding on the lightspears in the loft, rays entering the chinks in the wall of the loft and trying to pierce the protective layer of water that surrounds me.

Today I played Beethoven over and over and over and over, louder and louder, and I gave a superb performance as director, moving swiftly about the loft and even crashing into walls, but being careful not to step on Roberta, Jeannie, and Cheri, who lay before me like a passive audience. But even the music could not clear my head, and I left before sundown, thinking I would let the bug-car take me away into new fields. Instead I walked across the driveway, my feet crunchingly loud in the gravel. The elves turned in the garden and watched me with unblinking, accusing eyes. Why have they always accused me, telling me in their nonspeaking voices that I am wrong when I am not wrong, but have only been wronged. Why couldn't I have been righted? Uprighted, instead of always being downwronged in their eyes. They were all staring at me now, some with faces split in hideous grins and lit by the setting sun behind me.

"They are not your judges and you shall not be judged." I thought at first one of the elves was speaking to me, but it was Francis Macomber, his voice near and breathy in my ear.

"No, I won't!" And as I said it I knew I had shouted, but there were no curious manfaces here to turn and look at me with quiet repulsion in their eyes, only the elf faces, stone faces. I knelt slowly in the driveway and kept my eyes on the closest elf, whose bulbous bilious eyes watched me greedily, waiting to catch me unawares. My hand scrabbled in the gravel until I found a large smooth stone, and still fixing him with my power stare, I hurled the stone. An ear flew off and there was raucous laughter from Francis, hiding somewhere in the garden, but the elf never flinched, never altered his gaze. I ran past him into the house. No lightswords penetrated its thick walls; I was safe here. I walked softly down the hallway with its worn carpet, carefully avoiding the open traps, and looked into the dimly lit living room as I headed toward the kitchen. Mother was in the corner of the couch, a little blue ball over there illuminated by the blue tunnel light of the television. I found some milk in the refrigerator and was drinking it to whiten my insides when Francis, speaking very close to my ears, asked me when I was going.

"Going where?" I replied.

"To do what must be done." I didn't ask what he meant, because I knew. Francis and I had an understanding. After all, hadn't his woman killed him and hadn't I been appointed and anointed the revenger?

"Soon, soon, don't worry," I shouted, and turned back to the living room. My mother watched me with large eyes, elf eyes, as I came into the living room. I wondered if a rock would knock her ear off.

"What were you shouting about?" she asked.

"Was I shouting?"

"Don't talk in circles. Were you talking to me, or to yourself?"

I sat down on the couch near her, not wanting a confrontation. "Just myself, Mother. I had an idea, something came into my head, and I just shouted it out. Don't you do that sometimes, just shout ideas from your head?"

"No." She was watching me. I looked at the television tunnel of light, but there did not seem to be any news on. My mother loved the quiz shows and knew most of the answers, but tonight she seemed to be just watching me. I turned back to her and smiled.

"They had some more on the TV tonight about those girls that got killed," she said in a voice that swept toward me like breakers and then receded. I nodded and smiled at her because I wanted to make her happy. She couldn't help what she was.

"The announcer said they was looking for a young man named Jerry. Wouldn't that be something if they caught him?" I heard her talking from a great distance and I knew it was important to keep watching her lips and smiling or her voice might fade away completely.

"They're going to put a picture of him on the TV tonight. Something like what an artist drawed." Her voice swelled as if coming over a loudspeaker in an empty auditorium, and I put my hands to my ears to protect them. A single synapse popped at the very top of my spine. It sounded like someone snapping their fingers.

"The news said the sheriff's people was looking for a young man who drove a white Volkswagen." A neuron crackled in the center of my spine and made me sit up straight. Mother was saying something important, but it was hard to follow. Laughter rang in my head, but it wasn't Francis; it sounded like a girl, like Cheri.

"Sonny! Will you take your hands away from your ears? I swear, sometimes I can't understand what you're doing."

I smiled and moved closer to her, because I wanted her to protect me, but she leaned away and I felt her putting up protective screens.

"You've got to be going," Francis said discreetly from the hallway.

"I've got to be going, Mother."

"At this hour? Where? You just drift in and out of here and I never know what you're doing."

"I have so many things to do."

"Well, you're not out working, I know that. You spend all your time up in the old pumphouse loft, don't you? Seems like you've practically moved up there. Even got your tape recorder up there, don't you? I heard the music the other night through the bathroom window. Why do you want to spend so much time in that dirty old place?"

"It's not dirty, I fixed—"

"There's much to do tonight," Francis said.

"It's just a place for me to think," I finished. "Sometimes a person needs to get away, you know?"

"I try to understand, Sonny," she said, and put an arm around me. She drew me toward her skinpillows again, but Francis was demanding. "Sonny, now!" He was at the front door, waiting, and he called again: "Tonight we must get the lioness."

"Good-bye, Mother," I said, and pushed away.

"Sonny, where are you going?"

"I have things to do, that's all."

"You're just going off and leaving your mother, that's what. Well, go ahead and leave and have a good time. Don't worry about me being here alone. Don't worry about me having no company, no one to talk to. You just have a good time."

I ran after Francis' voice into the night, into the bug-car.

Yvonne Sills waited until she heard the Volkswagen pull around the driveway in a hiss of gravel, then slowly got to her feet. "Sonny runs from me like a stray cat runs from a mean kid," she said aloud as she made her way slowly to the kitchen. She poured herself another glass of Mountain Red wine and then leaned against the sink counter, running one hand absently through her hair.

"I don't like it a-tall," she muttered. "Them talking about a kid in his twenties who drives a white Volkswagen." She drained her glass in a moment of decision and made her way down the hall to the little table by the front door, where she found the flashlight. Outside, darkness slid over her, and the elves danced in the fringe of her light.

"Oh, Sonny," she breathed heavily as she walked. "Oh, Sonny." Her breath came faster now as she moved heavily across the gravel driveway to the pumphouse. She shone the light up the ladder nailed to the wall and shuddered at the sight of the thick cobwebs clinging to the joists around the trapdoor.

"What do you want to come out here for?" she said to Sonny; but Sonny wasn't there to answer. She eyed the ladder for a full minute and then stuck the flashlight in her robe pocket so the beam pointed upward. Grunting and panting, she made her way slowly to the top. At first she could not raise the trapdoor, and finally had to climb higher and lift it with her hunched back, inching it up until it fell back against the wall. She rested, still standing on the ladder but with her arms on the floor of the loft. Her breath came in gasps and she felt her heart pounding viciously. She took the flashlight, being careful not to drop it, and turned the beam into the loft. She was surprised at how clean it was, and at the worn old carpeting on the floor. The tape recorder rested on a crate to her right. She let the light beam swing slowly on around the room. There were some old clothes, some shorts and a shirt, a white sweater and skirt. . . .

"What would Sonny have such clothes up here for?" she said aloud, and heaved herself the rest of the way into the the loft. She ran the beam over the clothes again. Here was a blue workshirt tied in the front, and a pair of shorts right below it, even a gold earring just above the collar of the shirt. She bent and pulled back the shirt a little to reveal a flimsy brassiere inside precisely where the breasts would have been. "My God, my God," she breathed, and turned to the next arrangement of clothes—a T-shirt with a clenched red fist printed on it; but it was the last pile that made her head swim and made her feel she would faint. It was a cheerleader's costume with "San Miguel Frosh" in large blue letters on the front and "Yell Team" on the sleeve. The pleated skirt and boots were carefully arranged below the sweater.

Yvonne Sills held her hand to her mouth and stared at the clothes before her and tried not to think what kept bursting inside her head. Why, Sonny, why? Nausea rose within her, and she could taste the bitterness in the back of her throat as she haltingly made her way back down the ladder, not bothering to close the trapdoor. The walk to the house was agonizing as pain seized her legs and chest. Once back on the couch she sat for nearly a half-hour with head back and one hand inside her robe to calm her pounding heart. She couldn't think. Her mind filled with the terrible possibilities and then dissolved. But it was Sonny, it was; she wanted to cry, but there was nothing left inside her. Sonny, Sonny! Who will help you? It was a full hour after she had returned from the loft when Yvonne dialed the sheriff's department.

Dispatcher Margaret Richards advised Car 9 that a silent alarm was ringing at Covert's Grocery when the phone buzzed. She picked it up and glanced idly through the glass door to the adjoining room, where huge spools of tape that recorded all radio traffic and all incoming calls turned slowly. The voice on the other end was faint and muffled, talking of some girls who had died.

"One moment please." She hit the hold button and turned to the desk sergeant behind her. "Some woman talking about dead girls or something, Bill."

Sergeant Bill Fenton, nine years on the force and a man who felt he had seen it all, lifted the receiver while simultaneously lighting his cigarette. He blew smoke into the receiver and said, "Sheriff's department. Sergeant Fenton. May I help you?" It was a statement, not a question. Eight weirdos had called about the slain girls in the past week.

"You know those dead girls?" the woman's voice asked.

"What dead girls, ma'am?" Fenton said. He couldn't find his pencil.

"Those ones that been killed and all their clothing taken?"

"Yes, ma'am. May I have your name, please?" He lifted the log sheets but didn't see his pencil.

"Well, my Sonny, my baby, wouldn't do that. He just couldn't." The woman sounded as if she were crying.

"Yes, ma'am. Now, could you give me your name and telephone number, please?" He cupped his hand over the receiver. "Margaret, you got my pencil?"

"Sills. Still, I know he wouldn't . . . he just—"

"What was that name again, ma'am?" Fenton said as Margaret handed him the pencil that had fallen to the floor in front of his desk.

"He wouldn't, but he has these clothes up there. But he wouldn't, he just wouldn't."

"Now, wait a minute, ma'am, just take it from—" He stopped suddenly and looked at the receiver, dead in his hand. He put the phone down slowly.

"That was an odd one, Margaret," he said. "That one was definitely different than most of the others. The boys might want to check that one out." He made a note in his log: Woman called about dead girls. Name indistinguishable. No address given.

"Can't understand these old bags half the time, but I think she said her name. If one of us has a minute, Margaret, maybe we can get it off the tape."

Fenton sat a moment, then rose and started toward the tape when the phone rang.

"Sheriff's department, Sergeant Fenton. May I help you. . . . Yeah, okay, relax, lady, and give me the address." He cupped his hand over the mouthpiece and spoke to Margaret: "Family disturbance at 312 South Road. Better get someone over there quick." He turned back to the phone with a sigh, because the lady was begging him not to hang up until a deputy arrived at her house.

The bug-car took me to a pay telephone and stopped. I stared at the dark box near the gas station until Francis told me to call. I skimmed through the book until I found Eriksen's number and address. The telephone current sizzled through me when I lifted the receiver. I dialed, and each click triggered a nerve pulsation that began in my ear and ran down my spine. The mechanical bell whirred once, twice, and then the telephone lifted. The woman said hello, and my voice deepened of its own accord, took on the Arkansas twang of a CB radio operator.

"Uh, this here is John Hawkins. Is Detective Eriksen there, please? I have some important information for him."

"No, he's not."

"Well, Mrs. Eriksen, is there another detective there I could talk with, or a deputy?"

"No, there isn't. Have you tried to reach him at the office?"

"Uh, yes, ma'am, but he wasn't there. Do you know when he'll be back? It's real important I talk to him."

"No, I couldn't say. He's been quite busy. Could he call you back?"

"No, I'm moving around quite a bit myself, Mrs. Eriksen. I'll just try to catch him later on. Thank you." Click. Simple as that, I thought, and snapped my fingers to see if I could create a spark. I started back to the car and then returned and tore out the page with Eriksen's address, even though I knew his house.

Cynthia hung up the telephone slowly and looked at the large clock on the wall in the kitchen—9:27. She had talked to Dan just twenty-seven minutes ago and he had still been there. As she listened to the muted whir in her ear, she drummed her fingers on the polished bookcase and watched the second hand sweep around. When the phone had rung for one full minute she hung up.

Goddamn you, she thought as she stared at the clock. Oh, goddamn you. She grabbed the phone again, ready to dial the dispatcher and see if she could get him on the car radio, but if he was out there, she didn't want to give him the satisfaction. Still she held the phone and she thought of dialing that woman. Nancy. Nancy what? Nancy Hall, the attractive secretary that Mrs. Dewitt across the street had twice cattily mentioned as the person her son had seen Dan with in the Hilton bar after work. She had responded that Dan has many contacts to make and many places to check out in his work and he drew help from many quarters. Detectives often talked their cases over with their secretaries, she had said, and after all, they are just as informed as the detectives because they type all the reports. Mrs. Dewitt had smiled and nodded and said, "Oh, I see." But what if she called Nancy and he wasn't there? Or he was there? Then what? *Oh, hi, dear, just calling to see if you were having a nice screw. Denice and I are having a nice time here too, all alone, just watching some TV. Well, good-bye now, have a nice time.*

"Mom, bring me a Coke?" Denice yelled from the family room, where they were watching the movie.

"No. Your teeth will fall out."

"Well, I'm thirsty."

"Then drink some water."

"Oh, *Mom.*"

Cynthia watched the red second hand sweep around—9:29. Why had Hawkins called? Calls to

Dan at home were not uncommon, but they usually were from someone at the office. Hawkins. She had never heard of him before.

"Mom, *please?* It's a party night. We're watching a TV movie."

Denice? It could be. The man had wanted to know if Dan was there. Or another detective. And she had said no! She bit carefully at a tiny hangnail on her right index finger. Whoever called now knew there was no one guarding the house.

"Mom?" Denice stood in the living-room doorway, still dressed in the brown pleated skirt and the beige cashmere sweater she had worn to school that day. "I wondered what happened to you. Come on, you're going to miss the show."

Cynthia caught the hangnail with her incisor teeth and pulled. It hurt and she saw a tiny drop of blood ooze out. "Go ahead, get a Coke," she said. "I'll be right in."

She moved swiftly through the house, ensuring that the front door and the garage doors were locked, then went to the back door and brought in Spider, who was sleeping on the doormat. "Not that you'll be much help, you deaf old dog," she said as she ruffled his furry coat, "but maybe you'll be able to smell something." She returned to the kitchen and was about to pour herself a brandy when she decided she better stay awake until Dan got home. "Maybe it's dumb and running scared," she murmured aloud, "but I had better be more alert." She put some water on to boil for instant coffee and wondered again where her husband really was.

I drove by the house at a proper speed, not too slow and not too fast. Nothing anybody would notice. The porchlight illuminated the gleaming white door and spilled across the green lawn. Every light downstairs seemed to be on, and one upstairs, which I thought might be the bathroom. The garage, which was attached to the large two-story house, was closed. I couldn't tell if Eriksen was home or not.

"If he were home there wouldn't be so many lights on," said Francis with a derisive laugh. Two blocks from the house I stopped and parked, but then I realized that if I did get the lioness—no, *when* I got her—I would not be able to just carry her through the streets. I turned left to the alley and drove up behind their house with my lights off. My heart pumped hard as I got out, and the light gleaming through the curtains at the rear of the house seemed to fall upon me like a beacon. I half-expected a large dog to leap snarling upon me or Eriksen himself to jump from the shadowed bushes and thrust his gun in my face. But nothing happened, just the stillness of the night, a child crying in the house behind me, and a dog in the next block barking fitfully.

A six-foot-high chain-link fence separated their yard from the alley, and I was about to climb over it when I saw a gate at the corner, unlocked, and I simply walked through. I took a deep breath to calm myself, and avoiding the bars of light that fell across the rear lawn—they could have been lightspears put there by the lioness to trap me—I moved slowly along the row of bushes at the edge of the lawn until I was beside the house. My synapses were clicking rapidly, racing with the ferocity of a Geiger counter in a radiation field.

Francis hissed beside me in the dark: "Look inside. Find the gray lioness and capture her. This is your last chance to redeem men everywhere. You will be the savior, you shall be revered. Now, go on."

Why didn't they have a dog to bite me? Everyone had a dog. Even a little bitty one inside that made nasty barks at the slightest sound, but there was nothing. I rose carefully to the darkened window at the end of the house, and my eyes slowly discerned it was the kitchen, with light from another room spilling into the adjacent dining room. In that far room I could make out part of what appeared to be a robe and a bare foot that swung idly. The lioness? Ducking below the windows, I moved quickly the length of the house until I stood in the flowering bushes that flanked the corner room by the garage. The curtains were drawn, but I moved slowly along the window until at the center, where the curtains were not completely shut, I could see most of the room. I drew nearer the window, not wanting them to see me, and then froze, my breath stopping, for there they both were, at either end of the couch across the room, staring directly at me. I was paralyzed, but as I watched, the girl took a glass from the end table beside her, and still staring at me, took a drink. Only then did I realize—and now I could hear it—they were watching the television directly below the window. I moved to get a different perspective of the room and could see a large dog lying near the chair of the woman; the easy chair, probably for Eriksen, was empty. Then he really wasn't home! I backed away from the window and wiped the sweat from my face. This was it! This was my test of manhood, my warrior chance to face the gray lioness and defeat her. But how to trap her without being trapped myself? That was part of the test. I could not just charge into the house, break through a window or door, without falling into their trap. No, I must play her waiting game, wait until she came to me.

I returned to the window, watching and waiting, and within a few minutes Denice rose and left the room. She said something to her mother that I could not hear; her mother nodded slightly and continued to watch the television. Still I waited, and within one minute light fell across the garage roof above me. I backed away from the house, staying in the bushes that flanked the garage, until I could see the lighted window. The ruffled curtains were drawn, but I could see a shadow pass briefly back and forth. It was quite possible that was her room, so I studied the garage with fresh interest. At the corner grew a small fruit tree. Its limbs were slender, but they would be strong enough to hold me while I climbed onto the roof. And the peak of the garage roof came just below her window. I had to try. My energy levels rose as I watched her room until the light went out again. I peered through the window and saw her come back into the television room wearing a blue robe open in front to reveal blue silken pajamas.

"Now! You must go up there now!" Francis said in a terrible voice that spurred me on. Getting onto the garage roof was easy, but the window, as I had feared, was locked. I wanted to cry. Why couldn't anything go right? I tugged at the split window, but the rotating catch was firmly in place. Knowing I had no choice, I took my pocketknife and prepared to break the glass beside the catch. Surely they would hear me and bound up the stairs with that ferocious dog in the lead. But with the television on, maybe they wouldn't hear it. This was the worst part. Once I had the lioness, I would be calm, because then I knew precisely what to do, and once I had killed her she would not be able to turn the minds of others against me. When she was dead, the others would see how right I was. I wrapped my knife in my handkerchief and rapped sharply on the glass pane. Nothing happened. If I hit it too hard, the whole window might collapse on the floor inside. Damn! I gave another rap, a little harder, and a six-inch crack ran up the window. Well, if they hear me I will just run and capture the lioness another day. She might be someone else by then, and not a detective's daughter. She did this to me just to make it hard. I hit the window again, and the glass gave way in three large shards that left a hole large enough to put both hands through. The glass was caught in the curtains. It had not even fallen. I carefully removed the pieces, then turned the catch on the window, opened it, and went inside. I was in! I could hear the television below, and no sounds of turmoil. Light from the bathroom across the hall fell through the open door, and I glanced around. They had heard nothing. A large canopied bed stood in one corner; a closet with louvered doors was beside the door. There was a desk with books open on it near the window, and a bureau of drawers topped with Raggedy Ann dolls.

I went slowly into the hallway, where I could better hear the voices talking over the television.

"Oh, Mom."

"It's ten o'clock, Denice, and tomorrow is a schoolday. So please don't argue with me."

"All right. Good night." Her tone was surly. It's now, it's now, now, now, and I slipped back behind the door. I heard her slippered feet brush the carpeted stairs as she came up. It was dark again when she closed the bathroom door. My eyes adjusted, and in the darkness I could hear every sound within the house: the rasp of the toothbrush as Denice scrubbed her teeth; the wail of police sirens on the television show downstairs; the creaks of the house, like old bones resisting any movement; or were they anticipating the pain that was about to come? Why was she so long in the bathroom? The water stopped, and I heard the faint hiss and tinkle as she urinated. I could hear so much up here; wouldn't her mother and that beast of a dog hear everything downstairs? Maybe I should hit her when she came in, a single chop to the neck that would stun her. But if I missed and she cried out . . . No, I didn't know how to do that, I only knew how to apply the pressure, fast and hard, to the two carotid arteries. Why was she still in there? She knew I was out here, that's why. The lioness could smell me, she could smell the pores opening and my juices running, she could smell the electrical heat from my body. She planned to outwait me, make me move first. That's how the lioness was, always trying to lure the other into her trap, into her folds, her wet and enveloping folds, then snap! Snap, the door opened and light burst in a yellow rectangle across the floor before me, and I held my breath. My muscles strained until I thought they would unravel like old rope. Her shadow preceded her into the room, and now . . . Jesus! It's going away, she's receding, fleeing. I started to edge out from behind the door. I would take her in the hallway if I had to, pin her and kill her there. Maybe that would be best, a single quick struggle and be done, before her mother knew what was happening, and then I could burst from the house and run and run. But that wouldn't be right; the gray lioness had to suffer, suffer worse than the others. She must submit to my will, the will of all mankind, she must be punished by my flaming sword, her own trap burned and destroyed by my righteousness. Snap. It was dark again, and I heard the rustle of her feet over the rasp of my own breath. She was at the door. I held my breath and crouched. Snap. My synapses were crackling now. Snap. Light flooded the room, blinding me and sending light-shudders through me, and then she was right before me, her back exposed as she stood by the end of her bed and slipped the robe off, first one arm, then the other, bringing the robe around, her hair loose and flowing, halfway down her back, a blond mane. Here was the lioness, and I had to move, I had to. One step, another, and I was there, but she smelled me, felt the heat of my charged body as I approached, and she started to turn, but I had her, one hand over her mouth and my arm crooked around her neck, muscles of my forearm and biceps bulging to bite into the carotid arteries. I pulled her back until her feet swung clear of the floor and there could be no sound. I backed away a little as she swung out frantically with her feet and narrowly missed a small table with her reading lamp on it. Air hissed from her nose; a whimper only gurgled in her throat. Her feet flailed out again, and both slippers hit the far wall with a faint plop. She pummeled at me, but without strength. She was almost gone. There was a final convulsion, and then she sagged in my arms. Still I pinched her neck in my arm, taking her to a dangerous limit. She had to be out long enough for me to get her off the roof. I held her like a folded sack and carried her to the window and rolled her facedown onto the roof peak. I followed, and the air was cold on my sweat-slick body. At the edge of the garage roof I lowered her headfirst, holding her by one ankle, until her head almost touched the grass, and then, with a little swing to drop her flat, I let go. It was easy, easy; I had her, and soon it would be all over. She began rolling her head back and forth, her mouth working with small sounds, and I took precious seconds to put her back under again before we fled, she riding like a hunchback on my shoulders, to the bug-car, which gurgled in its bowels to see me safely back. I tied her hands, put her on the rear seat with a blanket over her, and we were gone gone gone.

"I did it, Francis Macomber, I did it, for you and for Ernest and for my father!" There was no answer.

Downstairs, the dog raised his head and looked at Cynthia, bright brown eyes alert and demanding an answer.

"What, Spider?" Cynthia said.

The dog stared at her for long seconds, then pushed himself into a sitting position. A flow of air with the smells of the night filled the living room. It filled the dog with unease. He stood up and stretched, then unhesitatingly made his way up the stairs. Cynthia watched him go, curious at what had motivated the old hunter. She had heard nothing, and certainly the Airedale had heard nothing. Still, he moved as if looking for something.

She quietly put down her coffeecup and moved to the foot of the stairs. Above her, softly lit by the wall-bounced light from Denice's room, the dog looked down at her. He watched for a second, then soundlessly turned back and entered Denice's room. Cynthia started to yell at Denice to turn out the light, but something made her stop. A queasy feeling filled her stomach. There was something different in the house, something cool. Air! Moving air. Denice must have left her window open. Lifting her robe, she ran lightly up the stairs, moving silently and not knowing exactly why. She eased up to the room and could see that the bed was empty, not even turned down. She glanced at the bathroom door beside her. No light underneath. Then boldly she pushed into the room and felt the bottom of her stomach fall out. Her knees nearly buckled. Spider stood with his head out the open window, his feet on the large broken shards.

"Denice!" Her cry echoed off the darkened houses outside, but there was no answer. She flew down the stairs and out the back, but there was nothing! No car, no sound, no daughter. Cynthia whirled and raced back inside the house. Flinging open the telephone book, she hunted for the desired number, then punched it out viciously on the touch-phone. A woman's voice, soft and immensely relaxed, answered after the third ring.

"Yes?"

"This is Cynthia Eriksen." Her words were hard and chopped. "Is my husband there? I must speak to him. It's an emergency."

"Mrs. Eriksen, your husband wouldn't be—"

Hot tears flooded Cynthia's eyes, and the room swam as she angrily cut the woman short. "Goddammit! I know he's there. Now, you tell that bastard to get home now. Now! You understand?" She was screaming and crying. "Tell him his daughter's gone. Kidnapped." She flung the phone against the wall and collapsed on the counter.

10

"Cynthia!" Eriksen bellowed as he burst into the house. There was no answer and he was starting up the stairs when he saw her sitting at the dining-room table. Her face was gray and both hands gripped the edge of the table in a futile effort to stop her trembling.

"Cynthia. What happened?"

Her voice was small and brittle. "While you were . . . were with that woman, your daughter disappeared. Someone took her out her bedroom window."

He stared unbelievingly at her, then raced up the stairs to Denice's room. The curtains billowed slightly as the night breeze coursed through the open window. He tore back downstairs and looked at the kitchen clock—10:48. Where the hell are those patrol cars I radioed for, he thought as he faced Cynthia.

"What time did this happen?" he asked.

Her eyes came up flat and hard. "Probably just as you were doing it with that woman."

"Goddammit, Cynthia, we'll settle that matter later.

Now, I want to know everything that happened, and I want it fast," he rasped, and saw her flinch at the menace in his voice.

"I sent her up to bed at ten sharp," Cynthia said in a voice that broke as she talked. "She wanted to stay up longer, but I wouldn't let her because it was a school night. And then, I don't know, maybe fifteen minutes later, Spider got up and went upstairs. I felt something was wrong. I don't know why, I just did. I went into her room and . . . and she was gone! Just that open window. I ran outside and looked all around the house and down the street and down the alley but there was nothing." Large tears slid down her cheeks.

Eriksen put his hand to her face, but she stiffened and turned away. He went to the bookcase and dialed the sheriff's office. Swing dispatcher Margaret Richards took the call and Eriksen tersely gave her the details and described Denice.

"Put out an APB on my daughter and advise all units to stop every goddamned white VW they see on whatever excuse they can think of. Tell them to say they thought the tires were too bald. You advise San Miguel P.D. and CHP. I'll call the sheriff." He depressed the receiver and dialed the sheriff. Conrad came on the line and Eriksen repeated his story.

"All right. Stay at home and I'll be there immediately. We'll make your home the operations base, at least for tonight, in the event phone calls are made to you." Eriksen started to protest that the killer didn't make phone calls but the sheriff had already hung up. The doorbell rang, and he went to admit the two deputies.

At that same moment, Larry Blanken lay on the imitation bear rug in his bachelor studio and fumbled with the clasp of Helen Marshall's brassiere.

"I think it's stuck," he said, and wished his forehead would stop sweating.

"Here, I'll do it," Helen said, half-turning on the rug, where she lay in just her panties and bra.

"No, I'll get it." He wiped his brow on his shirt sleeve and bent to the task.

"I thought you were experienced at this sort of thing." Helen giggled over the swell of Mantovani's orchestra.

"I am, I mean . . . well, a little. There." He removed the bra and kissed her, and she ran her hands up to peel back his unbuttoned shirt.

"Will you be loving with me?"

"Sure, baby," he panted in her ear. "Is this really your first time?"

"Yes. Does that bother you?"

"No, I just think of you as a national treasure," he said as he kissed his way down her neck.

"Why?" she breathed.

"You may be this country's last adult virgin." He slid his hand down to her panties and was about to remove them when the ringing telephone brought everything to a halt.

He groaned and let it ring three times in hopes it was a wrong number, but when it persisted he crawled across the floor to the end table.

"What," he growled. He listened in agitated silence as Margaret Richards outlined the situation and said the sheriff had ordered him, among others, mobilized for the emergency.

"But I'm really tied up," he wailed. "Get Pitkin. He's the reserve deputy, get . . ." He broke off lamely as Richards stressed this was an emergency and that he was expected to respond to radio calls within two minutes.

He slammed the phone down and turned toward Helen, who sat watching him with her arms across her pale breasts.

"You won't believe this, but I've got to go out in the middle of the night right now to look for some goddamn nut who kidnapped the daughter of one of our detectives." He went to the closet and began pulling on his uniform.

"Can you believe it? At this hour I gotta go out and look for some whip driving a white Volkswagen with a kidnapped girl in the back. Sure." He buttoned his shirt as Helen mused aloud.

"Sonny drives a white VW."

Blanken looked at her. "Who does?"

"Sonny Sills. Remember that guy who shot off his mouth in the restaurant that night?"

"Oh, yeah." Blanken was under the bed looking for his boots. "He was your boyfriend or something, wasn't he?"

"Not really, but we went to high school together."

"What was his last name?"

"Sills," Helen said. "He's weird, but I don't think he would go out and kidnap a girl. Although he choked me one time. Really scared me."

"I'll be darned," Blanken said. "Listen, you don't have to go home. Stay all night. I might not be out there too long."

"No, my parents would really freak out if I didn't come home."

"All right." He walked to the door with her and kissed her. "Drive safely going home, and I'll see you tomorrow. I've really gotta rush."

She saw him talking on the radio as he pulled away.

Fred Thomas, listening to the police scanner radio in the crew car, braked to a stop outside Eriksen's house.

"Come on, hook up, hook up," he urged as he led the cameraman and sound man toward the front door. "Hit the lights and start rolling now," he said, and punched the doorbell.

Eriksen flung open the door expecting the sheriff and was hit by a blinding light. It took him a full second to realize that there was someone standing in front of him with a microphone asking what was happening.

"For Chrissake, get that goddamn light out of my eyes." He stepped out on the porch, and Thomas backed down one stair but kept the microphone in front of himself.

"We need to know what happened to your daughter, Sergeant."

Eriksen advanced another step. "Listen, Thomas, I told you what I was going to do to you with that microphone, and I meant it. If you hadn't been sneaking around here taking pictures of my family, that asshole wouldn't have my daughter right now." Stepping forward, he suddenly seized the reporter by the wrist and drew Thomas slowly toward him.

"Dan!"

Eriksen turned to see the sheriff puffing across the lawn with arms windmilling.

"Let him go!" Conrad puffed. He pushed Eriksen toward the house. "Go inside and I'll be right there." As Eriksen walked away, he heard Conrad talking to Thomas.

"Naturally he's worked up about this, and I hope you'll take that into consideration when you edit this film. Now, as soon as we have something for you boys, we'll let you know. Meanwhile, let us do our job."

Conrad came into the house wiping his face. "Hell's *bells,* Dan, you did it again."

"The next time that guy even looks at me I'm going to punch his lights out."

"We'll talk about that later," Conrad growled. "Where do we stand now?"

Eriksen dug out a Camel and lit it. "Our department has patrol cars on every major street going out of town. P.D. has cruisers in San Miguel. CHP has roadblocks north and south on the freeway. Harris and his ID team are upstairs going over her room."

"But nothing hard so far?"

"They've stopped at least six white VWs, but nothing. No one resembled this Jerry, or Sonny, or whoever, and no Denice." He turned as he spoke and looked at Cynthia, who still sat at the dining-room table watching the wall.

This time I wasn't going to make a mistake like with Cheri and let the lioness escape, so we went up the ladder together. That way I could open it and keep a tight hold on Denice. "And I'll cut you bad if I have to," I whispered as we struggled up the ladder. She was so close I could feel her heat through her cotton pajamas. Her breath hissed next to my ears. We went up one rung at a time, and when we were close to the top I reached into the blackness to push the trapdoor back. We weren't as close as I expected. "Come on," I whispered, "and don't try any tricks." Her breathing sounded like a hissing cat. We went up two more rungs, and I knew this could be it. I reached up; again nothing. Then I felt the floorboards of the loft and suddenly realized that the trapdoor was open. But I never left it open! I jerked my arm down and froze on the ladder. My heart thudded in my ears; was that why I could hear nothing up in the loft? But someone must be up there waiting for me. Who? The police! Eriksen had already found us! But how could he? He couldn't! Who had been here? I always closed the door, didn't I? I felt a rivulet of sweat slide down my cheekbone and spin away into the night, and I wished I could disappear with it. I let my breath out softly, trying to breathe silently. If they were in there, then it was too late. Maybe I had left it open. I had to act. Pushing Denice before me, I entered the loft, which was as dark as a tomb, and I waited for iron fingers to close around my neck from behind; but there was nothing. I lowered the trapdoor and flicked on the light. Empty. I felt like a drowning man who suddenly bursts into the air. Breathing deeply, I dragged the girl across the room. She whimpered and mewed as I untied her hands and stood ready for her to fight or run, but she stood quietly with eyes staring at the floor. I tied one hand to a large nail driven into an exposed stud, then pulled the other hand up and tied it in a like manner. She stood in a modest crucifixion against the wall.

I turned on the tape recorder, and the strains of Beethoven's Fifth filled my tiny sanctuary. Beethoven. Beethoven understood the pain and suffering of mankind; he understood what I had to do now. I turned toward Denice, and her eyes, which had been staring at the clothes I so neatly arranged along one wall, came up to mine, and they were filled with fear and loathing.

"Do those clothes . . . aren't those Cheri's clothes over there?" I could barely hear her voice over the soul-sustaining music of the master.

"What?" I said, and stood close, watching her eyes

now, wanting to study the eyes of a lioness in her final moments.

"Don't those belong to Cheri?"

"Should they?" I wouldn't tell her anything. She was just trying to draw me out. "Why would you want to know? It's too late, anyway." I unbuttoned the front of her pajamas, and her fear boiled to the surface. She lunged forward, straining at the ropes, and tried to bite me, but I easily avoided her, and then she swung viciously at me with her foot, striking like a lioness. She screamed at me, throaty noises that filled the room and drowned out Beethoven. Too much, too much. I turned the music up louder to drown her, to smother her with the love and the hate that dominated Beethoven. The room trembled and throbbed so much with the sounds of the music that I could barely hear her.

Eriksen paced the living room, only half-listening to the dry voices that crackled from the portable radios. More white VWs had been stopped, but no Denice. He turned to Darby, who sat drinking coffee.

"We're running out of time. If they haven't stopped him by now, he may have already reached his destination."

Darby shrugged, not knowing what to say.

Eriksen dialed the patrol desk. Sergeant Bill Fenton was turning the watch over to the graveyard shift and was impatient to leave. "Sheriff's department," he barked into the phone.

"Eriksen here. Did you or Margaret take any strange calls tonight, anything that might be linked to this kidnap? *Anything?*" he stressed.

"Yeah, two of them talking about dead girls. I noted them both in the log for you guys to follow up on in the morning."

"Goddammit to hell," Eriksen yelled. "Why the fuck didn't you tell me! What time did they come in?"

"That's the point, Dan," Fenton said contritely. "Both calls came well before your girl was taken. I didn't think they could be related and I didn't want to both—"

Eriksen slammed the phone down. "They had two crank calls tonight dealing with the dead girls. I'm going to listen to the tapes."

"I'll go with you," Darby said.

"No, wait here in case something breaks." He walked into the dining room, where his ashen-faced wife still sat. The sheriff and deputies manning the radios discreetly kept away from her.

"Cynthia," he said, bending over her. "Hating me for what happened tonight is not going to make things better. It's not going to help us find Denice." He waited, but she gave no sign of hearing him. "Why don't you go to bed and get some rest?" He sighed. "I've got to go to the office for a few minutes."

Still she stared at the wall, and he prepared to leave.

"Dan." Her voice was small and tight. He turned toward her again as she continued. "If Denice is dead, I will consider you dead too." She spoke without taking her eyes from the wall. He turned and left.

Eriksen pressed the buzzer outside the patrol division's radio room and was admitted. Going straight to the watch sergeant's desk, he ran his finger down the swing shift's log notes. "Here," he said to no one. "At nineteen-fifteen Ernie Cahill, Hawkins Lane, says he has new information on Thomas and Chavez. My ass," Eriksen said, and kept going through the log.

His finger stopped and he read it aloud: "Twenty-fifty-three. Woman called about dead girls. Name indistinguishable. No address given." Eriksen returned the log to the watch sergeant.

"Find anything?" he asked.

"Some woman called. Probably a whip, but I'll listen to it on the tape," Eriksen said, and entered the tape room. He ran the swing-shift spool back at high speed and watched the counter until it registered 20:52. He listened to one minute of routine calls and then heard Fenton's bored voice on the phone. Then a woman came on, an older woman by her voice, Eriksen thought.

"You know those dead girls?" she asked. Eriksen could hear the hesitancy in her voice.

"What dead girls, ma'am?" Fenton's dry tone.

"Those ones that been killed and all their clothing taken?" the woman said. She sounded afraid, Eriksen thought.

"Yes, ma'am. May I have your name, please?"

"Well, my Sonny, my baby, wouldn't do that." Eriksen felt numb in his stomach. Sonny! He listened carefully. "He just couldn't." There were muffled sounds on the tape, and Eriksen thought it might be the woman crying.

"Yes, ma'am. Now, could you give me your name and telephone number, please?" Fenton's voice faded, and Eriksen faintly heard him asking about a pencil.

"Son of a bitch!" Eriksen said. "You weren't even listening to her." He fell silent as the tape rolled slowly forward.

"Sills. Still, I know he wouldn't . . . he just—"

Fenton's voice interrupted her: "What was that name again, ma'am?" Eriksen could hear papers on the desk being shuffled.

"He wouldn't, but he has these clothes up there. But he wouldn't, he just wouldn't." Eriksen held his breath.

"Now, wait a minute, ma'am, just take it from—" There was the sound of a dial tone. She had hung up.

Eriksen ran the tape back and felt his fingers tremble slightly as he listened for the name again. It was hard to hear because Fenton had talked about his goddamn pencil over that. "Sills. Still, I know he wouldn't . . . he just—"

Eriksen spun from the tape room and grabbed the telephone directory out of the desk sergeant's hands. He flipped it open to the S's and ran his finger down the listings. A roaring filled his head, and he found it difficult to concentrate. The woman's voice and two key words rang in his mind: "Sills . . . clothes . . . Sills . . . clothes."

"God*dammit!*" he cried. "Look at all these fucking Sillses. And no Sonny or Jerry Sills." The desk sergeant stared at him. Eriksen quickly counted the number of Sillses. Seventeen. "We'll just send a patrol car to every damn one of them, and the first place with a white Volkswagen in the yard is going to be blown away."

He crossed the room to where Sergeant Mott sat before the radio console. Eriksen slammed the telephone book down and pointed to the names, but Mott held up one hand to stop him as he completed a radio call: "Car 22; San Miguel."

"Car 22." Eriksen wanted to grab the mike, but he had to let Mott finish this one call.

"That old man Cahill, over on Hawkins Lane, is complaining again about loud music from a neighbor. If you get close to that area you might check it out, but considering what else is going on, I wouldn't give it too much priority."

Mott turned toward Eriksen as he finished, but the detective was moving toward the door. "Yvonne Sills, on Hawkins Lane," he shouted, and was gone.

I stood in the center of the room and let the waves of music crash upon me as I directed the symphony through the threatening third movement. I was very good tonight and I felt the violins sing within me as we moved as one into the triumphant fourth movement. Beethoven was triumphant, and I would be triumphant tonight. When the music ended I felt drained and sagged against the wall near Denice. When I caught my breath I turned to look at her. She stood with legs braced apart and her head forward so that her blond mane obscured her face. I stepped in front of her and with one finger to her forehead pushed her head back. Her eyes filled with tears, and great drops splashed on her pajama top. She said something but I couldn't make it out. Her voice was distant, like summer thunder in the foothills.

"What?" I said, and leaned toward her, but not too close. This lioness was still very much alive and dangerous.

"Are you going to kill me?" she said, and her swimming eyes came up to meet mine.

"Why do you want to know that?" I asked, on guard

immediately. Even now she couldn't stop spying on me, prying into my life. "Why?" I shouted.

She ducked her head. "Please, don't hurt me. Just tell me what you want."

"Tell me what you want," I mimicked. "Just tell the lioness what you want. Come into my web, said the spider to the fly."

"Why did you kill those other girls, and Cheri too? What did they ever do to you?" she said, and watched me with her cat-blue eyes. Yes, she had eyes like a Siamese. I should have known long ago who she really was. I saw her eyes cloud over as I laughed with the joy of my victory tonight.

"Don't hide behind your eyes," I said. "It's too late."

She started to speak, but seemed to think better of it and just stared at the floor.

"Naked came she into the world and naked shall she leave it," Francis said in a voice that filled the entire room.

"Yes," I said, and untied Denice's right wrist. Holding her tightly, I slipped her pajama top off that arm and retied it. She watched my every move, her breath coming in hot little pants, and I knew I had to be very careful. As I loosened the other arm she gave a powerful lurch and pulled her arm free, but the rope on the other arm held firm, and she came up short, like a puppy on a leash.

She screamed, a cutting shriek that ripped the room and split my mind. She must stop! I lunged forward and caught her by the throat with my hand and gave a violent squeeze that turned her cries into a gurgle. I held her until her face was crimson and she shuddered with repeated spasms. Her eyes glazed and she was going, she was going, but it was too soon. I knew it. She must be punished first, she must know how terrible she is, and I jerked my hand away.

She coughed violently and I heard the air rasping in her throat as she struggled back to life.

"One more time like that and you will be gone forever," I cried as I retied her wrist, but she wouldn't listen. She sagged on the ropes, head down and long hair swaying in front of her young breasts that were banded white against her tawny skin. I took both breasts in my hands and squeezed until her head snapped back in pain.

"You'll never suckle young lions again with these," I said through my teeth. She moaned but did not cry out. "You destroyed my father and you killed Francis and you wanted to take away my manhood, but you won't. You're finished." I shoved her back against the wall to display my contempt and then started Beethoven from the beginning again. The music would hide everything.

"Naked," Francis boomed over the sudden surge of music.

"Yes!" I shouted back, and stepped to Denice again. Watching that she did not strike me with her powerful hind feet, I slid my index finger in the elastic band of her pajama bottoms. Her breath caught in her throat and she swung her head back and forth, as a lioness will, but she did not resist.

"Good. You're learning," I said with a pleased laugh. Then slowly I slid her pajamas down while I watched fear unfold in her face. Her breath quickened.

"Oh, please, please, please don't, don't hurt me, please. I won't tell anyone," she said in short little cries.

Still I lowered the pajamas until the lioness stood naked and unprotected. She was vulnerable at last.

"Yes," I said softly, but loud enough for her to hear over the music, "I am going to kill you. But only after you have suffered all the pain I have." I sat before her, out of reach of her claws, and watched her die a little as the music swelled around us.

From the black depths of the screen porch, Yvonne Sills stared at the pumphouse. Streaks of light spilled between the warped redwood boards that her father and grandfather had nailed there so many years ago. The sounds of that long-hair music that Sonny liked so much cascaded from the loft and rolled across the dark fields. Her eyes were wide and her lips were wet as she listened. It had been the piercing shriek of a woman that had brought her first to the open bathroom window, then to the porch. But now she was not sure what she heard, for there was nothing but the music. But Sonny was up there, that she knew, and there were the clothes of three young girls up there. Three girls were dead.

"But Sonny, Sonny, you just have the clothes. Did you find them, sweetheart?" she breathed. *"Did you find them, my darling, and put them there because you liked the color and texture? You always were such a sweet boy, so understanding. You would not harm anything, Momma knows that."* The words kept moving through her mind, but there was something unacceptable about them. Her hands, now cold, moved up past her neck until they reached her ears, and she tried to stop the onrushing music, but she could not shut it out. Instead she opened the screen door and haltingly moved toward the pumphouse, even though she did not know what she would do when she got there. She was less than halfway, standing near a large stone toad, when she saw the beam of light stretch down the road and then wink out. She turned and waited, curious at the appearance and then abrupt disappearance of light, as if someone had cut their lights up the road. Maybe parked in front of old Cahill's place, she thought. She was about to continue on when she saw the sedan glide to a stop outside her gate and she saw the brief glow of a cigarette inside before it too disappeared. A terrible dread filled her as she knew someone had come for Sonny, come for her baby.

Eriksen was on the radio before he was out of the department's parking area.

"Four-oh-one; five-twelve."

"Four-oh-one. Go." Conrad's voice came right back at him.

"I think we've got a real possible. The home of Yvonne Sills at the end of Hawkins Lane. It's less than a mile north of the office. Get me backup units, but have them come in quietly."

"Ten-four, five-twelve."

Eriksen listened to the dispatcher's voice cut in immediately: "Cars 14, 15, 19, and 22 provide backup for five-twelve at the house of Yvonne Sills, end of Hawkins Lane. Code two."

Eriksen cut his lights as he passed the first house, Cahill's place, and drifted to a stop in front of the Sills' yard. He stubbed his cigarette and got out. The only streetlight was too far behind him to be of any use, but he felt reluctant to use his flashlight. *If Denice is in here and still alive,* he thought, *I don't want that asshole to know I'm about to blow his head off.* He moved swiftly toward the house, then dropped to one knee and drew his .357 as he saw a dark form moving slowly toward the lighted pumphouse, from where the symphony music blared.

He hit the light, and the beam jerked the woman to a stop. He saw a short, fat woman with doughy skin turn and shade her eyes. He ran to her.

"Sheriff's department," he said, and covered most of the light with his hand. "Are you Mrs. Sills?"

"Yes," she said hesitantly, and he watched her hand flutter to her mouth.

"Do you have a son named Jerry or Sonny?" he asked in a harsh voice.

"Why do you want to know?" she asked, and stepped back slightly.

Eriksen leaned forward and scratched the side of his head with the barrel of his pistol so she could not miss seeing it. "Just answer the question," he snapped.

"I don't have any boy named Jerry," she said. Eriksen was about to grab her by the hair and worry about the consequences tomorrow when the night was split by a yelper siren and a Blazer truck with the sheriff's badge on the side roared down the lane and spun into the yard. Deputy Larry Blanken, with all lights flashing, leaped from the truck with revolver in hand.

"You son of a bitch!" Eriksen screamed. "Kill those lights. You were told to come in here code two. God*dammit!*" He turned back to the woman before Blanken's headlights went out and saw a white Volkswagen parked beside the pumphouse.

He ran to the side of the Blazer and shoved Blanken away from the door as he grabbed the mike.

"Four-oh-one and all units responding to Hawkins Lane. The subject is here."

He turned and ran toward the pumphouse with the flashlight cutting a wide beam ahead of him. No need to be secretive anymore, he cursed, and then drew up short. Something was very wrong. The music. It was gone. Silence from the loft. And the lights were out too. The old lady came toward him in the dark. He heard her labored breathing and her feet shuffling in the gravel.

"Don't hurt my boy, don't hurt my Sonny, please. He don't know what he's doing."

"Sonny!" Eriksen shouted. "This is the sheriff's office. We know you are in there with the girl. We want you to come out peacefully. Do not harm the girl. Do . . . not . . . harm . . . the . . . girl. Do you hear me?"

He listened, but there was no sound from the loft. The woman, breathing in ragged gasps, closed in on him.

"Oh, don't hurt my baby. Sonny don't know what he's doing."

"Shut up," Eriksen snarled. She clutched his arm and held on to keep from falling. Eriksen shook her off and moved away.

"Denice! Can you hear me. Are you all right?"

"Daddy, oh, Da—" she cried before her voice was cut off. Eriksen plunged into the pumphouse, but the woman was on him again, pulling at his arm and pleading for her son.

"Blanken, get this whip away from me," he shouted, and shoved her back. She lurched and fell heavily.

He swung the light around to the ladder and started up. "Sonny, I'm coming up, but no one's going to hurt you. I'll come up and we'll talk."

"If you come up here, the lioness will die," Sonny shouted. Eriksen froze with one foot on the ladder.

"Sonny, it's too late. It's all over. No one—"

"It is *not* over! It won't be over until she is dead and Francis releases me," he shouted.

"All right, all right. Now relax." Sweating heavily in the humid night, Eriksen jerked off his jacket and threw it on the ground. As he stood thinking for a moment, four cars swung into the driveway and stopped.

"Dan?" Darby's voice called softly.

Eriksen ran toward him. The sheriff and Lieutenant Nye were getting out of their cars. Two more patrol cars swung in.

"Bill, put a car on each side of the pumphouse and get their lights on the top section. He's up there with Denice."

"She's still alive, still okay?" Darby asked.

"She's alive," Eriksen replied tersely.

As Darby moved away, Eriksen turned to Conrad. "He's got her and says he'll kill her if any of us go up there. Call Friedland. Better yet, send a patrol car to his house and bring him here immediately. We may need him to talk this son of a bitch down."

Conrad tilted his hat back and was about to say something when he caught the look in Eriksen's eye. He turned to Nye. "Get right on that, Harry."

Eriksen started back to the pumphouse, but Conrad held him. "I've ordered up three men from the Special Enforcement Detail. They'll be here any second."

"I don't know how we can use them. There's only that little window in the loft, and there's nothing high enough around here for a man to get a shot through it."

"He may show himself, or we might get a shot right through the wall," Conrad said.

"And put a bullet through Denice too?" Eriksen replied. "You tell those sharpshooters to stay out of this. I'll handle it myself."

He turned and ran toward the pumphouse. "Bill, light this place up." As headlights and spotlights bathed the old wooden structure, Eriksen took Mrs. Sills by the arm from where she leaned against a patrol car.

"Mrs. Sills, does Sonny have a gun up there?"

She shook her head and moaned. Eriksen gave her a shake and repeated the question. "I don't know, I don't know," she said.

"Does he *own* a pistol or a rifle or anything?" Eriksen said.

"Just a little .410 he uses for doves."

"Where does he keep it?"

"In his closet usually." She wiped her face with one hand and looked at Eriksen. "Please don't hurt my baby."

"Baby, my ass," Eriksen muttered as he turned to the nearest deputy. "Check his closet out and see if the shotgun is in there."

"Sonny Sills." Conrad's metallic voice boomed across the brightly lit yard. Eriksen turned and saw him standing with a bullhorn to his mouth and television cameras rolling on him. "Sonny Sills, this is Sheriff Conrad. This place is surrounded by my men. There is no escape for you. Send the girl out first and then you follow with your hands in the air. No one will hurt you." He paused and then asked: "Do you hear me?"

There was no answer from the loft. Behind the sheriff Eriksen saw three men in blue coveralls holding M16 rifles mounted with sniper scopes get out of a patrol car. He ran toward them, vaguely aware the cameras were swinging toward him.

"I don't want these men used, Sheriff. We can't risk it with Denice up there."

"I'm deploying them and they'll await my orders," Conrad said. A man scribbling notes on a pad moved in, and Eriksen shoved him back and stepped close to Conrad.

"I'll make it simple, Sheriff. If you use those men and Denice gets killed, I'll come after you."

Conrad flushed. "You just cool down."

There was a pregnant silence as the two men stared at each other; then Eriksen turned on his heel. "I'm going to talk to him again." As he walked swiftly toward the pumphouse, a deputy caught up with him.

"That .410 is still in his closet."

"Good. So at least it doesn't appear he has a gun."

"He could easily have a Saturday-night special," the deputy said.

"Well, we're going to find out. Besides, all the girls

so far have been strangled, which would give me time to get him first." He stepped into the pumphouse and turned to the ladder.

"Sonny. Denice. I'm coming up just to talk. No one is going to be hurt, so be cool, Sonny. We're just going to talk." He started up.

I heard his voice booming below me, the hollow ring of a man talking from the bottom of a well. He would be coming up that ladder soon, and I would see the door lift slowly and he would emerge like a trapdoor spider looking for a prey. Looking for me. But he should be helping me. He should know I have the gray lioness, and when she has suffered, when I have punished her, then there will be peace. Why don't they understand? But I knew they wouldn't. I knew it when I heard the siren and saw the first car pull in with its macho lights blinking and winking at me. And then more cars came and threw lightspears at me, darts that came through my wombtomb and tried to hurt me. There was no place to hide, they were on all sides. I took the lioness down from the wall and held her in front of me. She tried to cry out to her father once. Why should she have a good father? Where was my father? She had destroyed him, snapped his balls off, and driven him away. It wasn't right that she should have a father. At first I kept moving to dodge the lightspears, but finally there were too many. I felt the icicle pain shoot through me and melt my innards. Light is a very cold pain. The lioness struggled again when I freed her arms, and I thought of choking her out, but that would not be good enough. She must be awake to know the pain, but I couldn't inflict it on her now. I had to wait until they were gone and the lightdarts disappeared. Sitting down, I held her in front of me, one hand around her waist, and her skin felt warm beneath my cold hand. She struggled and tried to pull away at the sound of her father's voice below us; I pressed the edge of the knife against her neck to make her quiet again. We waited amid the lightspears for the door to open. Let him see her and be gone.

Eriksen, expecting the trapdoor to be latched, shoved on it violently; it flew back with a crash against the wall. He held his head down below floor level, waiting for a shot, but there was nothing. Absolute silence. He slowly raised his head. The interior was speckled with light seeping through cracks in the wall. The first thing he saw were his daughter's eyes, wide and pleading, and her mouth working soundlessly. Next to her throat the blade of a pocketknife winked at him, and right behind his daughter's head, the face mostly hidden in her hair, was Sonny. A streak of light illuminated the one eye Eriksen could see. It stared at him, unblinking. Eriksen, watching that cyclopean eye, rose a little more above floor level but kept his revolver below the opening.

"Sonny, I'm Sergeant Eriksen. And that's my daughter you have there. Put that knife down and—"

"The lioness will be punished and no one, no one is going to prevent it. Francis Macomber has assured me I'm right," Sonny said calmly.

Eriksen looked at him and felt chilled by his calmness. Denice's eyes never left him; he knew the terror she felt. Then he saw with a shock that she was nude. He had thought on first glance that the white bands were bra and underpants. He had never seen his daughter nude since before puberty, and he felt suddenly embarrassed for himself and for her.

"Denice, honey, are you all right?" he asked softly.

She started to answer, but Sonny yelled from behind the curtain of her hair: "The lioness will not speak. She cannot. It is forbidden."

Eriksen saw her nod slightly. He moved forward then, leaning his chest on the floor as he stretched out an arm. "Give me the knife, Sonny. Hand it to me and we'll go downstairs together. There's a doctor coming. He'll help you. He'll talk to you."

There was sudden rage in Sonny's voice as he shouted back, "My father would have helped me. But he's gone, because the gray lioness killed him. You had a father. Everyone had a father, but I didn't. Because of this bitch right here. And she's going to pay for it.

She is going to pay for my father and for Ernest and for Francis."

Eriksen saw him raise the knife until the point was digging at the flesh on Denice's neck.

"All right, all right. Relax. Now, what do you want to do? Just tell me." He held his breath as he waited, but Sonny said nothing, just pushed the knife point tighter against Denice's neck, until she was whimpering. He could hear Sonny laughing.

Eriksen felt the ladder tremble. He looked down to see the sheriff standing with Friedland. They watched him expectantly, and he signaled for Friedland to come up. The two men jammed the opening.

"Hello, Sonny," Friedland said cheerfully. "I'm Ben Friedland. I'm someone who can help you, just like a doctor would help someone who broke a leg." He paused. "I heard you talking about your father. Where is he now? Any idea?"

There was a silence, and then Friedland continued. "I know you must have loved him very much. And he loved you. Just because he had to leave so many years ago doesn't mean he didn't love you. And he wouldn't want any harm to come to you."

Sonny twisted from behind Denice until his face was exposed. "My father left me because this lioness bitch killed him. She did it and she is going to pay and no one is going to change that."

Friedland continued as though Sonny had not spoken. "If your father were here now he wouldn't want you to hurt that girl, he wouldn't—"

"He's not here because she killed him, can't you understand that?" Sonny said loudly. Eriksen gauged the distance to be no more than fifteen feet. Sonny's head was fully exposed. One shot. Right between his eyes. As if Sonny had read his mind, he slid his head back behind the curtain of hair so that just one eye glittered at them. The knife still puckered the skin on Denice's neck.

Friedland, still talking, eased himself higher into the loft and raised one knee to put himself fully on the floor. At that moment Sonny made a swift stroke with the knife, making a thin red stripe on the side of the girl's neck. It began to drip blood before Denice even reacted to the razor-sharp knife cut. Friedland froze, appalled. He backed up and put both feet on the ladder again. Sonny said nothing; Denice cried out and her body trembled violently. Eriksen jerked Friedland backward. The psychiatrist nearly fell to the ground below. "What the hell are you doing?"

"I felt he was being receptive," Friedland said as he regained his footing on the ladder.

"Get out of here. He's not hearing anything."

Friedland didn't move. "That's the problem. I think he might be hearing voices, audio hallucinations. He might even be following orders from those voices."

Eriksen pulled his eyes from the blood on his daughter's neck and looked at Friedland. "Well, you keep talking. Maybe he won't hear those other voices then. But don't make a single move inside again."

I heard them whispering and plotting against me. I knew they wanted to kill me. That's why they were throwing the lightspears through the cracks in the wall at me. I could no longer escape them, and the cold pain made me weak. They should be helping me, but the lioness had them in her power. They believed her, not me. I watched the new man, the man with the bloodred hair, move his mouth at me, but his voice was no more than the cries of monkeys, just rising-and-falling shrieks. But Francis couldn't reach me through those monkey cries, couldn't help me now when I needed him most. I realized I would have to deal with the lioness on my own. This was my final test. I must make her suffer and be done with it.

Eriksen, listening to Friedland's calm voice coaxing Sonny to release the girl, wondered if he could get a shot off. He dismissed the idea. Sonny was completely hidden behind Denice, except for that one eye. Suddenly he felt his stomach turn over as the knife abruptly made another slash along the side of her neck. Blood flowed even more freely; he saw it course down her neck, across her collarbone, and over her breast. He heard Friedland stop in mid-sentence and gasp. Eriksen clenched his .357 to stop his impulses.

Friedland whispered, "It looks terrible, Dan, but he hasn't cut the carotid artery. The cuts are really pretty superficial."

"Daddy!" Denice cried, but the knife point came up under her chin and she fell silent. Eriksen clearly heard Sonny chuckle.

"Keep talking," he told Friedland, and quickly descended the ladder. The sheriff and a dozen deputies holding shotguns and rifles ringed the pumphouse. Beyond them he saw ropes up to hold back newsmen and the growing crowd.

"Look," Eriksen said to Conrad, "that asshole has a knife against Denice's throat and he's cut her twice. She's bleeding bad. I'm going—"

Conrad interrupted. "Can we get a shot at him from up there?"

"No way. He's got Denice in front of him."

Conrad looked at the flaking red boards above him. "How about a shot right through the wall?"

"Shit. It would go through both him and Denice and out the other side. Even with a twenty-two or a shotgun we couldn't be sure of not hurting Denice."

Conrad eyed him. "You got another plan?" Nye broke away from some newsmen and joined them.

"Yes," Eriksen said noncommittally. "I'll tell you about it in just a minute." He went back inside the pumphouse. Friedland looked down as he started up.

"We're not getting anywhere. This is a very dangerous situation, Dan. This boy is completely unpredictable."

Eriksen was not prepared for the sight of his daughter; her face, her arm and her breasts, and one leg were smeared with blood. Sonny's free hand kept going to the side of her neck and rubbing the blood over the girl in slow sweeps. Even her hair was streaked with it. The right hand kept the knife point at the side of her neck.

"Denice," he breathed, and he saw his daughter's eyes open slowly and stare at him. He was not sure she recognized him. Eriksen turned to Friedland and spoke in a whisper: "This talking isn't doing shit, is it?"

"No."

"Well, keep at it. I only need a few more minutes." He took a careful look at where Sonny was sitting with his back to the wall, then hurried below and ran to the barn. There had to be an old fruit ladder around there somewhere, he knew. He found it hanging on the wall at the rear of the barn. And another on the ground. He called to the nearest deputy, and together they carried the long orchard ladder around to the back of the pumphouse. Eyeing the upper loft for the center point, the two of them eased the ladder against the wall.

"Careful! Don't let it hit. No noise," Eriksen said, and the ladder touched softly against the structure. It was not quite as high as he wanted, but it would do. He saw Conrad and Nye coming toward him, and he quickly turned to the deputy.

"Give me your Buck knife." The man unsnapped the tooled leather pouch on his gun belt and handed him the folded knife. Eriksen pocketed it and turned to face Conrad.

"What's going on, Eriksen?" Nye asked. His lips were flaked with tobacco leaves from the cigar he was nervously devouring.

Eriksen spoke to the sheriff. "Friedland says we're getting nowhere with the talking. He can't reach Sonny. Time is running out."

"So what's your plan?" Conrad rumbled.

Eriksen eyed him silently for a moment and then pulled the Buck knife from his pocket. He opened it, and the six-inch steel blade shimmered in the spotlights.

"Sonny's back is against the wall right there. Right in the center. The wall is made of one-by-six redwood. It's old and the boards have warped apart. So I'm going up and—"

"Jesus Christ, Eriksen!" Nye exploded. "You think you're going to stab that kid in the back? Just like that? Jesus, this community would land on us like a ton of bricks. I can see the goddamn headlines now: 'Deputy Sheriff knifes boy in back.' That's just going to be great publicity."

"That's my daughter up there," Eriksen snapped. "She's got two knife cuts on her neck now. She's bleeding, goddammit, and I'm going to end this shit now!" He moved toward Nye threateningly, and the lieutenant backed up involuntarily.

Conrad held up a hand. "Dan, it's one thing to shoot someone in a situation like this, but a stabbing in the back. I don't know. There just has to be another way. Get—"

He was interrupted by a shriek that at first Eriksen thought came from Denice, but it ended in a bass howl.

"Leave me alone. Go away!"

Eriksen spun and started for the ladder but Conrad's big hand stopped him. Eriksen shook it off. "I'm going to do it, Sheriff. That's all."

Conrad stared at him. "All right, but I don't know anything about this." He turned away, and Nye followed him.

Eriksen ran to the bottom of the ladder, knowing he was dealing in seconds, and started up. The old ladder quivered under his weight, and he was conscious of the voices in the crowd and the bright lights upon him. Then he could hear nothing but his breath coming in tight little gasps as he reached the top. Putting one hand against the rough boards to steady himself, he could hear Friedland inside still speaking calmly and steadily.

He peered at the spaces until he made out Sonny's blue denim shirt pressed against the boards. He measured from the floorboards up to where the middle of the back would be. One foot would be enough, he decided. He pulled the knife from his pocket, opened it, and felt the blade lock. It seemed unusually heavy in his hand. He had never stabbed anybody in his life, but he had read the blade didn't go in easily. Placing the point of the knife at what he thought was the center of Sonny's back, he slid the tip carefully through a space between the boards until it barely touched the denim shirt. He heard Mrs. Sills suddenly give a ringing shriek, but with no further hesitation he slammed the heel of his hand against the butt end of the knife and drove it in the full six inches.

The lightsword exploded in my back and I opened my mouth to scream, but there was nothing. Pain flashed red and filled my entire body until it arched me back like a fully drawn bow. The lightsword held me pinned; the sounds grew dim. Someone called my name, but his voice grew more and more distant, until there was nothing but the roaring of waves, so cold.

Eriksen heard Darby shout, "We've got her, Dan," as he dropped down the ladder and ran to the door. Two ambulance attendants were already starting up the ladder, and then Cynthia was clinging to him. His hand still tingled with the feeling of Sonny writhing on the other end like a great fish that had been speared. The knife was still in Sonny, and he heard someone on the ladder chopping a hole in the wall to free him.

Then he saw Denice being lowered, wrapped in blankets, and laid on a stretcher. An attendant swiftly wrapped her neck in gauze bandages and loaded her into the ambulance.

"She'll be all right, Dan," Darby said at his side, but Eriksen didn't hear him. He took Cynthia's arm and helped her into the ambulance. As he reached for the door he saw Conrad and Nye striding toward him. He pulled the door shut, and the ambulance, with a moan from its siren to clear the crowd, began to move. He looked at Cynthia. She said nothing, but only watched their daughter, who stared at the ceiling and looked at neither one.

ABOUT THE AUTHOR

T. JEFF WILLIAMS is in his late thirties and lives in northern California. He has worked as a stringer for the Associated Press and as a correspondent for CBS, covering the war in Cambodia and events at Wounded Knee. His first novel, about the Vietnam War, is called *The Glory Hole* and has been published recently. He is at work on his third novel.